Chapter One

Black Love in Innocence

All black love starts off innocently. I guess all love naturally does. black loves however whether in Baldwin hills California or in Brownsville Brooklyn has to overcome numerous pitfalls', roadblocks, and player haters by the hundreds. Black Love has to overcome self-hate and self-doubt from both parties. Cultural and semi cultural differences family, friends, friends of friends, in-laws, friends of in-laws, lovers, ex-lovers, and friends of ex-lovers seem to doom "Black Love" before it ever gets started.

Black people on a whole are very emotional people who base their whole existence on emotion rather than logic, and when you through "self-hate" on top of that you can have a very miserable person lying next to in bed as you wake up day in and day out. There are black people who really desire to be loved and give love, but base their whole existence on be jealous of those who have found love.

The first thing all the black woman in my family said as Barack Obama was being sworn in as President was:

"Look at that Bitch!"

"She ain't even Light Skinned!"

"She looks like she does her own hair!"

"That Nigger ain't got good taste! He won't last long!"

Instead of just being happy for them and seeing them as the first black president and first lady; for being in love and "Happy."

Black children are raised with all kinds of twisted distorted beliefs about love. Usually by some miserable older aunt who has always been single, miserable and who claims that "NO ONE" knows more about relationships and "Men" than she does. This aunt is usually the one who passes down the worst advice possible to the younger generation as she babysits the young boys and girls of her family.

Young black girls are taught to do whatever it takes to be as "light" as possible.

Everything is at least tried from sleeping with Noxzema on your face and arms, wiping your face with Clorox bleach, to avoiding the sun like a vampire and believe it or not this practice is done the most by young girls who society would already consider "light skinned".

3

They're taught hair straightening. This makes you a double threat. (The triple threat is having "light" eyes). From every young age, black girls are taught to sleep with their heads in a certain position to not mess up their hair. They are taught that working up a sweat is almost a crime. If the gas is off in a house it causes a panic not because the family will not be able to cook food, but because the hot comb now cannot be heated and the hair of the women in the house will be nappy. Curling irons are more important than water; and rent money is spent at the beauty salon. Needless to say at this point it's not hard to understand that a black girl no matter what shade, feels that her natural state is anything but beautiful; and if this is not enough then comes the Euro-American influence of thin being beautiful.

The black girl by adolescence has starved herself, learned to vomit after meals, and takes diet pills given to her by Spanish witch doctors in the neighborhood that practice in their Botanica's. Anything to look as un-black as possible then she feels that Maybe, just maybe she could find a Man who will love her; for who she is.

Young black boys are taught to....Do good in school, do good in school and do good in school! So that one day they could get a good job and maybe be able to purchase one of these young girls previously described once she's mastered the art of being near white and made it through to adult hood. Who will love them for being able to purchase them?

Black children on a whole are advised to aim their sights so high that if they cannot come close to achieving any of the examples described previously that they should just give up because "they ain't shit!" and never were meant to be shit and are probably like the absentee father whom they've never met and don't know.

Even with all of this incredibly ignorant non sense pumped into their impressionable little minds. Black people take it to the next level and forced these children into the ultimate school of confusion, self-hate, and sexual abuse....The black church. The black church reaffirms and compounds the ignorance that they are getting at home which makes these children think: "Okay mommy is right....I ain't shit".

On Sunday morning they put on their best clothes; some which took the very last of their money and hope that their appearance is pleasing enough on the most critical of eyes just to be welcomed into the house of the Lord. Mommy gives them enough change to put into the collection plate each of the five times that in is placed in front of them attached to long poles handled by the preachers goons who are dressed in wrinkled and matted old uniforms, wreaking

Black Church

Sex, Drugs, and the Holy Ghost

By

Michael "Mick Man" Gourdine

Index

of alcohol, and clearly hung over the usher is the one who always reassures them that they are dressed good enough to be in the Lord's house by always saying "Look at how nice you all look" as he makes his first collection round. Passing this inspection always makes mommy and the children feel good. They're all happily and add their money to the plate, while silently begging the Lord for forgiveness. On the way to church they were told they better not make a sound and better not try and keep any of the money to buy candy later after service. Simply to beg for forgiveness for being born out of wedlock, born poor, and most of all for being born black! For the most loyal sheep in the flock however there is yet one more hurdle to cross. If you really want to into heaven and are not on the fence or half stepping, the sacrificial offering separates you from the just run of the mill ghetto black folk. After all five collections are made, the Reverend asks everyone to dig just a little deeper and make a real sacrifice. You will then be allowed to come up front and hand over your money personally to the reverend and have him lay his precious hands on your forehead *(After taking you money of course)*, blessing you and wishing you well. You are then allowed to catch the Holy Ghost on your way back to your seat and stop, drop, and roll to the point where the women *(Dressed as nurses)* come and give you the only known cure for the Holy Ghost. Nooo, it's not medicine, or words of wisdom; it's just air from white hand fans with a red cross on them. Hot air from a church that is surely 95 degrees no matter what time of the year it is.

The worst part of black church for all children who attend *(besides the constant sexual abuse)* is the racial confusion. The black church has the poorest of the poor people spending most their hard earned money and competing against each other to look like they have money when both parties are well aware that they are both as broke as hell. To make matters worse they are both constantly on their knees begging for forgiveness, being broke and black to a gigantic picture of a blond haired blue-eyed white Jesus.

Children being children always find a way to live and have fun no matter how dismal or insane their circumstance. The sacrificial offering is a very fun time for children; they get to hear their mother and friends make fun of who had the nerve to wear whatever is seen as inappropriate clothing to church, who didn't get her hair done right, and who has the nerve to show her face in church when everyone knows she's a stripper etc,.; and then the Holy Ghost. Some children even fake the Holy Ghost just to have fun, let off some steam and to impress their friends. Some of the children become junior ushers, some join the choir, and some take part in the cake sale after church. It's the best hustle because the children learn the art of the skimming by stealing money for their personal use.

The black church with all of its faults serves an important function in the black community. For instance there are people who will only talk to you before, during or after Sunday service. On any other day of the week whether in front of their house or at the Pathmark, you had better not say a word to them. The black church is a place where you can get to know people in an informal manner surrounding. It's where children from different social classes can get to know each other. This socializing takes place during Sunday school, which starts an hour and a half before service.

At first it's all pretentious. Black children have the worst hang ups that are taught to them by the most confused people in the history of the world. Everything is a 'front'. Everything is pretend, which leads to emotional breakdowns during Sunday school and confessions of abuse at home. Boys who are up start pretend they want to be gangstas and try to be the toughest kid in Sunday school. All the while some 16 year old Sunday school teacher who is also the Reverend's daughter tries to teach these backward children about the word of God, knowing that none of them actually believe any of the stories of the bible; when she really does.

The kids themselves actually test her faith on a weekly basis. The Sunday school teacher actually starts to think 'How could there be a God if such things are happening to these children". She puts out graham crackers and juice every Sunday morning. She takes the time and puts together a lesson plan which always turns into a sort of 'breakfast club' for children with serious issues. The most seriously disturbed children are always the ones who are not allowed contact with anyone outside of the church because the parents are afraid of 'Unholy" contamination. These children are made to go to school and church STRICTLY! If they are not in one of the two places, they are home watching PG rated TV shows and studying for school or church. These children are undoubtedly on their way to being prostitutes and drug addicts when they get older. These are always the most mentally unbalanced children then adults in the black community.

The most stable of the children are those who understand that attending Sunday school is merely a formality. It makes their parents look good and like upstanding citizens in the community. These children are neither believers nor Atheist. They are really Agnostic, couldn't care one way or the other and really have no interest in getting to know God because after all they are children and barely know themselves. They become cynical after a while and start to become observant of the fact that the Reverend is always drunk, or is always taking a young girl in to his private office for special counseling. This in turn makes them complete non-believers who never trust anyone who may come across as too religious in their eyes. These children seem to find ways to just make time pass while they have to be in such a dismal atmosphere. This is the atmosphere where the seed of puppy love can first take place; where black love can grow to fruition in the most innocent of intention as it did with two childhood friends, Gifford Cook and Chinse McDaniel's.

Chapter 2

Black Puppy Love

Gifford and Chinse first saw each other while holding their mother's hand on the way to church. They were actually third generation congregants of the Burns Memorial Church of God and Christ. Their grandparents had come up from the south during the great migration in the 1940's. Like millions of other black people did during that time to escape the "Jim Crow" south. They sought to find a better life where the next generation could come closer to achieving the American dream than the last, while trying to hold on to some of the old traditions of the south like attending church. Both where six years old and Gifford winked at Chinse as they all crossed Sutphin Boulevard at the 'triangle' to walk through the front doors of the church. Gifford saw Chinse as a little angel that he wanted to be close to. Of course he couldn't imagine sex, but his instincts incited him to protect her as a possession, yet he would have to get to know her first.

There were four sections of church pews at Burns Memorial; four pews in each section. Gifford's mother sat him next to her all the way to the right in the first section and third pew. Chinse's mother sat her to her left in the third section on the opposite side of the church in the fourth pew. "Well at least she's not in the fourth section, I can at least see her face without straining," Gifford thought to himself. He knew he would be seen by nearly the entire congregation if he looked over his shoulder toward the back of the church to get Chinse's attention, but it would be a chance he would have to take.

During the second collection as the plate connected to the long handle went passed Gifford's lap, only after his mother nodded to him to place the fifty cents she had given him into the basket. Gifford looked back and waived to Chinse. She smiled revealing her adorable little dimples which made her even more appealing to Gifford; he was too preoccupied with Chinse he didn't feel his mothers' hand slap his thigh with a strong thud. Gifford was well aware as all black children are, causing a scene brings down the harshest of punishment from a black mother, especially in church.

The only thing that would make that punishment worse was to cry or actually make noise as you were crying, after being hit. It would make the original offense not just a felony, but an aggravated felony. In this case Gifford was well aware that he would at least get the slap on the thigh. Gifford just held his breath as he got the "look" from his mother. It is the look that children are familiar with and truly need no verbal assistance. Gifford only hoped that he had impressed Chinse with his willingness to receive pain in order to get her attention.

It was May 17, 1987 a sunny spring day in South Jamaica, Queens N.Y.C. and as usual on days like today the young girls of the church would be having a cake sale outside the church doorway to the left of the entrance to the church. They had different cakes for sale, but the only one everyone was interested in was the yellow cake with chocolate icing. It sold out in mere seconds as people rushed over after shaking hands with other church members who they hate and exchange phony smiles that their faces hurt. After the sacrificial offerings were collected and the 'nurses' finished fanning off the people who were lucky enough to catch the "Holy Ghost" and then there would be final words from the Reverend. Before the final words from the Reverend would be delivered, the young girls involved in the cake sale would be excused to get the cakes arranged into place at the side door.

Gifford glanced at his mother and in spite of the "look" he received from her earlier he looked back in Chinse's direction and saw that she was being led by her older sister Capalitana, to assist in the cake sale. After the Reverend finished his near endless final words, he gave the command to shake the hands of everyone to everyone's north, south, east, and west. Then and only then was everyone free to leave until they returned the following Sunday.

As Gifford, his brother Brian, and mother, Walani exited the church; Gifford was surprised to feel his mother leading them directly towards the cake sale.

"And what's this little dolls name? The one that has my Son's complete attention"
Mrs. Cook asked smiling at Chinse.

"My name is Chinse McDaniel's," she said smiling with her dimples even more pronounced than in the pew and causing the butterflies in Gifford's stomach to grow to the size of eagles.

"And what's your son's name? Chinse asked, looking squarely at Gifford who shyly looked at the ground.

"Oh don't be shy now boy! Mrs. Cook said, putting Gifford seriously on the spot.

"You know we ain't over here to buy no cake! This pretty little thing damn near cost you some teeth so you might as well speak up now!" Mrs. Cook said clearly joking.

"I'm Gifford, this is my little brother Brian and this of course is my mother Mrs. Walani Cook."

Gifford spoke very dryly and withdrawn, he felt as though the whole congregation was watching. He was also very small for his age which made him feel puny. Gifford hated feeling small in the world. Being big from a distance, like the stunt he pulled in church was easy. Once up close his courage always seemed to fade.

As the Cook's crossed Sutphin Boulevard, Gifford looked back over his shoulder at Chinse with a little smirk and shrugged shoulders was all he got in return from her. Then she went back to smiling at the approaching customers. At that moment a feeling of failure came over him. This feeling had come more and more frequently in his life. The feeling of depression was becoming a vicious cycle. He would get sudden surges of courage that would fade to cowardice even if he was being successful at whatever task he was attempting to tackle. Gifford would then shut down and have to wait for his courage to rebuild itself and take another risk; at that point he would seem to give up and would sink into depression. Even at this young age he was starting to recognize this pattern even though no one else seemed to notice.

Time seemed to draw out like a blade as Gifford waited for what seemed like an eternity for each day to end at the Samuel Huntington School on Union Avenue better known as P.S. 40. He would wait for his baby brother Brian by the kindergarten exit; where Mrs. Vickie Walker knew damn well that she shouldn't be turning a five year old over to his six year old, first grade brother, but did it anyway because it wasn't the first time she had done it and it damn sure wouldn't be the last time either. Mrs. Vickie Walker would just shake her head and say, "Now go straight home you two, I mean it! Straight home!"

The two Cook brothers would then walk northward on 109th Avenue toward the South Jamaica Houses or the "40 Projects" as they were notoriously known throughout New York City; to the Cook family it was home. After all it was a short walk to 6 160th Street, Apartment 3C; a safe one. They would debate back and forth about their favorite cars like the Pontiac Grand Am, Nissan Maxima, Volkswagen Jetta, Suzuki Samurai, and Gifford's favorite, the Jeep Wrangler Safari Edition. Gifford swore to himself that one day he would own that car. Once in a while during their walk home they would see cars they were scared to even dream of owning. One of the two of their favorites belonged to the "King" of their projects James "WALL" Corley of the CORLEY Brothers. It was a cream colored Rolls Royce. The car always seemed to float. The other belonged to the "King of Queens", Lorenzo "FAT CAT" Nichols. It was a convertible Burgundy Rolls Royce with white leather interior. Both cars were inspiring as well as breathtaking.

The church so far had done its job of destroying any White aspirations that Gifford or Brian may have had. It was hard to believe that black men owned such cars; but after all these were no ordinary black men; they were black "Gods". The most these two boys could hope for was that some civil servant who attended their church would take a liking to them and one day make a phone call that would enable them to become civil servants, then after find a girlfriend who was on the system and gain a project apartment so that maybe, just maybe they would be able to afford a Jeep Wrangler Safari Edition, of course.

As they strolled along the one block walk from the school to their building they milked it for all they could. This was down time where the brothers were allowed to bond and get a look at their world, make their own opinions, and dream about their futures. They would also sing the popular songs of the era like: Don't Be Cruel by Bobby Brown, Push It by Salt n' Pepa, and Paid In Full by Eric B. and Rakim just to name a few. Then it was straight into the house to watch two episodes of "Good Times"; depended on which episode was on. If the episode of Good Times playing wasn't a good one, then they would switch to Channel 5 to see what episode of "What's Happening" was airing. Then it was homework time.

Mrs. Cook would come home from work; she was a cashier at the Western Beef on the corner of Merrick and Farmers Boulevard. Walani worked long days and was scared to death about her young sons; not so much about their current situation, but about their futures. After their father Lance had received a twenty five to life sentence in 1983; Walani knew that she would have to raise her sons alone in the South Jamaica Houses.

Being from that place was not necessarily a death sentence; because many people from there made it and made something of them. Walani also knew that young black boys without a father would have a very difficult time just making it to adulthood even if they were raised in Beverly Hills. Walani swore to herself to have them boys in church every Sunday and Gifford and Brian involved with the church and its members as best she could. Only then, Gifford and Brian would stand a chance at survival.

On a good day Mama Cook would bring home four chicken wings and fried rice with extra soy sauce. The boys would split it in half along with half a can of Pepsi. Gifford and Brian would then clean up after themselves and bring the garbage to the incinerator. The boys liked to play a game they called "Criss Cross Crash" in the hallway of the building. After dumping the trash each would take off in a separate direction to the opposite walls usually giving the one holding the garbage a head start. They would then touch their respected walls and head back toward each other at top speed trying as best they could to turn inward to the main hallway without crashing into each other racing back toward the apartment usually with Walani standing their staring furiously at them to stop the horseplay at once. The boys would then be allowed to play their super Nintendo Super Mario brothers' game until about 9:00 p.m., then turn in for the night.

Apartment 3C was a quaint apartment with two bedrooms, eat-in kitchen and a living room. Gifford and Brian shared a bedroom where they had a metal bunk bed. Each had a four level dresser with a thirteen inch television on top. At night the boys would talk to each other about everything from what happened at school to what happened on an episode of 'Good Times".

"I still can't get her out of my head Brian," Gifford stated out of the blue and half confused at his infatuation with Chinse.

"I still can't get her out of my head Brian,"

Who Chimpanzee? Brian said in a joking manner

"Her name is Chinse, pronounced SHANICE" and I think it's a pretty name" Gifford stated in her defense and very seriously.

"I know nigger, I can tell you've been thinking about her since church. I was wondering when you was going to say something about her. I think it's a pretty name too. I also think she's pretty, but I know she's yours already. Even though you haven't even spoke to her yet she is your girl," Brian said assuring letting his brother know that he had his back and loyalty in only the way that a brother could.

"I can't wait to see her this Sunday. Every time I think about her I get a funny feeling in my stomach. I just can't wait Brian".

"I know Gifford, I know. Now get some sleep we gotta get up early"

Even though Brian was a year younger than Gifford he seemed to have more of a handle on the world. He seemed more mature. People would often confuse Brian for the older brother even though Gifford was bigger in stature. Brian seemed more confident and manly. Brian would council Gifford and make sure that Gifford would do his homework. Brian even stayed quiet when Mrs. Cook would refer to Gifford as the man of the house.

At the age of seven in South Jamaica one was well expected to be. Lance Cook their father would even tell him he was when he called collect from Clinton Correctional Facility in Upstate New York, but even he could hear who the man of the house was really the second he was on the phone with Brian.

As Gifford laid there he couldn't help but think about Chinse. What was her background? Where did she live? Did she live in the 40 Projects? Was she a real nigger like him or was she a snooty Bourgeoisie African American who lived out in Cambria Heights, Laurelton, or where the Super Uppity blacks live, out on LONG ISLAND! Because if she had been coming to church from all the way out on the island, surely Chinse would be too good to know him, be his friend and certainly not his girlfriend. After all Gifford had heard his mom, talk a lot about Long Island people. The more he thought about it that, it couldn't possibly be the case. Why would Long Island niggers, people of such standard and nobility come to a house of worship and pray to the same God as niggers from South Jamaica Queens; that couldn't possibly the case, even if she was bougie, she had to be a nigger from somewhere in Southeastern Queens, and not from the Far East either which made her fair game. After he did the math over and over Gifford came to the conclusion that Chinse had to be fair game, now all he had to do was come up with the courage to actually speak to Chinse to make this dream a reality. As he thought about it more he smiled and fell into a deep sleep.

Gifford's calculations however where 100% wrong; the McDaniel's' did in fact live out on Long Island. They lived at 808 Fullerton Avenue in Uniondale Village, Nassau County, New York 11553. Although they lived there, they were not from there. The McDaniel's where from South Ozone Park. Their father had hit the New York Lotto, the second prize for $560,000.00. Mr. Robert McDaniel's then grabbed his wife and two daughters and followed the African-American dream of every black person from Brooklyn and Queens (the low end of Long Island) and moved out to Long Island.

Mr. McDaniel's kept his job as a New York City Correctional Officer, so he didn't want to move too far out on the island and his daily commute to Rikers Island wouldn't change by much. The only difference would be an extra half hour; he would have to drive on the Southern

State Parkway and an additional fifteen minutes on the Belt Parkway making his extra commute a grand total of forty five minutes.

Unlike Gifford and Brian who were only a year apart, Chinse and Capalitana where four years apart. Which made Capalitana or "Kep" as people called her a very strong influence over Chinse. Sometimes Kep would be downright put in charge over Chinse by Mr. and Mrs. McDaniel's. Chinse was in the first grade as was Gifford and Kep was in the fifth. They also had only one block to walk to the Northern Parkway Elementary School at the corner of Fullerton Avenue and Southern Parkway.

The McDaniel's home was what society would consider upper middle class. It was green with white roofing and a matching garage on the northern side of the walkway to the street; with a comfortable amount of lawn on both sides of the house and a more than comfortable backyard which had a modern gas powered barbecue grill, lounge chairs and a swing set for the girls. Ralph and Juanita McDaniel's loved to watch the girls pig tails flop around the girls' heads in the breeze, as they would waive to their parents who were sitting by the barbeque. This was the African American dream.

In all the splendor and perfection there was a secret Juanita hid from Officer McDaniel's who worked four out of four at Otis Bentham Correctional Centre on Rikers Island or "O.B.C.C." as it was known to all on both sides of the law in New York City. Juanita had grown terribly bored with the perfect life.

For years the McDaniel's had made the long commute from Long Island to attend church services at the Abyssinian Baptist church at 132 Odell Clark place New York N.Y. 10030. To all regular black folk that was simply 138th Street. It was a simple choice for Ralph, The Abyssinian Baptist Church was the best black church in New York City and by best it is understood that this church was as bourgeoisie as it got. To Ralph this meant that it was the only place for his wife and daughters to attend. He figured that they should attend the best church so that they would be exposed to the best people thereby giving them the best chance of meeting the best man qualified to give Chinse and Capalitana comfortable lives.

This would seem like the perfect place for the family, but it was far from perfect for Mrs. McDaniel. Juanita's ex-boyfriend Eric Fickland or "Fick" as people called him lived in Rochdale Village just a five minute drive from the Burns Memorial Church on Sutphin Boulevard. Fick also helped Juanita out with another growing problem she had developed due to the terrible boredom of Long island. Juanita had developed a tad bit of a Cocaine problem that was more than her allowance from Ralph could cover. Juanita convinced Ralph that she and the girls didn't like such a long and traffic congested commute to Harlem every Sunday. That it would be much more convenient for all of them to attend church closer to home, closer to her old neighborhood that she missed terribly. The warm feeling of southeastern Queens, R.C.L. Soul Food on Rockaway Boulevard, The Rib Shack on Linden Boulevard, all of her friends and family, above all else her very strong jones for a sniff that Fick was more than glad to give to Juanita as he rode her from behind in that small coat room (called the office) right next to the bathrooms on the first floor of the Burns Memorial Church of God and Christ.

Needless to say two worlds were colliding. The Cooks, a small but virtuous poor family from the South Jamaica Houses and the McDaniel's, a small upper middle class family from the suburbs who were admired by all of the poor black people in Jamaica, Queens. The McDaniel's were in fact looked up to and admired but had a problem or two and were anything but virtuous although no one at the Church had any idea just how deep Mrs. McDaniel's indiscretions were, at least not yet.

Finally Sunday came. It had seemed like a month since Gifford was embarrassed at the cake sale by his mother. He felt like he could grow to love church. That Sunday could become his favorite day of the week. Gifford had begged his mother to spend some of her hard earned check to pay for fresh haircuts for himself and Brian from the barber shop on 165th Street across from the Coliseum. Gifford helped his mother lay out their clothes so that he could wear a nice pair of slacks out of the grand total of three and the one he thought looked the best on him. Gifford used a shoe shine kit that his mother had bought for her boys to shine his shoes; to a mirror shine. As he rinsed his mouth with peroxide and brushed his teeth with baking soda Brian and Walani looked on smirking at each other but happy to see Gifford take such care in his appearance. Both were concerned about his feelings. They both new he was going to try and approach Chinse today and rejection could be very painful to a boy so smitten at this age, especially, when his crush had yet to be elevated to the point of action.

As the Cook's walked under the underpass at 109th Avenue and 159th Street they were all laughing and smiling in the sunshine. Chinse with her little dimples had seemed to have bought happiness to this entire little family. None of the three were really interested in a single thing about any kind of scripture. All three couldn't wait to see what would happen between Gifford and Chinse. The smile was immediately wiped off Walani's face as the family turned the corner of Sutphin Boulevard toward the church.

Ralph had heard about the incident at the cake sale the week before. Where this street trash named Gifford had made eyes at his daughter and had been the talk of his McDaniel's household the entire week as it had been in the Cook household. The McDaniel's had gotten to church early just so that he could give the McDaniel's a hard cold stare giving the Cook boys the message to stay away from his daughters. It didn't work Gifford and Brian they just as confused by it and Walani just sucked her teeth and whisked by with her boys. Walani hoped as to not confront Officer McDaniel's not just because it would crush Gifford's feeling, but because Ralph was a good person to know if you could get close enough to know him. Although Walani knew as did everyone in the Burns Memorial Church what was going on in the back room between Mrs. McDaniel's and Fick. She loved just the idea of her sons being ingratiated with the haves. When Reverend Burns talked to Mr. and Mrs. McDaniel's he was much more attentive and much more respectful. After all the McDaniel's were the "Haves" and on top of that they lived out on Long Island which entitled them to more respect than most parishioners.

When Officer McDaniel's was able to escort his wife and daughters to church on a seldom day off everyone at the church showed him the utmost respect. Especially since when he didn't come the entire church was aware that Fick would stop in and have Juanita touching her toes in the office after he made a sizeable donation to the Reverend. The Reverend at times would use some of that donation to have Juanita touching her toes for him as well. Several other loyal parishioners had also been walked in on as they had Juanita touching her toes for a few bucks for them as well in the "back office".

As the crowd made its way into the church and pews, Mrs. Cook made her move. She made her way to the back office knocking loudly to make sure that she didn't see any 'Ungodly" activity in the back office to speak to Reverend Burns.

"I need a favor Reverend" said Walani in a huff.

"What could the Reverend do for you on the fine spring morning?"

The Reverend said showing signs of lust as he hoped that Walani was going to ask for some money to make it through the week.

"I need for my Son Gifford to be excused from service early along with the girls who do the cake sale so that he could help them," said Walani. Knowing that she was busting the Reverend's bubble but still showing that one day he might get some booty.

"Oh I see so that little Gifford can get close to Officer McDaniel's daughter, I don't think that he would like that" said the Reverend; insinuating that it may take Walani sacrificing her body for such a huge favor.

"I don't think Officer McDaniel's would like to know that you're fucking his wife either, or that you was letting that drug dealer Fick in here every week to fuck her" sneered Walani in a threatening manner.

"Well the good Lord smiles on young black puppy love and I see this as beautiful black puppy love. Yes ma'am in Jesus Name Gifford will be excused to help out with the cake sale" said the Reverend showing teeth in an open act of surrender.

"Well thank you Reverend Burns, I prayed this morning that the Lord would help you to see that it was the right thing to do. Yes Sir in Jesus name" said Walani smirking in his face knowing that she had the upper hand.

It took poor little Gifford all the self-control a ten year old boy could possibly have to wait for the last offering as he did the previous week before turning to look over his shoulder and see Chinse's pretty little dimples. Gifford expected to feel the same thud on his leg as he did before, he was aware of the consequences for interrupting the Lord's house especially when the Lord's money was being collected; but he didn't care. He had to see his darling Chinse who was already in his mind his girlfriend and future wife, even though he hadn't said more than ten words to her. This time however was different. There was no thud on his lap and he was allowed to stare as long as he wanted. Chinse looked back too. Time seemed to stand still. Gifford could hear his heart beating. He could even hear music in his head; it was a popular song at the time it was titled 'If Your Heart Isn't in It" by the group Atlantic Star.

This was the closest thing to Romance that Gifford had ever experienced. He felt like he was actually floating. Then to his surprise it was Chinse who got slapped on her thigh by Officer Ralph McDaniel's who was watching the whole exchange and wasn't the least bit amused. Chinse's smile dropped and tears welled up in her eyes. Gifford stared at Mr. McDaniel's with fury. He had never felt this way before and was outraged that someone actually put their hands on his woman. He gave Mr. McDaniel's a look of death. The stare was broken up by the announcement for the girls who ran the cake sale to excuse themselves to prepare the cakes for selling. The Reverend also announced that the girls had a lot of cake, I mean really a lot of cake this week and needed some help selling the cake outside at the side door.

"Is there anyone here who is willing to help our little sisters out selling this delicious cake here on this beautiful day?" The church fell silent as no one volunteered.

"Gifford Cook I see you have your hand up, thank you for volunteering. Everyone give a round of applause to this fine young man who has volunteered his services to help our young sisters in Jesus name Amen; God is good!"

The congregation applauded to what sounded like the crowd at a World Series game as a homerun was being hit. Reverend Burns looked over to Mrs. Cook and gave a nod as she nudged Gifford out of his seat as she was applauding. Mrs. Cook leaned over to give Gifford a kiss and whispered in his ear: "Go get your girl tiger!" Gifford smiled realizing that his mother had planned this whole thing. Gifford looked to Brian who winked motioning with his head to head out of the pew and go handle his business. All three then looked over their shoulders as the McDaniel sisters rose out of their seats to exit their pew. When they saw the outraged face of Officer Ralph McDaniel's who was not at all amused by this openly displayed crush that Gifford and Chinse had just displayed on one another. Officer McDaniel's had asked for "Time Due" with his captain just to come to this Sundays service to make sure that Gifford's displays of affection would cease and cease immediately. Now to further his outrage the Reverend had been coaxed into conspiring to bring this puppy love to the next level. Officer McDaniel's thought to himself: "No way. Not ever. I have worked too hard for too many years tending to "Care, Custody, and Control of little black pieces of shit that looked just like him and are in the same place that he is going to wind up more than likely. In fact ten years old is way too young to even have a crush on a boy for my sweet little Chinse. This shit will not be allowed to continue"

Officer McDaniel's sat there stewing as the Reverend gave his final drawn out sermon and asked for everyone to shake hands with everyone to the North, South, East, and West before freeing the congregation until next Sunday. As most people clear out there is always the usual faces of fans, which run up to the front of the church to clatter around the Reverend to ask for favors, money, and numerous other things. The Reverend knew it was coming so he just braced himself and turned toward the middle isle. The Reverend could see through the small crowd of people and sure enough Officer McDaniel's was on his way in a huff with his wife in tow. Mrs.

Cook with Brian in tow was also approaching the front but falling back at the same time to try and hear what was going to be said. Officer McDaniel's asked to have a private discussion in the back office with the Reverend and Mrs. Cook in Private. The Reverend put on a big broad smile and said. "Ralph, they're just children. Our church is about bringing people together of all ages. It's innocent; I have daughters of my own, older than yours who were acting in this same manner at that age"

The Reverend was trying as best he could to quell the situation while letting Officer McDaniel's know that he understood how he felt.

'That won't do Reverend, we need to talk" said Officer McDaniel's with authority in his voice as if he were telling inmates to be seated in the chow hall.

"Ralph I'm going to have to ask you to remember where you are; you are in the Lord's house. I am the authority here and you will be respectful."

"I'm sorry Reverend; I've been under a great strain lately. I've been hearing about this little boy all week and I'm worried about my daughters falling in with the wrong crowd" said Officer McDaniel's in an apologetic tone.

"I understand Ralph; right now both "children" are busy with a cake sale at church. Nothing bad is going to happen here. I guarantee it. Go outside and see for yourself and enjoy some cake in the sunshine with your fellow parishioners."

There was a silence as both men didn't even realize that about twenty five people had listened to the entire exchange and stared angrily at Officer McDaniel's with contempt because he had referred to a ten year old who had done nothing but smile at his daughter as the "wrong crowd". Officer McDaniel's was well aware of this look; he had received it numerous times by inmates, visitors of inmates, neighbors who he had threatened to 'lock up" for blocking his driveway just to name a few.

Officer McDaniel's motioned to his wife to follow him as he swung on his heels and brushed past the Cook's giving each of them a wicked stare, as he headed toward the front exit of the church. Mrs. Cook and the Reverend locked eyes and the Reverend gave a sigh of relief and wiped his head. The Reverend, the Cook's and all who had witnessed the exchange gave a nervous laughter together.

Now that he stepped out of the church in sight of all of his fellow parishioners he was still in Officer Ralph McDaniel's but was closer to Ralph until he was far away from their presence.

Ralph walked out in a huff with Juanita in tow pulling her hard to the point where she was on her toes trying to keep up. Pushing past the crowd as one or two people tried to greet them to no avail. As the two concerned parents made a sharp right turn to the side of the church, Juanita pulled hard on her husband's hand.

"Look at them Ralph, what could possibly be harmful about that?"

They both paused for a moment to watch the children selling slices of cake. All the children involved with the sale where behind the table laughing and giggling with each other and feeling important as their peers came up to the table greeting them with their parents like they were the little rock stars of the church. Although Ralph hated each and every moment of it and each and every person in that church, he couldn't help but enjoy seeing his baby girls laugh and be happy as Juanita said.

"You see baby, this is what it's all about, our babies happy, God has truly blessed us" Ralph bit his lip and mumbled in surrender, "I'll be in the car."

Ralph didn't look over his shoulder as he walked slowly to his white 1987 Nissan Maxima, which was costing him dearly, making him beg his captain constantly for overtime. Ralph was not worried about it being stolen even though he had dropped his full coverage to liability a week after he was granted the loan to buy it because the church was just a half block east of "Big Mack's Deli" which was the headquarters of the King Of Queens, Lorenzo "Fat Cat" Nichols; who had a fleet of the most expensive cars that money could buy. Every car from Rolls Royce's, Bentleys', Ferrari's, Mercedes Benz's, B.M.W's just to name a few where constantly wrapped around the block so his car was an absolute joke in this neighborhood. Ralph rushed to his car because he hated these people, everyone who lived in this neighborhood. He felt as though nothing made sense here, he worked hard and could only get respect by frightening people. Ralph felt as though no one respected his work ethic, or respected the fact that he was a law enforcement Officer. Ralph felt like everyone in this community where fools for giving their money to Reverend Burns who drove a "Big Body 500 Series" Mercedes Benz, and was loved. Drug dealers drove the same cars as movie stars and where idolized in the community where as hard working law abiding citizens where seen as suckers. This made Ralph furious and he was damned if he let his daughters get caught up in it. As Ralph sat in his car he remembered that Gifford and Brian's father was serving a life sentence.

"These little Niggers are going to be drug dealers plain and simple" Ralph mumbled to himself. "And I'll be damned if my babies become their hoes."

Juanita and Walani smiled and spoke cordially to one another while Brian stood by their side on the eastern corner of the triangle across from the church which is Shore Ave, directly across the street from where Ralph was parked. Juanita was as happy of the girls, Ralph figured. "She ain't no different from the rest of these ignorant niggers. Happy to be in this slum," Ralph once again mumbled to himself.

Juanita would look up and waive to Ralph, although her conversation which seemed to last forever to Ralph and finally in what seemed like hours which was nothing more than twenty five minutes. The crowed had dispersed and the girls were left with enough unsold slices of cake to each have one slice to take home, which meant that it had been a very successful cake sale. Then the girls which numbered four plus Gifford realized that there was enough for just one of them to actually have two slices of cake. Chinse proposed like she was holding her own little sermon in front of the girls, the Cook's, the McDaniel's, and the Reverend that the two slices be given to Gifford for working so hard without any prior experience and doing such a good job helping out this fine Sunday. Everyone applauded as Chinse handed the slices to Gifford and kissed him on the cheek. Gifford thought to himself that if there was in fact a God that he had surely smiled on him, because this was indeed that happiest day of his life.

The Cook's waived goodbye to the McDaniel's on the corner of Shore Avenue and Sutphin Boulevard everyone was smiling and happy except Ralph of course who sat sour faced in his car and itching to get out of this neighborhood of the damned as he always referred to it.

The Cooks walked home from church and today was a beautiful day it was around 82 degrees and sunny. In the winter this walk would sometimes be brutal, but not today. The family walked quietly as Gifford ate his cake and Walani and Brian shared the extra slice he was given of the yellow cake with chocolate icing; it was so moist and delicious. They headed east on Shore Avenue; then made a right turn on 154th to 108th Street where the made a left, then another right which took them back on to 154th Street, then onto 109th Ave which was a straight away for a few blocks past P.S. 48. You could see the projects in the distance under the Long Island Railroad tracks.

"What a beautiful day", Walani thought to herself thinking of how proud she would be if Gifford would grow older and be in a serious relationship with Chinse McDaniel's. A real have from Long Island, that would mean he would have a chance at being a real somebody, and maybe just maybe Brian would hook up with Capalitana. The only thing that would make their situation even more fortunate would be Ralph McDaniel's pulling some strings, by making a few phone calls and having her two boys become New York City Correction Officers. The thought made Walani giggle and smile.

"What you laughing at Mama?" Gifford asked, wondering if he had done something silly in all of his unsure actions of the day.

"Nothing baby, I'm just happy; and I haven't been for a long time" replied Walani smiling.

Gifford and Brian smiled at each other and then at their mother, it was a truly a fine day. Gifford thought to himself that he never wanted to wash the spot on his cheek where Chinse had kissed him. He could still smell the Pink Hair lotion that was in her hair.

Usually for outsiders, well outsiders that had any sense once you walked into the "Hole" on 109Th Avenue and 157th Street you put your game face on because things were damned serious. The hole was an open air drug market with no less than 50 drug dealers spread between the four corners and the side of the bodega at all times, along with a black numbers runner and the Dominican numbers runner on the inside in the back of the store; inside the door behind the cookie rack. The Cook's had known everyone and spoke to everyone. Queens differed from the other four boroughs in this respect. In all other borough's envy ruled over all meaning you have to be afraid to let black people see you happy especially, if you are a light skinned black person, because then the people watching would do all they could to wipe that smile off of your yellow face, but not in Queens. In the hole, happiness was smiled upon and encouraged. Everyone especially those in the drug game smiled and waved, even the prostitutes in P.S. 48 who plied their trade on a Sunday morning would smile and wave. So as the Cooks entered into the hole their demeanor didn't have to change. They laughed and smiled all the way throughout the projects to their building and up to their apartment; ending a perfect day.

Every night the whole week Gifford talked to Brian about the "kiss" he had gotten from Chinse that past Sunday, Brian told his classmates and Walani had told her co-workers at Western Beef. The whole family seemed to be on cloud nine. The future seemed so bright all because Gifford had been befriended and ingratiated by the "Haves" of Long Island. Walani even slipped a few steaks in her purse along with some stolen ice cream pops from work to make the meals at home extra special. The boys found themselves preferring to watch "What's Happening" over Good Times so that the subject matter wouldn't kill their moods. Gifford and Brian even found themselves watching the "Brady Bunch" just to get to know how the "rich" people lived. After all they had befriended the McDaniel's, hell the sky was the limit. The McDaniel's household however, was entirely a different story.

"Okay, he's light skin, but that's all that little nigger has!" screamed Ralph, who was incensed at the thought of his little Chinse being impressed by Gifford.

"And you kissed that little project skell! He's a future inmate and believe me he's going to be a little yellow homo. Those niggers in jail know just what to do with mother fuckers like him!" insisted Ralph.

This was just Monday morning after the whole "incident" had occurred. The whole family had to sit at the breakfast table as Ralph had come home from doing a "double" from 1500 hours the night before. Ralph had even called several times during the night to scream at Juanita and chew her ear off about the whole situation.

"Calm down baby, it was only a cake sale, my God it's three in the morning," said Juanita; trying not to kill her own mood because she had Fick on the other line talking dirty to her.

"She ain't going to marry the little yellow nigger, and besides didn't you say all the boyfriends they are ever going to deal with would have to be light skinned because you want your grandchildren to have a fighting chance in this world?" said Juanita, trying to work an angle she knew appealed to Ralph.

"That is true, but I want them to be from a good solid at least working class family," said Ralph in a much calmer voice; at least being happy that Gifford was light skinned.

Juanita knew she was reaching him, and thank God Ralph had nearly blown her damn high and sensitivity. Before Ralph had called she had almost climaxed between all of the dirty talk from Fick and the cocaine she had sniffed thanks to the money from the cake sale.

"Try to get back to work with a clear mind, I got to get these girls out to school in the morning and get to work on some more cakes baby," said Juanita trying to get Ralph off of the phone.

It worked and she clicked back over and Fick was gone. Juanita just laid there and fell asleep.

"At least I still got my buzz," thought Juanita as she drifted off.

The rant went on at the breakfast table as if that whole conversation hadn't happened. Ralph was built something like Officer "Winslow" from the TV show "Family Matters" and people like that always have a problem with hyper tension and high blood pressure so they can never let something that's bothering them go.

Finally it was Sunday morning, Walani thought that maybe she should get her and the boys to church early so that she could have a word with Reverend Burns to make sure that Gifford would be excused to help with the bake sale as he was the Sunday before. Walani even took the measure of "Short changing" customers especially the senior citizens who really didn't know any better on top of stealing from other cashiers registers as they took bathroom breaks to ensure that she could offer extra "tidings"; sort of like a bribe if need be to make sure that Gifford would be able to help out with the cake sale.

Everyone was up early and nervously getting dressed. Walani even put more than the usual amount of hair gel from her $1.99 one gallon jug, which she used ever so sparingly. One could feel the tension in the air as they walked to church. The feeling as if everything should go right, but expecting something to go wrong everything rode on Officer Ralph McDaniel's allowing everything to go smoothly.

As the Cook Family made the right turn from Shore Avenue onto Sutphin Boulevard they saw the White Maxima parked across the triangle. Ralph was sitting behind the wheel looking deadly serious and Juanita and the girls had already crossed the street to go into the church. As Juanita held the door for the girls, Gifford and his family saw that Juanita had a swollen shut left eye and lip. The Cooks paused for a moment as if afraid to walk another step toward the church, but then continued as if they had no choice, as if somehow the three of them had created this whole mess and must see it through; hopefully clean it up with the hope that life could go on the way it was before what happened last week happened. The Cooks silently filed into the church not knowing what they were going to hear or see.

"Reverend Thomas I do want to sell my Cakes I do. I know everyone loves them and my girls love selling them, I just won't be able to let them if you allow Gifford to assist them" Juanita said to Reverend Burns with her voice cracking outside the back office.

"Juanita they are just children, and I can't ostracize a boy because he comes from the projects and his father is serving a life sentence. This is a church and I must show fairness," said the Reverend showing sternness because he saw the Cook family approaching down the hall.

"Is that what this is all about?!"said Walani in disbelief but knowing damn well that was why Ralph had a problem with her son.

Before the Reverend or Juanita could say anything Officer Ralph McDaniel's who had followed the Cooks in the church thundered in his most menacing Correctional Officer in the Rec Yard voice. "Back up off my Wife! Back the FUCK UP! Take those damned kids to the pew and Juanita take the girls to the pew and I'll speak to you two and the Reverend and tell you all how things are going to Motherfucking go around here!"

Everyone stood there in shock because everyone knew how close to being 'Unhinged" Officer Ralph McDaniel's had become, but he had never acted this belligerently.

"Get Moving I said GOD DAMN IT!" thundered Officer McDaniel's again to make sure his orders where clear and understood.

"Look Officer McDaniel's this is a church and my church understand. My name is on the Deed. I am responsible for my parishioners who worship here. It's bad enough your wife's face looks as if she's been in a car accident"

At this point Juanita interjected."No….No Reverend I fell down the stairs, I'm fine it was an accident honest to God."

"Look if that's how it is then that's yawls business understand?" the Reverend said calmly.

"BUT? Walani Cook and her boys are standing here and are now afraid. This Family has done nothing to you Officer Ralph McDaniel's and don't deserve this treatment. I won't allow you to treat them in this manner," the Reverend said with his anger rising.

"Reverend I will apologize to you and that is all. I want to speak to you, my wife and Walani in private" said Officer McDaniel's sounding almost, but not quite apologetic.

"Ralph what is wrong? Is everything alright at work? Do you need private prayer sessions?" asked Reverend Burns, hoping to somehow reach this man who seemed very close to the edge of insanity.

"Reverend Burns, I think it's a bad idea for my daughter and Gifford Cook to interact with each other at all. My girls are good girls who live out on the island. They are Long island girls, with futures, The Cooks are street people. Everyone knows who their father is and what he's done. Their father is a drug dealing murderer, He killed a thirteen year old boy for GOD's SAKE. I don't want them corrupting my girls and dragging them into the gutter and off to prison where they are sure to wind up"

Mrs. Walani Cook was absolutely incensed by such disrespect, and the look of hurt and confusion on her sons faces made her take this to a level even she wasn't sure she was accepting of, but a mothers instinct to protect her young is something more old and primitive than church with no complexity. Thought isn't involved in that equation so she just spoke.

"NIGGER, If ya'll are so hot shit then you wouldn't be selling cakes to begin with! I'll tell you what! Keep your funky little black bitches away from my sons! You hear me nigger!" As she spoke those words Walani couldn't believe they were being yelled from her own, but it was too late now war had officially been declared.

"Okay, okay. Mrs. Cook," pleaded Reverend Burns.

"Let me remind you that you are in the Lord's house and we shouldn't let our emotions get the best of us."

Reverend Burns was sweating because he was afraid that in her state of rage Walani would call out Juanita for the whore that she was and even worse let it be known to her husband that she was also sleeping with Reverend Burns. Juanita was as quiet as a mouse during this entire exchange.

"Do I need to remind you that I'm a New York City Correction Officer, which is like a police officer but works in the jails and can have you arrested" said Officer Ralph McDaniel's in a menacing last warning tone.

"Arrested for what? Nigger PUH-LEEZE!" hissed Walani as she spun on her heels grabbing each of her sons by their hands and leaving the church. Chinse and Capalitana were still sitting at their pew next to the cakes which had been bought in for sale. Gifford looked at Chinse and shrugged his shoulders as Chinse tried as best she could to force a smile; while Gifford was nearly being dragged to the front door. Gifford whispered to his mother:"Mama aren't we staying for services and the cake sale?"

Walani stopped in her tracks and said low but loud enough for others to hear, "Not today Gifford, some things are more important than praising the Lord, and that's being respected. If I ain't being respected somewhere then I'm not staying, not even for the Lord." Walani then took a deep breath and made the next statement loud enough for all to hear: "And we ain't buying their cakes no more either! They taste like Shit anyway!" Walani looked everyone square in their eyes, even her sons before finally exiting the church furiously. Walani decided that it was time to let her sons know a little bit about themselves, where they were from, and about their father. Walani hailed a dollar cab and told the driver to take the three of them to" Carmichael's" Diner on the corner of Foch Boulevard and Guy Brewer where they would have some soul food, hear their story and afterward she would buy all three of them some new sneakers from the Coliseum on 165th Street. Walani figured that that was the best way to spend the money she had stolen from Western beef all week. Her family's spirit was low and to all good black mothers that is a crisis that needs immediate attention. Walani and Brian could tell that Gifford was very sad. Gifford had imagined all week that he might possibly be invited to the McDanaiel's house in Long Island for supper and a ride in Officer Ralph McDaniel's 1987 Maxima; instead they were getting out of a funky dollar cab on Guy R. Brewer Boulevard . For the first time in Gifford's young life he felt poor. What happened next seemed to shock Gifford and Brian. Walani knew not only exactly what he was thinking, but how he was feeling. "This is home Son. Fuck those Bourgeois niggers from Long Island," stated Walani, in a tone that was foreign to both sons. Gifford and Brian had never heard there mother talk like this. As they were being seated in Carmichael's.

"Them little dark Black bitches wish they could get their little funky hands on my light skin sons," said Walani in a flat, cold, cocky voice.

Gifford and Brian looked at each other kind of puzzled. It was the first time their mother had ever mentioned skin complexion. This was also the first time she had sounded "color struck" to them. It was strange to hear her sound so discriminatory because Walani was dark skinned. What Walani was doing was teaching the boys to be proud of whatever they had. To feel better than anyone who was black and had more than them because they were "Light skinned", closer to white, superior. This lesson has been taught to light skinned children since the days of "Willie Lynch". It even let the boys know why their mother had picked their father to be their father.

Walani wanted her sons to be light skinned so that they could have a better chance at life then she did.

"Mama, what's Bourgeois? asked Brian in a curious but cautious voice.

"Oh that's when black people get a little money and think that they are better than all other black people" said Walani with the confidence of a scholar who was reading directly from Webster's dictionary.

"If that's true, then why should we feel better than other black people because we are light skinned?" asked Brian, as if he were on a debate team in Harvard and was about to "Stump" his mother.

"You'll always love me and not feel better than me because you fell out of my ass" sounding foreign and almost "Street" to her sons.

"As far as everyone else; ou are better. You two are just set back right now. We weren't always poor. You were just too young to remember how well to do we were. We lived in Hollis, but it was close to Murdock Avenue. Close enough to be considered Saint Albans. Our address was 188-40 Keeseville Ave, on the corner of Hannible Street who was a great black ruler by the way. Your father was a MIGHTY MAN; fuck what that asshole had to say. You always remain proud to be the sons of Lance Cook. He was a self-taught man who stopped at nothing to get what he wanted; he would have died to take care of us. Lance Cook is spending twenty five years in prison for taking care of us and to make sure you two would have a future. Whatever stood in your father's way, Lance Cook either went through it or found a way around it, which is just what we're going to do. Now Gifford, you like this Chinse right?
There was a pause from little Gifford then: "Yes mommy I do"

"Then we're gonna find a way for you to spend time with her. Don't you worry about how, you leave that to me. Just know that mommy like your father Lance Cook finds a way to get what they or their children want; one way or the other. But first I need to finally tell you about your father and I and how he really got sent away. He didn't kill no thirteen year old boy, it was an accident."

Brian asked sternly, "But was daddy a gangster who sold drugs mommy?"

Walani slanted her eyes to damn near Chinese slits and gritted her teeth and said
No different from CEO's of fortune 500 companies like A Philip Morris who sells cigarettes to children or Anheiser Bush who sells beer, which was once illegal to children at every corner

store, and no more of a gangster than powerful politicians who kill each other constantly for control. That's just how things are done in the grown up world. One day you will understand more. For now, just know that you will see those little chocolate girls very often and real soon.

Walani noticed that she was still loud from being shaken up by earlier events. People in the diner were staring, so she toned it down and began to talk in story telling mode.

Chapter 3

Lance & Walani

Walani Stevens came from a "cultured family in Brooklyn. Her mother was from the Marcy projects. Her father was from the Sumner projects just a few short blocks away. Due to her father being a Jazz musician he was able to earn enough money to move his family to Cambridge place in the Clinton Hill section of Bedford Stuyvesant, where they were able to give Walani a comfortable upbringing.

In 1979 Walani's life changed forever one day when she went with friends to the Jamaica Roller Skating Rink on Jamaica Avenue in Queens. Being of athletic build, statuesque, and dark skinned. She was a sight to say the least wherever she went skating. On this night Walani, Nicole Dash, and Tracy Brooks were as dolled up as much as they could be. All three young "Phillies" wore corn row braids in three different zigzag patterns with red, black, and green beads in them. Each wore a sweat shirt with iron on designs that made them unique. Walani wore a pink sweatshirt she had made just for this occasion with "Brooklyn Gurl" ironed on the front, Capricorn, ironed on one sleeve with the symbol of the zodiac on the other and a big arrow pointed down on her back emphasizing her biggest "asset". She wore Jordache jeans, which were the hottest jeans out at that time and of course her skates, she wore them everywhere even to Clara Barton High School as she rode the bus.

It was Easter Sunday 1979 and the local Queens D.J., Kendu was set to battle Grand Master Flash who had traveled from the Bronx to teach the Queens kid a lesson, but the big draw was the Sugar Hill Gang who was there to perform their new hit single, "Rappers Delight".

On the line to get in Walani sensed something different about Queens people. They didn't seem as grimy as Brooklyn people or as stand offish. They seemed friendly and outgoing. Queens's people didn't seem to be hungry or aggressive, but for some reason they seemed more dangerous. The appearance of very expensive cars riding up to the front of the roller skating rink filled with young black people only made Walani more curious about these 'Queens' people.

When the girls got inside they were taken aback by the size of the crowd in attendance. The place was filled to capacity most certainly violating any fire code that was supposed to be in effect.

"Let's go over to that game room area," said Walani in a huff to Tracy and Nicole.

As Walani leaned up against the Pac Man arcade game, she noticed a small crowd of young men coming down the walkway toward the game room. Everybody seemed to know them, and the even larger crowd surrounding them looked more like security or body guards than friends just hanging out with them. One in particular really caught Walani's attention. This light skinned fellow had crisp 360 waves *(which was an old hair style and not worn in Brooklyn, but was becoming a popular hairstyle in Queens because of an up and coming hustler who was popular, named Kenneth "Supreme" McGriff)*, he wore a red fisherman's Kangol hat with a crease on all four sides, a black mock necked shirt, black pleated pants, and red topped, black bottomed British walkers. This young man also wore something Walani had never seen before. It was a gold chain that looked like a rope and on the end of it like a medallion was a square piece of gold the read "1 oz.", needless to say Walani was more than impressed.

Lance made his way over to Walani an introduced himself, and time seemed to stand still. Walani didn't even see all the faces around him holding the crowd back giving him space to speak to her. It was as if the two of them were all that existed in the skating rink. Walani felt herself being nudged by Tracy, and Nicole to introduce them to some of the people around him. Walani asked: "Do you have friends for my friends?" Lance smiled and tried to give a few names. They were very colorful and unlike names any of the girls had heard before. The names sounded like weights, measures, and tools. All they could grasp were the names like Chico, Kilo, and Cool-Aid. This made them giggle as they heard them, so Lanced just stopped and asked for Walani's number, he then promised to call. Lanced reached for her hand and kissed it as he left with his "ante rage". This was also something that Walani had never experienced before, the Chivalry of Queens Men.

The thick smell of marijuana smoke made Walani choke but it all seemed so exciting. She went round and round counter clockwise on the floor to all of the best skating music "Chic's Cheer, Roll Bounce Rooooccck Skate, for the sake of God" just to name a few. The skaters would go to the middle of the rink to show off their moves they had been practicing all week. At about 11:00 p.m. the M.C. of the club would announce that it was "Couples" only time. Walani frantically looked around for Lance. He was up by the front with around 30 members of the Southeastern Queens Cartel. Walani had thought that because Lance was at the club that Lance was himself a skater. This was never the case in Queens, some men; macho men did in fact skate, but not the most serious of Queens gangsters who had an image to uphold. Walani relented to a well-known skater and staff member named "Wolfie" to skate slowly with. Walani felt almost depressed.

"This would after all be the best time to talk to him and get to know him," Walani thought to herself.

The third time around the rink Walani looked up and saw Lance and his crew at the side of the rink looking intensely at her. "Always and Forever " by the group Heatwave was playing as Walani waved and Lance waved back and signaled with his hand in the shape of a Phone and whispered, "I'll call you."

Walani had a smile on her face for the rest of the night; she had never felt so happy. Out of all the girls who were smiling in Lance's face all night, he had remembered to look for her on the floor. The night for both of them felt magical. Walani grinned all the way back to Brooklyn on the "F" train. Always and Forever would be their song, even until today. Lance grinned all night on the corner of 157Th Street and 109th Ave where he made his money. Lance who was actually twenty eight making him ten years older than Walani was part of the growing and recently independent 'Southeastern Queens Cartel". This crew; had its roots in Harlem where some of them including Lance was from. They worked for the infamous Leroy "Nicky" Barnes and were sent to South Jamaica Queens to expand his empire. The people he sent that were in charge were named "POP Freeman" and "Skinner" who bought younger underlings with them to help recruit local people to work for them and to ensure them that they were about business and helping the locals, not running them over.

In 1978 Nicky Barnes was given life in prison and his empire was left to a man named Gut Fisher, who was a lot younger than Nicky Barnes and didn't warrant as much respect. The crew who had been sent to Queens under Pop Freeman declared their independence and claimed Queens as their own. Guy Fisher did not try and stop it. Guy Fisher had become more concerned with rebuilding the "council" and the Apollo Theater. He saw Queens as a wasteland with no potential.

"So let them have the sticks, " Guy was reported to have said.

In the spring of 1978, Liberty Avenue on the eastern side of the Van Wyck Expressway was the original drug block, in the door ways of the factory buildings. Lance would drive his 1978 Eldorado Cadillac all the way from his building at 605 West 142nd Street, Apartment 23 to the pick-up spot which was a club named "Mr. Uglies" on Linden Boulevard. He would pick up his 'pieces' of dope, go to Liberty Avenue and start selling hand to hand in the doorway of what is now the Van Wyck sports bar.

By the fall of 1978, Lance had become tired of the long commute over the Triboro Bridge every morning. Lance had built quite a clientele by this point. He would have to "re-up" several times during the day at Mr. Uglies, which he didn't like because it telegraphed how much money he was making to the other workers, dope fiends and the police from the 1-0-3 Pct. Who were paid to look the other way, but would ask for more money if they thought you were making more money. One of Lance's customers was an old lady name Mrs. Francine Timms, who had started off taking morphine due to a hip injury; after falling off of the Q3a bus. After a while the morphine wouldn't help and her tolerance had grown. Mrs. Timms' doctor would make her wait for thirty days in between prescriptions as per the law and her little yellow bottle wouldn't last the month. This led Mrs. Timms to self-medicate with heroin, which was a heroin and an opiate derivative as heroin is. Mrs. Timms had become one of Lance's most loyal and favorite customers. Lance needed a "stash spot", a bank of sorts to hold his money and drugs so that he would not have too much cash on him, because he would be in serious peril if he were to get robbed and come up short with Pop Freeman, and not have enough drugs on him which would make him a violator of the Rockefeller Drug Statue which carried mandatory drug sentences with the minimum being twenty years for four ounces or more of heroin.

Mrs. Timms seemed like the perfect answer, she had a project apartment in the South Jamaica Houses, 6 160th Street, Apartment 3C is where she called home. Her rent was a whopping $28 dollars a month and Lance promised to pay it along with her utility bill, groceries and free heroin if she would let him use her apartment as a stash house.

After a while there was competition on Liberty Ave. Lance couldn't call them rivals because everyone fell under Pop Freeman's umbrella in one way or another. The competition was friendly mostly because there was way more demand than supply in the late 1970's. This competition actually complemented Southeastern Queens. When one dealer or group of dealers would run out of heroin or powdered cocaine then another dealer or group of dealers could sell in the same area letting it be known to all of Southeastern Queens, East New York Brooklyn in the West, and Eastward from Nassau & Suffolk Counties that this was the area to come too for drugs. The drugs sold on Liberty Avenue had the best prices and the best quality. It is rumored that they best "batch" of heroin ever sold on Liberty avenue was named "THE HANGER", sold in 1978 by Perry Burns who was a POP Freeman Lieutenant.

Liberty Avenue by 1979 had become a very, very hot spot and the Southeastern Queens Cartel had begun to expand. Pop Freeman and the original suppliers had relented control to certain areas to local that were from Queens with Pop Freeman still being the supplier. This put Lance Cook in a vicarious position. Although Mrs. Timms' apartment was his stash house he himself was not from the South Jamaica Houses. People took offense to him trying to sell his drugs in the park on the inside of the projects on the corner of 159th Street and 107th Avenue. Lance found the ideal location so as not to offend anyone. It was the corner of 109th Avenue and 157th Street right outside the projects with a walkway in on a dead end street. The intersection was perfect for lookouts to be able to warn dealers if any police were coming and there were many avenues for escape if it came down to running from the crime scene for whatever reason.

After a while Lance was making so much money there he invited dealers from the neighborhood who weren't from the projects to enjoy his corner as well. By Easter of 1979 the corner was full of dope fiends around the clock. The corner was making approximately one million dollars a day that was split between about thirty dealers. The corner was christened, the "Hell Hole" by locals who avoided it like the plague and was later shortened to the "Hole" by everyone in Queens New York.

Walani sat by her phone at 42 Cambridge Place all night hoping that Lance would call. She couldn't even concentrate in school for three days. Finally on Thursday Lance called.

"Hey Pretty Girl," said Lance in a raspy voice

"Hey Lance!" answered Walani, who had planned to "Pratt" and play hard to get, but couldn't help herself"

"When can I see you?" asked Lance, cutting right to the chase.

"I go to Clara Barton High School in Crown heights, you know where dats at?" asked Walani, praying that he would agree to pick her up from school. Knowing that if everyone saw her get into that Cadillac that her status and popularity in school would go into outer space

"Yeah I know where that is, why you want me to pick you up from school?" asked Lance like it wouldn't be a big deal.

"If you caaaaan" answered Walani, with the most seductive plea she could make with her voice.

"What time? Whenever it is I will be there," answered Lance like he would make it even if she had said 6:00 a.m.

"I get out at 3:20 p.m., meet me at the front of the school on Ocean Avenue."

"I'll be there tomorrow beautiful, at 3:20 p.m. sharp," answered Lance knowing that Walani could tell that from how much attention he had gotten at the Jamaica Roller Rink, that wherever Lance went he was sure to put on a show, and if it came down to impressing a young lady that he would really pull out all of the stops to make his appearance a spectacle.

"Okay, bye," said Walani giggling knowing she would be on pins and needles until 3:20 p.m. the next day.

At 3:03 p.m. Walani asked for a bathroom pass and went to freshen up for Lance's big arrival outside the school. Walani knew her time was short so she freshened up as fast as she could. On her way back to the classroom she heard a commotion in the hallway. Walani walked pass not paying attention to all the fuss that was being made about some spectacle outside. When Walani entered her classroom she was stunned to see everyone including her teacher looking outside the windows down in front of 901 Classon Avenue. There were four white Cadillac's which gave the appearances of a wedding motorcade. Each car was filled with men of different ages, but all unmistakably gangsters. All of the men stayed inside the cars except Lance who was leaning on the hood of the first car looking at his watch. Lance was dressed in a white Adidas sweat suit with blue stripes, white shell toe Adidas with white and blue laces that were made in design of a checkerboard and untied; with a white Kangol pull over hat. Walani was bought to by her teacher saying: "Who in the world is he here for? I wish it was me," as the whole class laughed.

Walani stood there quietly then went to gather her things. Walani was never one to show off and then the bell rang.

"Make sure you read chapters 26-29" said Walani's teacher as the class emptied out. No one even heard the teacher. Everyone was in a haste to get to Classon Avenue to see who these men where and more importantly, who were they here to see. When Walani exited the building she saw Lance looking at her through the crowd. He began to wave his hand moving people out of the way. Everyone seems to part like the red sea did for Moses, as she walked toward Lance. The crowd fell silent as Lance reach his hand out to her to bring her close and give Walani a slow kiss on the cheek. Lance then opened the door to the front white Cadillac and held it for

Walani to get in. The crowd watched in awe as he two men in the back seat introduced themselves to Walani as Lance jogged around to the driver's side, got in and let the motorcade toward Washington Avenue.

At first Walani was afraid to speak so Lance broke the ice, "You hungry?" he said with a smile.

"No, just glad you didn't stand me up," said Walani nervously trying to show appreciation for the status she was just given at school.

"What would you like to do?" asked Lance letting Walani know that they were officially on a date.

"I like to walk on the promenade, have you ever walked on it?" asked Walani.

"No I haven't, but I want to," answered Lance. Letting her know that he was willing to do whatever she wanted.

Lance then signaled out of his window with his hand for everyone to pull over. The motorcade stopped at Washington Avenue and Eastern Parkway. The two men behind Lance exited the car. Each gave Lance a hug and nodded to Walani. The men got into separate cars in the motorcade. The motorcade made a left onto Eastern Parkway to head toward Queens, Lance and Walani headed northward on Washington Avenue toward Brooklyn Heights and the Promenade.

The two of them strolled along the promenade looking at the Manhattan skyline and felt almost too comfortable together. They both felt like they had known each other their entire lives, but were for the first time about to hold an actual conversation. Each was nervous that they would say something, or hear something that would ruin how they felt or was being felt by the other.

"What kind of school is Clara Barton? I mean is it a regular public high school, or does it specialize in something?" Lance asked to break the ice.

"I had to take a test and be selected to be admitted. It's a school that specializes in nursing. Clara Barton worked at the patent office in 1863 when a train of union soldiers arrived in Washington DC that had been attacked by confederate soldiers. Clara Barton attended to them and was recognized by the President for doing so. Clara Barton was also friends with Frederick Douglas, a civil rights activist and founder of the American branch of the Red Cross," Walani said beaming with pride in her school, her knowledge, and her knowledge of Clara Barton's history.

"Wow, some lady" Lance replied taking a long and hard look at Walani making her look away in shyness.

"It's befitting that you attend that school, I see you and her share some traits," Lance said with confidence.

"Oh how so?" said Walani curiously.

"You can already tell my heart needs tending too," said Lance with a big broad smile. Walani placed her hand in Lance's and pulled herself close.

"What about all those girls I saw trying to get your attention at the roller rink, I'm sure they could tend to your heart," Walani said, while already displaying jealousy before the relationship could get started.

"None of them attend Clara Barton High School, nor tell me about Clara Barton. That's the kind of woman I need," replied Lance while letting Walani know that he placed a lot of value on people with brains.

Walani and Lance took a seat on a bench in front of the playground on the promenade and talked until the sun went down. Lance then drove Walani back to Cambridge Place and kissed her on the cheek. He gave her his phone number and a number where he could be reached or to leave a message twenty four hours a day. The number was 1-718-454-8271 was a special number to Walani. Lance kissed her on the cheek once again and watched her walk inside, before pulling off in his white Cadillac.

When Lance arrived back at the "Hole" his good friend Pearl informed him that Mrs. Timms was looking for him and that she seemed to be stressed out.

"She must be feigning," Lance said coldly.

"Naw man, seems like something was really wrong" Pearl said with a tone of concern.

Lance decided he should pay Mrs. Timms a visit so he drove around the projects from the Linden Boulevard approach and parked in front of 6 160th Street, after all his stash was inside. If Mrs. Timms was feigning then it wouldn't be a good idea to have her responsible for his money and dope, and besides he had given her more than enough earlier in the day to hold her for the next two days if need be.

"Lance! my sister died in Soperton, Georgia. Oh God! I got to go down home and see her off. I ain't got the money to go, please Lance help me go see my sister off!" she begged.

"Okay, I'll help you but with you gone I legally don't have the right to be here. If I give you the money, I need you to put my name on the lease so that I have the right to be in your apartment," said lance as Mrs. Timms sat silently with tears rolling down her cheeks.

"Okay baby, whatever you say. Thank God for you Lance. I prayed this morning that you would help me. I also prayed that you would come to church with me and meet my Reverend, Reverend Burns. The Reverend is a good man and understands people from all walks of life, he could really help you Lance. Would you please escort an old woman to church this Sunday, and then to the Greyhound station to see me off?"

"Sure Mrs. Timms I can do that," answered Lance with a heavy heart. Lance had always hated church.

Lance then gave Mrs. Timms a 'dime' and told her to get some sleep. Lance went home to Harlem after the long and eventful day that turned out to be more fruitful than he had planned. Of Course Pearl had made a ton of money, but Lane had also acquired a new girlfriend and an apartment to boot. Things seemed to be alright in Lance's world.

The next day Lance picked up Mrs. Timms at 8:00 a.m., Pop Freeman had taught everyone in Queens to do their most 'heavy" business early in the morning especially as cops were changing tours. The "B" squad or day tour starts at 0700 hours and ends at 1535 hours. The "A" squad gets off at 0735 hours so that the tours overlap never leaving the streets unprotected was the reason the tours where designed this way. However it doesn't work when the midnight tour always heads in early to do paperwork which is referred to as 10-62 at the "A" station house assignment, and the "B" squad ends Muster and heads out to get food for themselves and all at the station house. With this being the way it is to this day, all real movement of narcotics are done between 8:00 a.m. and 10:00 a.m. because there are no police and no conditions or split tour Police on the street. Lance knew that with Mrs. Timms along for the ride it gave him even more protection from prying eyes within law enforcement.

As Lance helped Mrs. Timms in the car he said: "We gotta make a little stop before we go to the housing office, it won't take long."

"Okay baby, I ain't in no rush, I just been praying and crying all night. By the way can you give me a little something to get me "Started" this morning? I'm in such pain" said Mrs. Timms in a begging voice.

"Sure Mrs. Timms, no problem," Lance said as he dug into his pocket and pulled out a whole gram wrapped neatly in a one hundred dollar bill. Since today was the day that Mrs. Timms was legally making him part owner of the apartment Lance thought that he ought to be generous with Mrs. Timms medicine.

"What up "HEAD!" Lance said to a friend as he exited his car at the "Hole". Lance went around to his trunk and lifted up a beach cooler, placed it on the ground lifting a handle up and rolled the cooler to another car. The Mark VII Lincoln Continental popped its trunk and the owner got out and hugged Lance. It was his cousin Leon from Chicago.

"How was the trip from Chi-Town?" asked Lance.

"It was good Cuzzin, longer than usual, but peaceful. The longest part was Pennsylvania. no scenery"

"Well I'm glad you're here on time" Lance said, as both men looked inside the cooler, then at each other. Afterwards Leon put the cooler in his trunk, he dipped his finger into one of the kilos then he and Lance sat inside of the Lincoln Mark VII. First Leon held his finger to his wide open mouth and inhaled letting in much more air than a person normally would to bring a sense of bitterness to the back of his tongue. The more bitter that taste. The better the dope!

"Good shit Cuzzin, always the best from my main man Lance," said Leon with a big broad smile.

"Glad to hear that Cuzzin, I hope the good people of "Woodlawn" appreciate it," Lance said smiling back.

Leon then put a big brown paper bag on his lap. He began counting off one hundred dollar bills then handing the stack as it reached a thousand over to lance who then in turn re-counted it. This process takes some time, but is standard to all drug dealers. Since they were at the "Hole" which was Lance's territory and the police were in between tours there was no rush. After the final count of fifty thousand dollars was reached for the two kilos of heroin, the cousins hugged and went their separate ways. As Lance entered his own car he found Mrs. Timms nodded out with white powder on her nose. Lance just started the car and made his way to 11645 Guy R. Brewer Boulevard, the housing authority office for Southeastern Queens, in the Baisley

Park Houses. Mrs. Timms nodded and bobbed and weaved the whole time they waited to be called and when they were Mrs. Timms spoke with a slur to her case worker.

"This here is my nephew Lance Cook; Imma put him on my lease. He's gonna be staying with me and helping me out"

The case worker looked over to Lance who just smiled and shrugged. The case worker was of course no stranger to such dealings and usually would demand a bribe to allow this to happen, but this was open and shut. Mrs. Timms had lived at 6 160th street since 1950, and knew people in the church, who knew powerful people in the community like Reverend Burns and Reverend Flake. So Lance Cook was simply allowed to add his name on the lease making him a legal tenant and heir apparent to the apartment. Lance held Mrs. Timms up and half carried her back to the car.

Walani was all the rage at her school ever since Lance had showed up to meet her. Even the teacher seemed a bit jealous. All of the girls asked Walani how the two had met? Was he from the Legrand family? What did he do to warrant so much protection just to go to a Brooklyn High School?

Walani didn't know the answers herself to most of the questions so she mostly shrugged off the questions, and gave off the impression that it might be dangerous for someone to know the answers to these questions. In short she loved it. The mystique of it all really appealed to Walani. She also felt, if Lance did come back he should do it alone and not make such a spectacle. Walani was a low keyed person who didn't like too much attention, but liked that people would now know that she was to be taken seriously, in short feared. In their nightly conversations from the pay phone at the "Hole" to Walani after homework Lance convince Walani to attend church that Sunday in Queens with Mrs. Timms. Lance thought that he might be able to meet Walani's parents and what better circumstance could there be then taking her to church. Walani had attended Church before but was no regular by any means. Her last experience was attending Girl Scout meetings at the Apostle Church at 245 Lafayette Avenue. Walani told her parents who gave their blessing and looked forward to Lance picking her up Sunday morning.

"How old are you?" asked Mrs. Stevens when she opened the door for Lance. She looked alarmed by his White Cadillac and expensive suit as he stood in her doorway.

"I'm twenty eight ma'am," answered Lance with confidence as if his age shouldn't be an issue.

"Do you know my daughter is eighteen and plans to go away to Lincoln University in Oxford, Pennsylvania in the fall?"

"I do ma'am and I hope she does well. I am very much interested in her and by no means want to stop her from achieving great things, academic or otherwise," answered lance to Mrs. Stevens rolling her eyes.

"Come in I'll let you meet her father." said Mrs. Stevens coldly as if Mr. Stevens would cut into this young buck and knock his cockiness down to size in short order.

"So this is the fellow my little girl has been on the phone all week with, and interested in taking her to church?" said Mr. Stevens. He impressed with the innocence of church as a first date.

"I see no harm in that," said Mr. Stevens smiling.

"Do you know he is twenty eight years old, and drives a car that costs damn near as much as this house?" asked Mrs. Stevens nearly pissed by this point.

"Well I'm seven years older than you darling and don't see that much of a difference" said Mr. Stevens looking at lance and winking,

"Besides church will do Walani some good, I loved church as a kid. It gives you direction and character. I've been trying to get the Mrs. to go for years. To no avail as you can imagine. Do you promise to bring her straight home Lance?"

"I sure will Sir. That is a promise" he said with a broad smile.

"Then you have our blessing" answered Mr. Stevens.

Mr. Stevens was impressed by a young Man who was obviously successful and interested in church. Mr. Stevens was also aware that Walani was smitten with Lance and if all she got out of the date was exposure to church then that was fine with him. Walani then walked over to Lance and stood in front of him as if to be inspected hoping to pass. She was wearing a pink one piece dress that hung off of her shoulders, black plain flats and her hair was neatly done with a curling iron "Tommy Boy" style with no ends meaning she closed the curling iron and ran it over the top of her head to smooth everything out. Walani's outfit and hair really went nice with her shiny dark skin. That really appealed to lance as it does most light skin black men.

"Are we ready to go to Church?" asked Walani, while smiling at Lance to break his hypnotic stare at her.

"Oh yes Walani, It was nice meeting you both Mr. and Mrs. Stevens," said lance almost embarrassed as he gave Mr. Stevens a firm handshake.

As the White Cadillac pulled up in front of 6 West 160th Street, Walani wondered what in the hell they were doing there.

"Oh, I promised my Aunt Francine that you and I would escort her to church this morning. Aunt Francine made me promise her. I thought the three of us would go then have some really good soul food at Carmichael's," said Lance almost apologetic, hoping that Walani didn't mind.

"Oh that's fine," she said; trying to hide her disappointment, bad enough this was a first official date, and now this old lady was along for the ride.

Both went upstairs and met with Mrs. Timms. Who was rushing them back toward the stairs.

"Come on youngins', we gonna be late, Lance be a doll and grab my bags."
Lance turned a and grabbed two little suitcases as Walani held Mrs. Timms arm and lead her down the stairs. On the way down Linden Boulevard Mrs. Timms began to speak.
"I can't wait to get to Georgia to see my people; I hope ya'll enjoy the place while I'm gone"
Walani looked over to Lance and smiled. She realized that she was part of some con, and just decided to play along. The three sat in church and really enjoyed the service. The Reverend had them stand and introduce themselves to the congregation. Lance made sure Walani saw him put a twenty dollar bill each time the basket went around and put a one hundred dollar bill for the sacrificial offering which allowed Lance and Walani go up to the front and have Reverend Burns put his hand on his head and slightly push it back. When the Reverend did this to everyone else on line they began to drop to the ground with the "Holy Ghost" roll around and scream "Thank you JESUS", but not Lance and Walani they just nodded to everyone as they smiled and make their way back to the pew where Mrs. Timms was holding her hand in the air with her eyes closing quietly "Testifying".

As the service ended Mrs. Timms grabbed lances hand and instructed him to stay seated because she had a surprise for him. Lance just sat stone faced wondering what this could be about. After all the pews emptied out Reverend Burns approached the three of them sitting in the pew.

"So this is the lovely couple you were telling me about?" said the reverend inquisitively. Mrs. Timms went on telling the Reverend about how she had a sick sister down in Soperton and that her nephew Lance and his wife were going to be at her place. Then she got kind of serious. Mrs. Timms let the Reverend know without telling him what Lance did for a living. Mrs. Timms also let Lance know that the church was having problems with a local drug dealer named "Reality". At this point Lance got the reason he was at church and because he was getting an apartment. Mrs. Timms wanted a favor in return, which was to ward off harassment from this character named Reality. The Reverend went on and on about how Reality was terrorizing everyone as they left the church, begging for money and sometimes taking it from parishioners. Reverend Burns had even tried to talk to the people at "Big Mack's" Deli on the corner, but no one would listen.

"I think I know this Reality character," said Lance assuring them.

"I think he also has a twin brother? I'll take care of it Reverend. Don't worry," Lance said as to assure them.

"PRAISE GOD!" I asked for his Holy Blessing today, and he it came in the form of You Son.......PRAISE THE LORD!" screamed Reverend Burns.

Walani sat there beaming and proud that she was accompanying a man who was so powerful that even a Reverend who drove a brand new Cadillac came to for a favor. Lance looked down his shoulder to Mrs. Timms who held his arm and winked. Mrs. Timms winked back and both understood that to get you must give.

Lance, Walani, and Mrs. Timms then had the best soul food Queens could offer. They ate at a reserved table in the back room of Carmichaels'. The room hat was only opened on special occasions. Lance had turkey wings, collard greens, and macaroni and cheese; Walani had the B.B.Q chicken, collard greens with candy yam juice on top, and macaroni and cheese, and Mrs. Timms had hog maws, collard greens, and macaroni and cheese. They all had Carmichael's famous warmed sweet potato pie with cool whip on top for desert. Lance made sure that Walani saw him tip the waiter a fifty dollar bill. Walani was very impressed. After the meal they all laughed all the way to Kennedy Airport where they waived Mrs. Timms as she went up the escalator.

Later that night after Walani was returned home and was doing her homework for Sunday. Lance drove to Harlem and collected a few belongings to move into Mrs. Timms apartment. When Lance was settled in he phoned his friend Cornbread and got the lowdown on Reality and his twin brother. Cornbread informed him that they lived in circle three of Rochdale Village and was associated with a heavyweight named "Himey".

"Reality has a three bedroom apartment in Building 10 Section C Apartment 13C, that he had inherited from his mother. Both brothers lived there. They had once been pretty successful base dealers, but had gotten strung out on their own drugs. Now they robbed people to maintain their habits. All they had left was a van that they sometimes slept in within circle three. I can introduce you to a friend of mine named Derek who lives in Building 11 he can get you access to this guy," said Cornbread in a deadly tone.

"Let's make it happen," said Lance in a cold tone.

Lance pulled into circle three and parked on the ramp alongside Building 10. Waiting in the lobby was Derek. Derek pointed for Lance to walk around to the side door because there were cameras hooked up in the lobby and if anyone tuned in to channel three on their televisions and God forbid taped it; it would show who came and had left the building. On the long walk to Section C, which was a long walk neither man said anything. Once on the elevator Lance mentioned that Derek could be his little brother. Derek then began to talk.

"I've known Reality for a long time. He's not the Reality he was. His brother will be back soon. I sent him to get me a veggie patty from the small mall, we don't have much time. Straight down the corridor inside the apartment is a terrace. I'm going to knock on the door and run past him to the terrace saying I have to show him something and that there's an emergency. Then you will follow and through him off the terrace, just make sure you don't grab me by accident……..adding the last part as a cautious after thought." Lance nodded and Derek nodded back.

Frantically Derek slammed his fist on the door screaming "YO REALITY…..YOOOOOO!" in seconds Reality opened the door. Just as according to plan Derek went flying past him down the corridor with Reality in hot pursuit. "What the Fuck Nigga? What the fuck is going down!" Reality screamed as he ran behind Derek. "LOOK! Your brothers been shot!" screamed Derek.

As Reality looked over the side Derek lowered his pointed finger even lower than it had been originally pointed to get Reality to look further over the side of the terrace. Reality noticed that his finger had changed direction and looked up at Derek curiously. At this point Lance came from behind like a linebacker sacking a quarterback and grabbed Reality as if to bodyslam him W.W.F. style, but bas he lifted Reality grabbed Derek's left arm then the sleeve as Derek's arm slipped away.

"What the Fuck "D"? You'd do me like this?" begged Reality.

Derek struggled to get his arm loose.

"This came from up top Nigga…..you done fucked up!" screamed Derek frantically freeing his arm. Lance with tremendous force flung Reality over the side and grabbed Derek's waist to keep him from going over. Lance's grip slipped to his knees while it appeared that the three of them might go over the side. With all the screaming going on Lance figured he had to silence this in any way that he could. At which point Lance reached to the small of his back and pulled out a black 38 special that he had gotten from a correction officer who had developed a drug habit. He reached past Derek and shot Reality in his right arm making him let go of Derek. Both watched as Reality fell all the way down. People who had watched the struggle were shocked as were Derek and Lance to watch Reality bounce about two stories back into the air before landing. Miraculously Reality jumped to his feet and ran past the crowed who just stood in shock as he ran diagonally toward the Rochdale Power Plant where he collapsed and died. Derek and Lance then scrambled to get out of apartment 13 C as fast as they could with Lance attempting to wipe anything that might have his prints on it off with a rag from his jacket. Both Men then ran down the stairs and out the side door to his car parked in the ramp of Building 10.

Someone screamed out, "Derek! What the fuck is the deal My Nigger?!"

Derek just screamed back, "Not my problem! Got to Run!"

Both Men screeched off, up Bedell Street and made a right turn so hard one could hear the tires screech for blocks. When they arrived at Reality's body, only a few people where standing around. Derek immediately recognized a brother of his good friend was standing there.

Lance said: "Is that one of the Cherry Brothers?"

"Yes it is" answered Derek confused

"Tell him to tell them that there's a big shootout going on in Circle three" said Lance in a calm tone.

"YO Niggas is shootin' up circle three Yo!"

As Derek said that the small crowd went running down 130th Street. At which point lance pulled out two guns.

"If you want to live nigger you better make sure he's dead," Lance said holding a 357 magnum. Lance placed the 38 special into Derek's hand. That same gun had already shot Reality. Derek didn't waste time, he was aware that time was very short at this point. Derek just leaned over and pumped two bullets into the chest of the already apparently dead Reality. This was not just to make sure that Reality was dead, but to make sure that Derek would stay quiet, and it worked. Both men ran back to the car. The car drove smoothly toward the small mall "Man, you ain't got to worry about me. Cornbread and Himey will vouch for me. I'm good" Derek said assuring lance that all would be cool.

'I know "D" everything is cool.......where's the small mall?"

"Oh I almost forgot!" said Derek as he instantly started giving directions. As the car pulled into the parking lot Derek saw another friend named 'Poppy"

"Where's Born?" asked Derek in a hastily tone as he jumped out of the car

"Oh that Nigga said you would be looking for him. He done copped a dime with that money you gave him for the veggie patty. I think he headed toward Baisley Pond. Born had the Van parked there since earlier, they ran out of gas." Poppy said to Lance as Lance jumped back in the car once again screeching off. As the car turned onto Baisley Boulevard Derek heard people screaming across the parking lot that Reality was dead, this made him nervous. Numerous people would know that he was in fact somehow connected to all of this mayhem. Lance was calm, deadly calm as he drove with murderous intent toward Baisley Pond.

The car came to a stop on the side of August Martin High School which was directly across the street from Baisley Pond.

"Is that the van parked facing the water?" Lance asked looking through his rear view mirror. Derek sat quietly and nodded his head.

"That nigger don't know me so I'm gonna go into the park. If he's in the van I'll motion across the street to you to come get his attention. At no time to you look in my direction. understand?"

Once again Derek just nodded not even looking in Lance's direction. Lance then exited the car and disappeared into the darkness near the water. Derek then walked up to the van and knocked on the door.

"Born you in there nigger?" screamed Derek

"Hold on!" Born screamed, back at which point he jumped out trying to explain him-self. "You ain't gonna believe what happened man, I was on my way to buy your veggie patty when I heard that you was in some kind of trouble. I ran toward the buildings when I saw the cops I then ran......."

At that point a very loud gunshot went off and Born's lifeless body fell to the ground. Derek stood there almost in shock. His ears were ringing kind of like the sound of when the national anthem would play at 2:00 a.m. and the T.V. would go off and all you saw were the rainbow stripes on the screen. Derek was frozen he could tell Lance was talking but he couldn't hear anything but that sound "OOOHHHHHHHH". Everyone who's ever heard a gun go off at point blank range knows that sound. Since Born was shot in the side of his head some of the blood sprinkled on to Derek's face. Lance once again was talking.

"Come on little Nigger help me!"

Derek just stood there motionless. Lance then grabbed Derek's arm and lead him across the street and sat him in the back seat and laid him on his side. When Lance was sure that no cops were responding from the 1-13 Precinct, he trotted back across the street. Lance grabbed Born by his shoulder and dragged him back up into the van. Born had a "Scooby Doo" kind of van with a raised bed in the back. As Lance tried to lay Born on the Bed a girl jumped up from under the covers.

"Please Mr. Please. I ain't seen nuffin!"

As the girl begged lance in a smooth motion bought the 357 from his waistband and shot her point blank in between the eyes. Lance then laid Born next to the girl who was bleeding out all over the covers. Lance the peaked his head out of the van and was thankful that no other cars were in the parking lot which was a known 'Lovers Lane' he also knew that it was getting late and would soon be. Lance then grabbed a rag that was on the floor and wiped any place his hands had touched as fast as he could then walk back across the street. Derek was still lying in the back seat in shock. Lance slid behind the wheel and rolled off toward Rockaway Boulevard and made a left toward the Van Wyck expressway.

"You okay, little fella?" Lance asked in a jovial tone.

Derek sat up and nodded like someone waking up from a long night sleep.

I 'ma put you up in the Jade East Hotel. I'll give you something for your trouble. You can't go back to Rochdale tonight. They'll be cops everywhere, okay?"

Once again Derek just nodded. It was clear to him that Lance was no amateur and meant business. Derek was just glad that Lance didn't kill him.

Lance drove the car onto the Van Wyck Expressway headed north and then made a U-turn on Liberty Avenue, got back on and exited onto the Belt Parkway headed east. When he pulled into the Jade East parking lot; he pulled out 10 one hundred dollar bills and handed them to Lance and told him to wipe his face off and sit in the car. Lance then went into the lobby and paid 'Linda' in cash for a room. Lance then came out and handed the key to Derek.

"Stay there until check out tomorrow, understand?" Once again Derek just nodded.

"You did well. I'll put in a good word for you with Himey. Stay cool "D"

Once again Derek just nodded and walked off toward his room.

Lance on the other hand was too smart to assume that it was all over. No one could know for sure if there were or weren't witnesses or if anyone was or wasn't talking to police. In Queens, New York this kind of recognizance is always protocol after a multiple murder shoot out, or sloppy hit job is done if for no other reason to kill anyone else who might become a threat.

As Lance pulled up to the "Hole" everyone was talking about what had happened in Rochdale.

"Rochdale's on fire YO! I heard Born got high and jumped out the window! Ain't nobody seen Born, niggers is wondering if he pushed him or some shit"

A man was heard talking loudly. Lance began to relax. It was always better when the story was far-fetched and was no way near what really happened. What made Lance even more comfortable was that he had no connections to Reality or Born. Hits are always better when the work is fanned out to non-connected people with no motive.

Lance then called Cornbread from a pay phone and thanked him. Who in turn thanked Himey. Himey wanted the apartment because it was a known drug location that made a lot of money before Reality and Born had lost their way. Himey and Cornbread then put a young

dealer named Eric Fickland or "Fick" into the apartment to start selling weed, coke, heroin, and base. The money that was made in that apartment in Rochdale is legendary To this day.
Lance feeling secure retired to Mrs. Timms apartment, took a shower, and then went to sleep.
The next day after picking up some weight from Mr. Uglies Lance drove by the Jade East Hotel to see what time Derek had checked out. Linda was very pleasant and helpful to anyone in the hustling game and made more money for doing gangsters favors than anything else.

"The police came by and asked if anyone checked in after 11:00 p.m. I told them no and that your friends room was vacant. They just left after that and your friend left at noon." Linda said with a big smile. Knowing full well that the two of them had something to do with the two deaths the night before, she knew she was getting a big tip. At this instant Lance pulled out three one hundred dollar bills and handed them to her.

"Thank you Lance" Linda said with a big smile and a hint of flirt.

Lance then drove past August Martin High School and saw the van with yellow tape around it with a small crowd gathered pointing and talking. Lance figured he would stand in the crowd and see what the cops knew and what the people were saying. Lance was pleased to hear all kinds of tales that couldn't be further from the truth. Lance was also glad that the cops were talking openly to each other in front of people as if the case was closed.
"Looks like her boyfriend caught them in the act, and enacted some justice of his own," one plain clothes Detective said out loud.

Lance breathed a sigh of relief and walked off. As he pulled up to the Hole everything was running smoothly, Pearl, John, were standing on the Southwestern corner with their hands moving a mile a minute collecting money in exchange for drugs that appeared to come out of their sleeves into their hands to disappear into the junkies hands. Hollywood lounged on a beach chair with a cooler filled with bottles of wine and vodka. Selling drugs from an inclined position, Lance just smiled and didn't care. Money was being made and everything seemed to be falling into place. Lance decided to check on Walani to see how his pretty little "Chocolate Princess" was doing. Lance figured he had put on enough of a show to impress her friends so this time he would just go by Clara Barton alone. It felt good to feel as though the future held so much promise. "Mary Jane" by Rick James played on his 8-track while he drove north bound on the Interboro Parkway on his way to Clara Barton High School. This time he would even park the white a block away and wait for her on Classon Avenue on foot.

As Walani walked out of school Lance couldn't help but imagine her out of her clothes. Walani was a beautiful girl. Her Afro-Puffs went perfectly with her round chocolate face. Her shirt was folded into a knot at her stomach above her belly button exposing her washboard stomach and her jeans fit her low-rider style showing the top of her waste and thigh's. This site was almost too much for lance who tried not to stare too hard.

"I was hoping I would see you today" said Walani with a big broad smile exposing her beautiful white teeth.

"I'll come every day I'm able to. That's a promise," Lance said smiling back.

The two walked off holding hands for the first time which made both of their hearts pound in their chests. At that moment Lance felt as though he loved Walani. He had to possess her at all costs, and was ready to die if need to be or any harm threatened to come her way. At the car Lance held the door for her which made Walani blush. As they drove off she placed her head on Lance's shoulders and looked up into his face with dove like eyes and ran her fingers along his eyebrows and whispered.

"I missed you" Lance replied

'I missed you too," Walani then reminded him to keep his eyes on the road before he killed them both. As the two of them laughed, Lance asked Walani if she would like to go to church again this Sunday.

"I think my parents would like that very much. I'm no real fan of it though" said Walani flatly.

"Maybe just a few more times so that your parents will feel comfortable about us, I don't think your mother likes me and as long as church is in the equation we have your fathers blessing. We could even cut out early, what you think?" asked Lance.

Walani just smiled and nodded liking the fact that Lance was showing his ability to read people and manipulate situations. The two of them walked again on the promenade and this time at the end by the park Walani pulled Lance close and gave him a long deep kiss. The two of them were in their own world. There could have been a tornado touching down and neither of them would have noticed. Lance made sure to get Walani home no later than 7:00 p.m. as Walani walked inside Lance waved at Mrs. Stevens who just rolled her eyes and slammed the door in his face. Lance just silently walked back to his car.

The week went by smoothly with Lance making his mark everyday like clockwork. The three workers he employed were allowed to close shop each day when their pieces ran out. Each man was handed what they would be selling at 8:00 a.m. at the Hole. Dope fiends need a fix to start the day very early so it was best for the dealers to get out early as well. A "bundle" was a decagram which is 10 grams. Each gram cost $50.00 a piece if that's what someone was buying they would see Hollywood who sold "Grams". Hollywood would be in possession of 5 "Bundles". Pearl and John sold 'Dimes" which were a tenth of a gram for $10.00 dollars and sold in glassine envelopes whereas grams were sold in a 'Chiclet" box. Pearl and John were both also in possession of 50 grams, if someone where buying dimes it made the gram worth $100.00 instead of a wholesale $50.00. After Hollywood sold his five bundles he would be in possession of $1,500. Pearl and John would be in possession of $3,000.00 after each man sold their respective 50 grams a piece. This would bring the days total to $7,500.00. Each man would be paid $500.00 for a day's work which was good pay in 1979. Lances' cut was $6,000.00 a day.

Lance paid Pop Freeman $20.00 a gram. Lance purchased 150 grams at a time for $3,000.00. So it would appear that he was only doubling his money. Since Pop Freemans dope was almost pure Lance cut it 4 times with either quinine or bonita. Everyone else in queens was cutting their dope 8 times. This meant that lance had the best 'package" around with it only being cut 4 times. It meant he made less money, but had more customers. This also meant his workers would sell out the fastest and be off of the street limiting Police exposure. Since he would 'Step" on it 4 times he would only have to "Re-up" every four days and his profit was quadrupled. Lance would pay $3,000.00. Make $6,000.00 a day for three days and on the fourth he would re-up spending $3,000.00 and only making $3,000.00 on that fourth day. In short he would spend $3,000.00 and after expenses make $21,000.00 dollars every four days. Lane needed Mrs. Timms apartment to stash his drugs and money. Lance was aware that his workers who lived in the projects were aware of his intake of cash and needed to not place all of his eggs in one basket. Lance figured he would try to settle this problem this Sunday with reverend burns.

Sunday Morning was a rainy one. Lance arrived on time and this time had flowers for Mrs. Stevens, who hesitantly accepted them. Mr. Stevens was even more jovial than the week before. Lance noticed that Walani was wearing the exact same outfit as the week before. As beautiful as she looked, he really didn't mind, but made a mental note to make sure that Walani never needed for clothes again as long as he had something to do with her. The two of them took off and parked immediately around the corner on gates and Green and tongue kissed for a long an feverish 15 minutes. Lance could tell it wouldn't be long before they would become intimate. Walani was really opening up to him.

Lance and Walani sat in the exact pew where Mrs. Timms had sat with them the week before. Lance remembered that she would be returning that Wednesday and to pick her up at "J.F.K. at 4.00 p.m. at Gate 17. Lance had never actually listened to a Reverend preach before but today as he sat with Walani he really enjoyed Psalm 37. Lance felt as though it was chosen just for him. Because of this he was extra generous with his tidings and at the sacrificial offering he let Walani see him give a $100.00 dollar bill, it also occurred to Lance that Walani had never asked him for a dime, which is something that all Hustlers take note of and appreciate in a woman.

After the service, Lance asked to have a word in private in the back office with Reverend Burns. "I need help Reverend?" asked Lance.

"Whatever makes your heart heavy my dear child the lord had led you this way for guidance"

Lance began: "I need a letter from you to file for a tax return. I need you to say that I give a donation of $300.00 a week which would come out to 20% of my annual income from my dry cleaners on 135th Street in Harlem. I also need you to find someone who is renting out a garage. I need to keep my classic car in a safe place where it won't get rained on, preferably an old lady who never leaves home where she could keep an eye on my car." Lance waited patiently for answer.

"Neither will be a problem my young man, I can tell you are gonna be just fine here in the church............Just fine. Just leave me with a number where I can reach you in case I hear something immediately for the time being your car can be kept right here. There's a garage around the corner with a lock on the front. I'll speak to the people in Big Mack's Deli and ask if they can keep an eye on your car for you. Those young men owe me a favor and your car will be fine" said the Reverend with a hint of sinister in his voice.

"Here take mine as well, that's my home number you can call twenty four hours a day if need be. I really appreciate the donations you have made to the church. I thanked the Lord last night for Mrs. Timms bringing you to our church, the church need more young men such as yourself. Next week I'm going to ask you to join our church in front of the entire parish. If you accept just come forth and be recognized. The Baptism will take place after the service in our basement" Lance just rose and shook the reverends hand and nodded his head. "Thank you Reverend, Thank you"

Walani was outside talking to another young woman who was introducing her to other members of the church.

"I think I like it here" said Walani to Lance as they walked toward the car.

"Let's go shopping," said Lance, abruptly.

"I want you to have the finest of things Walani. I love your outfit, and I also love you. I want you to have the finest of everything".

Walani stopped and looked deeply into Lance's eyes.

"I Love you too."

The two hugged and kissed being mindful that they were still in eyeshot of anyone outside of the church.

It was Walani's first time at Green Acres Mall. Coming from Brooklyn all she had known was Downtown Brooklyn, Delany/Orchard Street, and Kings Plaza on Flatbush Avenue when it came to buying clothes. Walani had never even heard of "Cinnabun". Lance let her buy whatever she wanted with reckless abandon. The two had to bring numerous bags back to the Cadillac numerous times. Lance urged her to keep shopping each time she bought something. Walani asked numerous times if she should stop and Lance would just encourage her to keep going. This was totally new to Walani, she was blown away. When it was all said and done Walani had bought 20 pairs of jeans. Everything from Jordache, Sasoon, to Calvin Klein, 30 tops all kinds of sweaters, pullovers, tube tops, 5 pairs of sneakers; and 6 pairs of shoes, 3 bags of under garments and lingerie were bought from Victoria secrets to top it off. Afterwards the two ate at Red Lobster which was also a first for Walani because Brooklyn had no such place. Then they watched the "Black Hole" at Sunrise Movie Theater.

By the time the movie let out it was 8:00 p.m. Walani knew she couldn't bring these entire packages home, her mother would never allow it. Lance told her that she could leave them over Mrs. Timms house and that he would bring her there as she needed even during a school day if need be to retrieve any and all of them as she pleased. As they dropped them off at Mrs. Timms apartment Walani said, "I got a little time. I want to try on some things. You want to see a show?" Lance salivated at the mere thought of it.

"Okay." said lance in a deep hungry voice.

Walani took some of the bags into Mrs. Timms bedroom and tried on some jeans and a top.

"Very nice, beautiful" said lance as she walked out and paraded outfit after outfit. Walani really was beautiful and it was really quite some show. Walani decided it was time to really surprise him and this time she put on a Victoria secrets Panty and top and walked out. Lance was stunned and sat there silently. Walani walked over to the couch and sat on his lap and whispered in his ear.

"Thank you Lance"

Lance sat there quietly. With the life he led he was without a doubt a cold blooded killer, and a hardened criminal. However he was a lonely man who shared his thoughts with no one. Walani made him feel as though he could trust her, as if he could confide with her. These emotions he had been feeling toward Walani were a first for him. Lance was twenty eight years old and had never been in love. Lance felt like he wanted to ravish Walani's body at the same time he wanted to respect it and nurture it. This all made him confused so he decided to let Walani take the lead whenever and if ever this very moment had presented itself. Mrs. Timms had a nice 'Hi-Fi" system in her apartment and Walani walked over to turn it on. The quiet storm had started and "You and I" by Black Ivory started playing which set a very romantic mood. Walani walked toward Lance knowing that Lance saw her as something more than just a sexy girl he wanted to screw. Women have an 'Instinct: a sense of when a man is sincere and when he's just "Lusting" after a Woman. Lance continued to watch her approach, Walani seemed to be floating in a black and red two piece thong and licorice top covered by a black see through slip. Her hips appeared to sway as she floated toward him. The moonlight caught a glimpse of her body through the window as she walked across the living room and her shiny black skin shined with an oily glow. Walani stopped in front of Lance and went down to her knees looking up to him with seductive eyes she said, "I will Love you forever Lance. Please don't look at me differently after what happens tonight."

Lance with butterflies in his stomach nodded much the same way Derek had nodded after he shot Born.

With that understood Walani sat on lance lap cowgirl style ad began to kiss him passionately. As "Heaven Must be like this" by the Ohio Players began to play. Walani sat straight up and slipped her succulent nipples which were even darker than her from behind the dental floss wide licorice and let her breast on display for lance to examine and pleasure himself. Lance first tasted each one and watched as they became erect. Lance then held them together with each hand going from one to the other sucking desperately as if he were a starving calf under his sow mother. With his left hand he reached around to feel that magnificent backside he had been forced to admire for the past few weeks from up close but might as well have been a thousand miles away with him not being able to touch them. Her buttocks were silky smooth to the touch full and firm just as lance had imagined them to be. Lance let his fingers front to be slide down her beautiful posterior crack to her warm slit. Lance felt the warmth and mist of her lips parting as he looked for salami's opening with his middle finger. Walani's lips puckered opened and let out a muffled 'Hiss" as Lance let his middle finger feel for Walani's clit as he entered her. Walani leaned forward and began to kiss lance as her breath became heavy. Lance sucked on Walani's tongue as if he wanted to suck it completely out of her head, he kissed he so deeply that he never forgot the taste bud configuration on her tongue. Walani got so wet that her juices leaked all the way down lances arm as he continued to have her ride his middle finger. Walani then stood up legs agape, she leaned down and began to pull Lances pants down to his ankles, then his boxer shorts, then his Izard shirt, then his tank top. As Lance sat there fully erect she gave him a long and hard kiss then turned around to sit on his manhood to ride it. Lance decided to give her a surprise that he knew she wouldn't expect him, Lance put his entire face right into her full firm backside. As Walani squealed with delight Lance bent her over and gave her a full "Analingus" then "Cunnilingus", then ran his tongue frantically from one orifice to the other. Walani's love juices were flowing down her legs at this point Walani was so excited that she had orgasm before the actual love making had started. Lance then pulled Walani back toward him so that she could mount him reverse "Cowgirl" style. When Walani sat down she was so wet that lance thought that she had urinated on him. Walani leaned back and jolted with aftershocks of her orgasm so violently that the back of her head was slamming into lance's mouth that lance just took in stride as any Man would. Walani rode violently and began to scream "OH!!!!! OH!!! OH GOD!!!!! OH!!!!," very loudly this only excited Lance more.

At this point Lance was so excited that he lost his gentleman composure and stood up, while doing so Walani slumped to the floor. Lance leaned down and grabbed her by her hair and walked her to Mrs. Timms bedroom and to the bed by her hair. Lance shoved her backward on to the bed and stared at her intently in silence as Walani stared back. Lance then rushed her pulling all of her sexy lingerie off violently as Walani squealed in delight. Lance then laid Walani on her back lifting her legs to his shoulders, entered her, and thrust with all of his might over and over again. This time both of them screamed.

"OH OH OH!!!!! OH GOD!!! OH GOD!!!! OH GOD!!!!"

Then Walani legs began to spasm uncontrollably as if she was having an epileptic fit. Walani's body jerked back and forth an in the night Lance could tell she was foaming from her mouth, although dark Lance could slightly see her in Mrs. Timms room from the streetlight outside. Lance looked down and Walani was squirting all over his stomach saying almost in tongue

"Thank you Jesus! Thank you!" In the same way the women had said it at church after catching the Holy Ghost, this made Lance smile.

Lance then turned Walani around and gave Walani a Loud 'SMACK" on her sweet chocolate backside and said, "Give me that Ass Girl! Give it to me!"

Walani turned around in haste as if she couldn't wait to feel Lance's penis from this position, as if she was hungry for it. Lance entered Walani 'Doggy Style" and pounded as hard as he could while pulling Walani's hair. Lance then maneuvered his legs to "Froggy Style" then climaxed himself inside of Walani. Lance then fell beside her and both kissed until they fell fast asleep.

Lance jumped up, "OH SHIT! It's twelve o'clock girl!"

Both looked at each other in a panic. Walani ran for the shower as Lance put his clothes each trying to figure out what they would say to Mr. and Mrs. Stevens when he came to an answer. Lance reached into his back pocket and retrieved Reverend Burns' home telephone number and reach for the phone next to the bed.

"Hello......Reverend Burns?" whispered Lance.

"Yes...Yes this is in fact Reverend Burns. Who may I ask is calling at such an ungodly hour?" answered Reverend Burns clearly annoyed.

"Sir, its Lance Cook. I was at church earlier. I was introduced to you by Mrs. Timms. Francine Timms, sir." Lance waited to see if the Reverend Burns did in fact remember him.

"Oh yes. The young man who is watching over Mrs. Timms home, the man who has been of so generous, and the man who helped us with our little problem"

Lance sat silently for a moment. It was good that the reverend knew that it was he that took care of the "Reality" problem, it was also not a good idea to talk about it over the phone so he interrupted quickly'

'YES, Yes Sir, That's me"

'Well what can I do for you young man" asked the reverend now jovial.

"I kept my girlfriend out kind of late and her parents are God fearing people can you please vouch that we were in fact with you painting the office at the church."

First there was silence, and then the reverend continued, "Of course I will, just give me the phone number and thank you for volunteering to paint the office or at least contributing for the painting supplies my good man" Lance answered almost sarcastically.

'Oh yes Sir, It will be taken care of you can mark my words. I will have a man to you first thing tomorrow for the job"

"Like I said God has bought you home Son......he has bought you home and we are glad to have you here at Burns Memorial Church of Christ."

Lance thanked him repeatedly. Lance then explained the alibi to Walani as they rushed to the Cadillac. Both held hands as they drove down the Belt Parkway toward the Conduit. When the Cadillac arrived in front of 45 Cambridge Place, the porch light was on and Walani walked nervously toward the front to just to have it opened by her smiling father who whisked her inside waving to Lance. Lance breathed a sigh of relief and made a mental note to call Cornbread first thing in the morning to request the services of Derek once more, this time for something way less sinister. Derek seemed like a good guy who only wanted to make a few bucks. Painting the office at the church seemed like an honest gig, something right up Derek's alley. It would also give Lance a chance to talk to him to see where his head was at and give him a sense of what the people of Rochdale Village were talking about. It would give a definitive answer to Lance's inner question 'Should he kill Derek or not".

The following morning after buying an old 1965 corvette (that needed a ton of work so no one would be interested in stealing it), Lance put in in the garage the Reverend had given him on 150th Street with $200,000.00 cash in it. Lance then went, parked his Cadillac and was waiting outside of the American Airlines Terminal at J.F.K. airport waiting on Mrs. Francine Timms It seemed so much had happened while she was away. Lance had made sure to move all of his belongings out of her apartment so that Mrs. Timms would not feel encroached upon. Mrs. Timms had a big broad smile on her little round face as she approached the Cadillac.

"Good to see you sweetie! I missed you" Mrs. Timms beamed at lance. Who gave her a big hug and kissed as he took her luggage and placed the suitcases in the trunk.

"That trip sure upset my pressure; you've got any medication for me? I ran out of what you gave me last night," Mrs. Timms said as soon as lance got in the car. Knowing that her habit was increasing before she left Lance already knew to have at least a gram on him when he picked Mrs. Timms up from the airport. Mrs. Timms wasted no time pulling out her works to shoot up right in the car as the entered on to the Van Wyck Expressway. Lance just sat quietly and turned on his radio to WBLS and coasted as 'Sweet Sticky Thang" by the Ohio Players was on. When the Cadillac arrived in front of 6 West 160th Street Mrs. Timms looked up with glossy eyes and exclaimed.

"Home sweet home" in a grandmotherly voice.

"I'm sure everything is exactly the way I left it. If you need anything just give me a call baby," said Mrs. Timms, as he dropped her luggage in the hallway.

Lance then drove to pick up Derek and drop him off at the church. Derek was glad he could be of help and to make a few bucks. Lance could tell that there was no need to worry about him. Derek was just a local kid trying to make his way in the world. Reverend Burns was happy to have the job done for free and also asked Lance if Walani would be "Baptized" this Sunday as he was scheduled to be. Lance told him; "Absolutely!" still wondering how Walani was going to take this news.

After Lance picked up Walani and the two of them were taking their usual walk on the promenade Lance began

"I told the Reverend that we would both be saved this Sunday"

"What do you mean, saved?" asked Walani in an angry tone.

"I ain't into all this religious shit!" said Walani angrily.

"Look the Reverend saved our asses the other night with your folks, and he's doing some favors for me and I'm going to get more out of him. There's no real longevity in what I do and He knows people, people who could get me out of trouble if trouble comes. I don't really know anyone from Queens and he could introduce me to influential people. I'm not asking you to believe in God….just me. Understand?"

Walani walked for a bit and said: "Okay, I Love you Lance and I'm sure you know what you're doing." Lance grabbed Walani, gave her a big kiss and the two of them walked to Montague Street for some ice cream.

Sunday Morning came. It was a Hot Sunny day June 23 1979. The Reverend Terry Burns was ready to wash Lance and Walani in the blood of the lam and all were eager to see. The Reverend led the entire congregation to the basement, to a cross shaped tub in the middle of the floor. The Reverend wore under his black gown, and fireman boots. The good Reverend stepped into the tub screaming for everyone to take their seats in the folding metal chairs. There weren't enough so the rest of the people who came last had to stand. Lance and Walani were taken into a back room where they took off their clothes and put on a white sheet with a whole in the middle to put their heads through to cover their bodies. They were then led to the front of the audience where Mrs. Timms sat who was their 'Sponsor" into the church.

"Let anyone who thinks that these two should not be washed in the blood of the lam and become members of this church speak now or forever hold their piece." No one said a word because no one really knew either of them. All the locals knew was that lance had money and was heavily connected to the street scene around the church. It was also rumored that it was he who took care of the 'Reality" problem, so not only were the local church folk afraid of him, they were also glad he was becoming one of them because that meant safety in and around the church. The Reverend then called Walani down into the tub. The Reverend cradled her in his arms and leaned her back and said to her. "Into the water you shall go a heathen when you return you shall be born again." With that Walani was leaned all the way back under the water and quickly returned to the surface to joyous applause from the crowd. Then it was Lances' turn who before he went under winked at Mrs. Timms who waved back proud of her adopted son. After Lance and Walani were toweled off and back in their Sunday clothes they were told that everyone was waiting in the pews for them. The two of them stood at the front of the church with Reverend Burns a half story above at the pulpit and ordered the entire congregation to come forward from the furthermost pews to the front and greet their new fellow members of the Church.

Lance told Walani to wait with Mrs. Timms outside while he had a word with Reverend Burns. Inside he sat with Reverend Burns in the back office and thanked him for covering for him on Friday. Lance also inspected the job Derek had done painting the office and asked the

Reverend if he was happy with the job. The Reverend then informed Lance of a certified public accountant in Brooklyn that he could use to establish an income history with. Someone who would have a yearly W-2 form, 1099 form, and use the Reverend's name to vouch that Lance contributed 20% of his income to the church where he was listed as a Deacon. Lance gave a very broad smile and said, "Thank you Reverend Burns. I have a most generous contribution to make today."

"Oh your usual tidings were more than enough."

The Reverend pretending to refuse

Then Lance pulled out ten one hundred dollar bills and handed them to the Reverend. Who hugged Lance and informed him that there was a safe at the bank that Lance was more than welcome to use at his leisure. If Lance wanted he could have a key to the church and the combination. Lance asked the Reverend if he would mind if a separate safe could be put into the basement that only he could have access to. Not only that he didn't trust the Reverend; he just didn't want the Reverend getting into 'trouble". With that said Lance didn't have to explain anymore. The reverend just waived his hand silencing lance and instructed Lance to follow him into the basement.

"You can put it here. No one will know it's here, but you and me."

The Reverend then extended his hand to shake lances hand and instead of a shake Lance hugged him.

"Thank you Reverend," said Lance humbly.

"It's Gods will young Man, the Lord bought you to us. Thank the Lord." Both men smiled then went back upstairs.

On the way to Carmichael's for Sunday brunch, Lance and Walani barraged Mrs. Timms with questions about Soperton, Georgia and her family there. Everyone laughed and smiled while they ate. Afterward Mrs. Timms was anxious to see her apartment.

"I hope you took good care of my place," asked Mrs. Timms, half joking knowing that Lance was a responsible Man and would most likely have hardly used her place.

'You know I did Mrs. Timms," Lance said to Mrs. Timms with a big smile. Before Lance could give Mrs. Timms a big hug and leave Mrs. Timms pulled him close to her and whispered in his ear. "I need some medication Lance, I'm in pain, I need to get well."

Lance looked over at Walani who looked puzzled and instructed her to wait downstairs while he spoke with Mrs. Timms about something important. Lance had noticed over the past few weeks before Mrs. Timms left that her appetite for heroin had been increasing quite drastically to the point where he worried for her safety. Lance had no idea what her intake might have been while in Georgia. Of course one could get heroin anywhere.

"Sure thing Mrs. Timms," Lance said with a smile, "You know I got you covered."

With that Lance went into the closet where he had hid his stash. He had also put a lock on it and retrieved a gram of heroin in a Chiclet box and handed it to Mrs. Timms who smiled warmly at Lance and said, "Hurry up after that pretty little thing now, you don't want her downstairs by herself too long. It's getting dangerous out here." Lance spun on his heels and headed for the staircase and met Walani with a big hug in front of the building.

As Lance and Walani arrived back on Cambridge Place, they were surprised to see Mr. and Mrs. Stevens, waiting in front of the house; "You little bitty, you have been running with a GANGSTER!" screamed Mrs. Stevens as Mr. Stevens just stood there looking down. "You decide right now! You either tell this no good Nigger good by right now or pack your shit and get out of my house."

Walani looked at her father who just looked away, she then looked to Lance who just stood silently, and then she walked over to his Cadillac and got into the car.

"You can go get your things," Mrs. Stevens exclaimed in a softer tone. She had expected for Walani to beg and plead, or maybe even tell Lance good bye.

'I don't need any of that shit Mommy," Walani said from the car.

"My man will take care of everything!" With that Lance just walked back to the car and drove off. As lance and Walani drove toward Green Avenue, Walani could see her parents arguing in the side view mirror and watched her father wiped away tears. Black parents pull this stunt a lot, a lot of times it backfires. Instead of telling their children that they are making a mistake and trying to show them the best and most intelligent road to take in life. They threaten them and attempt to leave them with no choice but to take to the streets. That bluff is sometimes called with a terrible outcome lying in wait for the parents, and the child.

Early the next morning, Walani awoke in lances Harlem apartment and started making him breakfast.

"You going to be late to school," Lance said dryly.

"I'm with you now; I'm grown, too grown for school," said Walani, with a hint of womanly pride.

"That's right; you are with me, so trust my judgment, finish school," Lance said in a fatherly tone.

Walani sucked her teeth and started getting ready. Lance dropped her off to school in time then headed to Queens. After stopping by Mr. Uglies, meeting up with the crew, and washing his car. Lance headed over to Mrs. Timms. To add some money to his stash that he had collected from Pearl. Lance was shocked to see that his closet was ransacked with all of Walani clothes thrown about, his shoe boxes were laying around with cash strewn everywhere. Lance then realized that his drug stash had been tampered with and at least 5 grams were gone. Lance immediately drew his 357 magnum from his waistband and went into commando mode on his knees around the house, so that if he were to come in contact with anyone he would be shooting upward as they shot downward giving him the higher probability of striking his opponent. The House didn't appear to be broken into which was puzzling, so Lance called out, "MRS. TIMMS?!"

With no answer Lance crawled over to her bedroom and saw her hand hanging over the side of the bed. Lance stood up and saw her there laying in her Sunday clothes from the day before, with a spike sticking out of her left arm where she had rolled up her sleeve. It was obvious the gram Lance had given her was not enough and Mrs. Timms had dipped into Lance's stash not realizing that the diesel that was there was uncut which made it lethal. At this point Lance put the 'Oaktown' back in his pants and cleaned up the house. Putting all the drugs, money and guns into garbage bag and loaded them into his car. Since Lance used this apartment as a stash house he didn't want to make it hot by making it a crime scene so Mrs. Timms had to be moved. Lance place a call to Linda at the Jade East Hotel and asked her for a room that no one was using that she could say must have been broken in to. Linda gave him Room 406 facing the rear parking lot. The room had been rented three times for four hours a piece in the last twenty four hours. The last couple that rented it had left after just one hour. Although their time had expired they never returned the key. Lance then went and picked up Pearl and John and told them of the situation. It was only about 10:00 a.m. so things were pretty dead at the projects and this time literally. The three of them would have to be careful, but there wouldn't be too many witnesses. Mrs. Timms had an old trunk in her closet that was full of clothes. The clothes were taken out and just stacked in the closet. Mrs. Timms was then literally folded in half as Lance, Pearl, and John stuffed her in the chest. Rigamortis had already started to set in so gasses had been building up in her body and starting the decomposition process. As Lance placed Mrs. Timms head to her knees, she defecated letting out a terrible odor. Lance felt terrible that such a nice woman would be treated in the afterlife this way, but felt as though he had no choice. John then looked outside to see who was around beside people trickling in and out of the bodega down the block on the corner of Brinkerhoff and 160th Street; things looked kind of dead. The three then carried the chest to the car and placed it in the backseat. The Cadillac made a stop at the corner store of Linden and Merrick so Lance could buy some bleach, sponges, and a bar of ivory soap. When they arrived at Room 406 the door was ajar waiting for the delivery. They carried the chest inside and all held their breath knowing the smell would be awful as the chest was opened. Lance carefully sat Mrs. Timms up and placed his arms under hers, lifting her straight up. Pearl then grabbed her ankles and the two of them swung her to the bed. They checked to see if any fecal matter had dropped to the floor in the process, thankfully none had fallen. Lance then instructed John and Pearl to help him carry the chest to the bathroom so there would be no drag marks.

In the bathroom Lance scrubbed the chest with bleach, then washed his hands with his own soap and scrubbed the entire bathroom with bleach. He then instructed John and Pearl to wash their hands with the Ivory soap and wait outside. Lance then continued to wash down all of the door knobs, sink, and again the tub with bleach; then making sure to keep the sponge. The door was closed from the outside with the sponge on the knob. The trunk was bought back to Apartment 3C and Mrs. Timms belongings were placed where they originally had been. Mrs. Timms bed was made and wiped with bleach to cover the smell of human waste; Lance then sprayed it with Lysol.

"Not exactly the cover up of the century, but it would have to do," Lance thought to himself.

The three men then went back to the car and were dropped off at the 'Hole" to resume their daily routine. Lance then went to Walani's school to pick her up. Walani seemed withdrawn. The realization of what had happened in her life was setting in. As they drove toward the promenade for their usual walk Walani began to cry. She didn't realize that she would miss her parents and that growing up could be pretty tough. Walani also felt like it was too late to talk to her folks about coming home. The truth was that Mrs. Stevens was jealous of Walani and had wanted her out for some time. Walani's presence made her feel old. Black woman are notorious for feeling this way and even competing with their daughters. This leads to the young girls being thrown out of their homes at a very early age continuing the cycle of self-destruction that plagues the black community to this day.

They walked silently along the boardwalk; Lance making sure to be a good listener if Walani started to open up and to support whatever decision she would make.

"Lance I have something to tell you." He took a deep breath wondering if his day could possibly become any more complicated and stressful than it had already been and the answer was yes.

"I'm pregnant."

Lance just listened and didn't show any emotion.

'Well, do you Love me or not," asked Walani choking up.

"Of course I do. You, me, and the baby will be just fine"

Lance placed his arm around Walani and the two walked silently along the boardwalk wondering what the future held and what the name of their child would be. Lance said.

"My grandfather's name was Gifford. If it's a boy his name will be Gifford"

"And if it's a girl?" Walani said sheepishly.

"Then you name her whatever you want," Lance said with a big smile. Walani placed her head back on Lance's shoulder and realized that as scared and unsure as she was about her life. Something felt right about Lance. There was no doubt in her mind that Lance would take care of, kill, and be killed if necessary to take care of her and her child, and she was right.

Lance and Walani stopped at "One Fish Two Fish" on 93rd and Madison on the way home for some clams and two- one pound lobsters to celebrate the good news. When they arrived at home the phone was ringing off of the hook.

"Yes Reverend, I'll come out to Queens this instant! That's terrible news, does anyone know what happened?" asked Lance sounding as shocked a humanly possible.

"What is it?!" exclaimed Walani.

"My God! Mrs. Timms was found dead somewhere! I have to head out to Queens to find out what happened"

Lance assured Walani to do her homework then get some sleep for school the next day. Lance didn't want any undue strain being put on his little Zygote. Lance pulled himself together not knowing what to expect. Lord knows who had witnessed what during the course of the day. Lord knows who had told what, and Lord only knew if the Reverend was only speaking on behalf of the police to get Lance to come to Queens to lock him up for murder.

Lance went straight to Mrs. Timms house. That seemed the place where an innocent party would go under such circumstances. Just as he thought there was a marked police car outside. Lance approached the car.

"Sir is everything all right? I heard that Mrs. Timms in 3C had passed"

'Who the fuck are you boy?" The operator said from the driver's side window in a very nasty manner.

"Sir, My name is Lance Cook, I'm Mrs. Timms nephew. I stay here with her from time to time. My uncle, Wilford London is a police officer in the 8-3 Precinct in Bushwick. His tax ID# is 864596. If you could please show a little discretion I would greatly appreciate to hear what has happened."

With the magic word of discretion being said, this is a code word amongst all cops and relatives of Cops. The police officer softened up and said that Mrs. Timms had been found dead in the Jade East Hotel off of the South Conduit, apparently of a drug overdose. The officer also informed Lance that the police did not have access to the apartment and had to wait for one 'Lance Cook' (whose name was the only other name on the lease) to arrive to ask permission to come in and have a look around. Lance was completely aware of his rights and gives the okay for the cops to come in, since he felt he had reached some kind of rapport with them and would only arouse suspicion if he didn't.

Lance unlocked the door and two white police officers went in before Lance cautiously looking around. Lance feigning fear said, "I'll wait out here in the hall so you guys can make sure all is well," to make it look as though he was so appreciative of the safety and protection that they were providing.

The two cops came from the back room and said, 'The place is clean as a whistle. Mrs. Timms sure kept a nice place…..where you aware of any drug abuse?" asked the first cop curiously.

"It's sad you know, Aunt Francine complained about being in pain a lot, being a nurse and all I never suspected that she would abuse her access to medicines at work."

The Cops faces turned to stone. "According to reports from responding officers Mrs. Timms had track marks on her arms, no needle was recovered either. This could turn into a homicide investigation. The manager at the hotel said no one had any idea when or if she had checked in. Your aunt wasn't even registered, can you tell us when, was the last time you saw your aunt?'

Lance knowing that this was a trap stayed cool and gave smooth short answers. Although it's not smart to answer such questions getting defensive could open up a can of worms.
"I picked her up from the airport yesterday. She had just come back from visiting family in Soperton, Georgia. My fiancé and I took her to eat at Carmichael's then dropped her off here. That was the last time I saw her."

Lance stayed cool praying to God that no one had already identified him as moving a God damned chest from the apartment earlier that same day. Lance also made sure to take note of the cops names so that he could cross reference with Cornbread to see if these cops could be paid off if need be, their names where Officer Poje, and Officer Gudersky. The two cops then made notes in their memo pad and told Lance that he might hear from them or detectives handling the case.

The cops then gave their sympathies and said into their radios, "Central is advised that sector George is resuming patrol and to mark the job 90 yellow."

Lance sighed in relief as soon as he was alone, he walked around the apartment making sure that everything was as he left it and that there were no clues that he may have left behind, something he could now take his time in. Lance then drove over to Holliswood to visit Reverend Burns.

"My God son, I'm so sorry to hear about what has happened. I've called all of her kin in Georgia. They are on their way. Is there anything I can do in such a terrible time of sorrow Lance?"

Lance just handed the Reverend a brown paper bag with $15,000.00 in it.

"Make sure she gets a magnificent sendoff," said Lance. The Reverend could see that Lance was genuinely hurt. A drug dealer is faced with a situation from time to time where he or she has to accept and live with the fact they have in fact contributed to the demise of someone who meant them no harm. Not a peer in the business or 'game' as it is sometimes called, but a person who was an addict, who helped you, become who you are. Who pays your rent and feeds your family. It makes the drug dealer realize that he or she is in fact human. The fact that society or your own shortcomings have lead you to believe that engaging in a trade of vice is your only or most fast means to the good life and doesn't negate the fact that you sucked the life out of this person to better your own. The people who never feel this guilt are the hardest of dealers, but not Lance. He felt guilty, so he did what all dealers do in such a case, they rationalize their role.

"She was using before she met me, wasn't she?"

"If she didn't get it from me she would have gotten it from somewhere; would she have not?" Lance repeated these lines to himself over and over until he believed them, and they made complete sense. Lance then drove back to Harlem. Walani was waiting at his usual parking spot on Riverside Ave and 141st Street. He usually parked there because no one else would park their car there, but Lance paid local dope fiends who slept in the park at the end of 142nd to keep an eye on his car overnight.

"The Cops been by here asking questions about you," said Walani looking shaken "What were their names?" asked Lance also now shaken.

"They wanted to know if I was with you on Friday. I told them you picked me up from school. I told them you didn't feel well so I think you stayed in the bed all day."

"Good job baby girl," answered Lance. He walked Walani back to the house and then paid Vickie Walker a visit on the third floor. Lance gave Vickie $1,000.00 to say to whoever asked that she had prepare Lance two meals that day and witnessed him in the bed sick. Lance then told Walani about Mrs. Timms terrible sickness.

"Then why did she check into a hotel?" asked Walani.

"Who knows baby girl, sometimes these people lose their minds. The drugs make the do crazy things. Promise me you'll never do drugs."

"I promise," said Walani who started to cry.

"I can't believe that nice old lady is gone," sobbed Walani as the two embraced.

Lance knew that Walani was scared and worried about her own future. Lance had bought her engagement ring weeks earlier, but couldn't work up the nerve until now. Lance then dropped to one knee right there on 141st Street and Riverside Drive. He said, "Would you marry me Walani Stevens?"

Walani started crying and said, "Yes, Lance Cook."

The two kissed passionately there under the moon. Lance knew that this would ease Walani's nerves and make her sure of her decision to be with him.

Reverend Burns stretched the fifteen grand that Lance had given him pretty far. There were five Limousines for Mrs. Timms family who flew in from Soperton, Georgia courtesy of the good reverend, two flower cars for the large assortment of flowers including five bleeding hearts, a plot in Evergreen cemetery under the Brooklyn-Queens expressway under a large maple tree, and a Mahogany casket. The Reverend didn't try to pocket any of the money. The good Reverend knew that there would be much more to come via Lance Cook. The food was prepared by the woman of the Congregation who had been friends of Mrs. Timms for decades now. No one talked about the way she actually died which is customary amongst black folk. Only the good times were talked about at the wake, the night before as each of her friends got up to speak their peace. The Reverend held the audience in a trance as he screamed and shouted for two hours about how sweet and graceful Francine Timms was and how much everyone including himself was going to miss her, but of course God works in mysterious ways, and only he decides who to call home and who not to.

The Funeral the next morning was even more of a spectacle. It seemed as though the entire South Side of Jamaica Queens had ground to a halt to say goodbye to such a special lady. Walani stayed home from school, dressed in black cried like a baby. Even ice cold Lance found himself wiping away a tear as Mrs. Timms casket was lowered into the ground and everyone filed by to drop their rose into her final resting place.

Lance purchased 188-40 Keeseville Ave., from a realtor on Farmers Boulevard for $63,000 cash. Reverend Burns helped him out with all of the necessary paperwork to make everything look legit. It was a very warm and comfortable house. The house had a finished basement where Lance put a washer/dryer. It had an attic which Lance had insulated and carpet laid so that it could be a playroom for his expected child. There was a living room, dining room, and kitchen on the parlor floor, and three bedrooms on the second floor. Lance joked that he wanted a lot of kids that's why he bought such a big house. Lance bought a twenty five inch floor model Zenith television, which was shaped like a 'C' and included something that Walani had never even heard of. It was a little brown box that was called 'W.H.T' which stood for Warner Home Television. It showed movies for pay; known as pay per view. Lance also bought a brass king sized bed, leather sectional sofa, a dishwasher, and had the baby room ordered out of a magazine down the cherry oak crib.

Lance had Walani close her eyes after school as he got off of the Van Wyck expressway onto Liberty Avenue on his way to her surprise. Lance was proud of himself that he was able to put this all together by himself. Lance also expected to make changes.
"Woman can be funny that way," Lance thought to himself.

Walani squealed and ran through the house inspecting everything down to the last detail. Lance stood in the middle of the living room as Walani went from room to room screaming louder with every step. When she was done talking with a look of wild excitement on her face Lance stated, "I got one more surprise for you!"
"WHAT IS IT?!!!!!!" squealed Walani jumping up and down.

Lance took her by the hand and led her outside the side door from the kitchen to a 1980 Datsun 210, complete with a baby seat.

Walani jumped up and down screaming so loudly that the neighbors up and down Keeseville Avenue and Hannible Street looked outside of their doors and windows. Lance handed Walani the keys and asked if she could take him for a ride. "Jamaica Funk" by Tom Brown played on the radio as the two of them drove up and down Farmers Boulevard examining their new neighborhood. Walani was happy and that's all that mattered to Lance. With all that had gone on in the last few weeks, Lance was sure glad the he had his three soldiers Pearl, John, and Hollywood, because the three of them held everything together on a daily basis while Lance had to get rid of, and bury Mrs. Timms, get engaged and buy a house and car, and lastly hearing that he was expecting his first child. The first day back at the hole after leaving Mr. Uglies, Lance found out that there was new competition in the area. Not at the "Hole" but on South Road. This new crew seemed more vicious than any other that had come up in the area thus far. This crew was split in two. The first group sold on 155th Street and South Road and the other sold on Montauk Street, 122nd Ave, and Farmers Boulevard across town and christened that corner the square because it was actually a crossroad where numerous streets came together. Their leader as Lance's crew put it was a guy named "Half Key" who was from Queens and knew a lot of people. He got his weight from the Italians at a bar called the "Gemini Lounge" in Canarsie, Brooklyn. This crew seemed to have an endless supply of product and itching to expand.

On the third day of Lance being back in full swing and while talking to his crew in the white Cadillac, Half Key drove up to the car in a white Audi 5000 four men deep and asked if he could have a word with Lance, just the two of them. Lance agreed.

"I heard you're the man to see about the Hole," assked Half Key in an overly friendly voice.

"This is true," answered Lance very flatly.

"Is it possible to pay you a tax to have some workers sell on your corners after dark when you guys have tapped out and are home for the night"

"I don't see a problem with that. After you've tapped out and have covered expenses, what do you think your take will be?" asked Lance unequivocally.

"We don't tap out, and we sell boy, girl, dirt, dust, and hard. I will work the corner until you come back out to claim it which is even better for you because I will increase the flow out here, and when you are we will retreat to 155th and South Road. For that I offer $10,000.00 a day." Lance started laughing as he stared into Half Keys now ice cold eyes.

"Come on nigger! All of that and all I get is ten grand a day with you making at least one hundred and fifty grand! I'll tell you what make it twenty thousand and we got a deal." Half Key was confused. With all the theatrics he thought that Lance was going to go hard on him and attempt to charge at least $50,000.00, but the truth is Lance knew he didn't stand a chance against Half Key and would have been happy with the ten grand, but had to put up a front not to look soft. Lance also knew that he would have to handle the Half Key gingerly. Lance knew that one day this relationship was going to get ugly, the question was, how long could he make this current agreement last, it was a sweet one.

Lance walked back to his car and explained the new deal with the crew who all seemed apprehensive at best about it. Lance told them the arrangement was for $15,000.00 a day and that they were all getting an instant raise of $2,500.00 a day. Which gave each of his boys two thousand a day extra and double what Lance was netting every four days; Lance had been wondering how he would re-pay his boys for the loyalty and hard work that they had been putting in over the last year. Lance figured that this was as good of any other way he could think of and at no cost to him, but what Lance had no idea how this would turn out in the long run. All he could do was hope for the best.

By July of 1983, all was magnificent in the Hole after a small disagreement that left the Streets of Queens littered with bodies over a four month period. An agreement was made over which crew got what territory and who did business with whom in Queens. Half Key had his rent raised quite a few times although just modestly to keep up with the enormous amount of money that he was pulling in. By 1983, Half Key was paying Lance and his three lieutenants $75,000.00 a day for his working the Hole and it was beginning to get old with him and everybody knew it. Lance had kept a pretty low profile and each of his lieutenants did as well. The four of them were barely on the street anymore they had four workers doing what the four of them had done that first year. Lance, Walani, Gifford, and a second son Brian who was born in 1981 lived extremely well at 188-40 Keeseville Avenue. Lance had even purchased a movie projector, 100-inch television that was so big he had to knock down a wall and connect the guest room to the master bedroom to fit it. The four of them went to church and sat in the same pew every week. Lance had been given keys to the church so that he could have access to his safe that he had installed in 1980. Mr. Uglies had burned down and Pop Freeman had passed of old age and now Lance was getting his weight from Italians on Pleasant Avenue in Harlem that Reverend Burns had introduced him to. Every four days Lance would go to "Rao's" on 115th Street and met with a guy named "Mattie" to get 500 grams; with Pop gone, so did the good prices; although not entirely.

The prices Italians were charging were a little steep, but the comfort of dealing with Italians was worth it. The 2-5 Precinct in East Harlem was completely paid off. Cops didn't even walk down 115th Street, never. You were also guaranteed quality. This would cost Lance a handsome forty five dollars a gram, but it was worth it. If the prices went up for Lance he did what any good business man does and that is to pass the price difference on to the consumer. In Lance's case he shorted them with quality instead of quantity. Everybody's dope in Queens was taking an 8" cut and Lance was previously cutting his at 4"; now he would step on his dope '6' times, which means he wouldn't hurt from the inflation at all. Lance had also begun to cut his heroin with Morphine and quinine, instead of Bonita. Quinine was need because every dope fiend looks for the hot flash immediately as they are injecting themselves and Morphine then would give them a concentrated kick instead of a drawn out one. Lance also noticed a tapering off of users the dope business is a "Blue Chip" business that will have the loyalty of those who already use. So Lance wasn't worried. His outfit was small after all. Lance did notice however that free-base cocaine was growing wildly popular among new users to narcotics. It was becoming phenomenal. In fact, cocaine which was once seen as a white Ivy League drug was in the ghetto now and being used at an almost alarming amount. Half Key's business was booming. Half key had started selling heroin with an "8" on it for rock bottom prices just to keep the clientele happy while he made a ton off of powdered cocaine, and Freebase cocaine. This also helped Lance, because they knew that only when Lance's crew was out there was the only time the dope any good.

By August 1983, Half Key just stopped paying. Lance would drive up to 155th Street and South Road and ask for him, and would be greeted with shrugged shoulders, snickering in the background, and an even more slap in the face of "What you asking me for?" from Half Key's soldiers. Lance did however still get respect from these same soldiers when they would start to show up in the "Hole" and Lance was there collecting the days take from his workers; then and only then would they still acknowledge him as someone to be respected. Walani could tell that something was bothering Lance each night as he came home and kept to himself. Lance would just sit out back by himself. Lance knew that he was being squeezed by the up and comers on top of having to compete with a whole new product put him in a very tight spot. Walani had graduated from Clara Barton and was a stay at home Mom with Gifford and Brian. Walani was doing all that she could to make Lance happy and with his family he was. Lance had stashed away 1 million in cash and was very pleased with his success. Lance just felt the walls closing in as all hustlers do when the old "Shakespearean" struggle of Young Lion versus Old Tiger is playing out in the streets. It's not that Lance was old; in 1983 he was thirty two years old, and by some standards he was pretty youthful, but if you evolve in the streets, you grow old fast the endless game of cops and robbers assisted by the advent of free-base cocaine made things change real fast during that time. Lance had also made an age old mistake of not being as visible as he should have been in the 'Hole." Allowing his new workers to fall under the influence of Half Key not to mention that his workers grew up right there with Half Key and went to school with him, while everyone still viewed Lance as an outsider. Lance pondered this for a whole evening in his backyard one night and came to one conclusion--Half key had to go.

Labor Day weekend 1983 was a hot one, the Jamaica Roller Rink was the place to be on a hot night on Jamaica Avenue. Everyone who was someone was there. All the top hustlers, all the pretty woman dressed in the latest fashion of the day. From sweat suits made by Lecog

Sportif, brand new Gazalle shades, Kangols, Stan Smith Adidas, and rope chains. One could say it was a real show. "Games people play" was thundering from the gigantic speakers as the skaters rolled round and round as fast as they could. All the hustlers convened at the front left side of the stage showing off watches and rings and pulling at every girl who walked by when Half Key made his dramatic entrance. Half Key was flanked by at least twenty soldiers who were dressed fresh out the box to say the least, causing the whole place to quiet to a whisper as they strolled down the aisle toward the front left where their peers had gathered. As everyone paid homage to the recognized new KING of South Jamaica. Four masked gunmen burst through the entrance fire shots almost indiscriminately. The entire club including the skaters as if out of instinct ran to the front left where the hustlers were seeking protection from the masked madmen. Two of the gunmen stayed at the entrance while the other two ran into the crowd grabbing people and throwing them aside trying to get to Half Key. A little boy named Hans Elder got in the way and fell to the ground in the mayhem. At which point a Half Key henchmen ran across the skating rink trying to seek refuge in the back lounge area. The masked gunmen looked down at Hans, put his foot on his chest and said, "Stay still little nigger, I ain't gonna hurt you" Hans just turned his head to the side and watched the gunman with an M16 shoot with military precision across the floor. The shots were so loud little Hans's hearing immediately seized. Everything went into slow motion as the man's shirt turned red as the bullets seemed to chew him up and spit his body to the ground. In all of this confusion Half Key ran out of a back door that he had paid a bouncer to have ready if just such a situation where to ever occur. The second gunman who had ran to the front let loose with a barrage of gun fire killing three additional Half Key henchmen before turning and running toward his friend, pulling him off of Hans and heading back toward the first two gunmen at the entrance where all 4 headed to the White Cadillac around the corner.

The crew of four headed back to the South side knowing that they had made a terrible error in misjudging Half Key.

"We should have planned this better, we really fucked up by not getting Half Key," Lance said while pulling off his ski mask.

"Head back to the house in the projects. We can see the corner of 160th Street and Brinkerhoff from there. I got a feeling that nigger might show up there to see if I came to the projects, thinking that I would never make a move on that corner because of all the people that be out there." Lance knew how cocky and unassuming Half Key was and was right. Half Key was from Queens and use to playing by certain rules. Hustlers from Harlem are used to changing the rules when need be when survival calls for it.

"Look Pearl, drive my car to the garage on 150th"

When the crew of Desperado's arrived on 150th Street the corner was buzzing with at least 50 hustlers who were making money a mile a minute. Lance knew he could trust everyone out there to stay quiet. They weren't fans of Half Key either. They were loosely aligned mostly through unknown agreements made through the Reverend of the Burns Memorial Church. Everyone out there looked the other way as if the four men were invisible as they rolled the corvette out on to the street and pushed the white Cadillac inside. After which Lance told the three men to wait around the corner on Sutphin Blvd. While he crossed his fingers and placed the $200,000.00 in the white Cadillac hoping the cops didn't find it, or the crew across the street took it upon themselves to investigate the car stumbled across it. Lance was in a tight spot and knew it and knew he had to take his chances.

Lance then ran back around the corner to Sutphin Blvd. Lance knew that he had to move, He and his crew might possibly be 'hot' right now and there were plenty of witnesses that knew where he and his car were. Lance used his key and went into the church. Lance opened his private safe and retrieved a sawed off 12 gauge shotgun, and three handguns for his crew. Lance then headed out of the church with this armory damned near in plain view. Lance handed each of his men .38 caliber handguns and put the sawed off shot gun under his arm.

"We gonna have to hoof it back to the projects," Lance said as he looked into the eyes of his loyal men who seemed a bit uncertain, but loyal to the hilt.

The four men then headed to 109th Ave and toward the projects. They spread out to not bring attention to themselves. They kept apart as if scattered and didn't make eye contact with anyone. They approached the projects from the Linden Boulevard direction so that they could see who was in front of the store on Brinkerhoff. The crew decided not to try to get to the buildings in fear of running across Half Key himself and a murderous crew vastly outnumbering them; hell bent on exacting revenge for what had happened.

After about two hours of just sitting in silence, kneeling close to the ground around four different parked cars. Pearl whispered, "Lance you was right Nigger…there he is." Lance

74

surprised his crew by saying, 'Ya'll stay here until I'm done, when I am going up to my apartment and lay low in 3C."

Lance then gave his keys to Pearl, his most trusted comrade. Pearl seemed surprised and said, "You sure?" Lance just nodded. He figured that with what was about to happen that chaos would ensue and he would need a head start and didn't want anyone knowing of his whereabouts, or even which way he had ran. Lance then walked slowly down 160th Street on the western side of the street to be shielded by the projects. Half Key was talking loudly to underlings with his back to the projects when everyone scattered from around him. A man named 'Chino" screamed, 'WHATCH OUT!!!!!"

Half Key fell flat to the ground and rolled toward the curb and disappeared under a car in an instant. Lance squeezed the trigger and the 12 gauge roared, "BLOOOOOOMB!"

A young boy 13 years old was lifted off of the ground and thrown against the wall reversed spread eagle as the Buckshot made a direct hit to his chest. Chino squeezed back with a .25 caliber Saturday night special, hitting Lance twice in the stomach. Lance fell to the ground in obvious pain. Half Key then jumped up from the curb wet with the blood from the young boy; whose blood had rolled into the gutter. He reached for his waistband and .38 caliber gunshot erupted from down the block causing Half Key to flee northward on 160th dodging bullets like a hall of fame running back. The three gunmen firing the rounds were wearing ski masked and picked up Lance's shotgun before disappearing into the projects and stalking into Building #6 and up to 3C.

Lance was arrested in the ambulance while being rushed to Jamaica Hospital for the murder of the 13 year old boy. Lance swore that he was just walking to the store and was cut down by bullets. When the police asked Lance where he lived he refused to answer. When the police refused to let the medics work on him if he didn't answer; he caved in in agonizing pain he said, "6 160th Street, Apartment 3C." Lance knew he was done.

The police let the paramedics go to work and jumped on their radios, "Central is advised that the alleged shooters in the killing on Brinkerhoff are held up in 6 160th Street, Apartment 3C."

The door was rammed down, Hollywood, Pearl, and John were arrested and charged with murder, conspiracy to commit murder, attempted murder, reckless endangerment, possession of unregistered firearms, and conspiracy to distribute narcotics *(Since 500 grams or a half kilo of heroin was found in the apartment)* in total all men were facing life in prison without the possibility of parole. There was one way to save his loyal boys and Lance knew it. Lance told his lawyer that the drugs were his and he did indeed shoot the boy by accident trying to shoot someone else over a gambling debt. Lance agreed to do this if the charges were dropped against his boys. They hadn't shot anyone. Their shooting stopped Half Key from killing him. Lance "bit the bullet" as they say and was sentenced to two 25 years to life sentences that were allowed to run concurrently. Along with the plea deal Lance had to forfeit his house on 188-40 Keeseville Avenue.

Lance kissed Walani in the court room as her soaked filled face begged in confusion. "What will I do? Please don't leave me Lance!"

As the Court Officers pulled them apart and walked Lance away. Lance looked into the court room to Reverend Burns and Pearl and nodded toward his wife as if to say "Take care of her." They both nodded.

Pearl went back to the garage on 150th Street and found the $200,000.00 of which he gave $10,000.00 to Walani along with the keys to 6 160th Street, Apartment 3C, and gave John and Hollywood $50,000.00 a piece and kept $90,000.00 for himself. Reverend Burns got word to Lance that his safe would not be tampered with and would only open it with Lance's approval. Walani moved into the projects an attempted to raise the boys as best she could. Walani also stayed close the church now that was the only family she would know.

Chapter 4

God helps those who help themselves......And Juanita McDaniels

Walani was well aware that the McDaniel girls went to Sunday school every Sunday, and now so would her boys. Without anyone being aware of her plans, she woke them up bright and early Sunday morning and dressed them in brand new outfits that she had purchased from an escalated amount of money she had stolen from her till at Western Beef. The radio played 'Man in the Mirror' by Michael Jackson as Walani thought to herself, "Yeah, make that change."

Walani was hell bent at making a good life for her boys and she would have to make due with where she was and what she knew, and of course what Lance had taught her.

Walani was all smiles as she and her boys walked pass the bodega on 157th Street and 109th Ave in the Hole.

"The wind and the sunshine is making my boys glow in their new clothes," Walani thought to herself and then said out loud.

"MY SONS!!! My gorgeous SONS! I don't call each of You SON cause you MINE! I call you SUN because you SHINE."

The Cooks all laughed together in unison at Walani's rare attempt at rhyme and humor. At the entrance of the church Walani said, "Don't worry it's only for an hour. You'll like Sunday school. I promise. I will be back for service in an hour; now be good Rockheads."

Walani spun on her heels wondering just how she was going to approach Juanita about her problem of their children being together when God showed her the light. Unbeknownst to Walani, Fick hadn't met Juanita at the church his morning for their usual toe touching exercising in the back office, and Juanita appeared to be "Jonesin" something awful. Walani saw her walking briskly toward the church minus her kids with her arms folded tightly and her lips twitching in every direction at once. Walani recognized this as the tell-tale sign of coke addict who at this very moment is open to about the vilest suggestion that anyone could come up with in order to scratch that uncontrolled invisible itch.

"Hey girl! Where the girls at?" asked Walani curiously.

Juanita stopped cold for a second, "Now you know more than anyone that Ralph or *(eyes rolled)* Officer McDaniel's don't want his babies around the locals. I dropped them off and made a run, have you seen Fick?"

Walani though that her action were typical. Juanita could only focus on anything other than getting high or the person responsible for getting her high for no more than thirty seconds. The question was could she cop and be back before Fick would show up, so that Walani could blow her God damned mind with some ice cold crushin' blow from the 40 projects. Walani figured that she had to try.

"Juanita! stay inside the church. Don't go anywhere okay? I'll be right back. I'm going to take care of you okay."

Juanita puckered her lips like a scorned little girl and said. "I ain't gotta stay nowhere, I'll go where I want," in an almost flirtatious way with Walani. Walani figured that she wasn't thinking correctly. Coke heads usually display this behavior almost advertising them, to whoever might be interested no matter what sex. Walani also knew that since this was the case almost anyone was allowed to step out of bounds with them so she answered the "Subliminal" flirt.

"Bitch get your ass in the church! I'll be right back!"

"OOW Walani. I ain't know, I'll be in the office waiting on you," whispered Juanita. She was feigning so bad her mind was damn near numb.

As the door closed Walani stood still for a minute knowing where she had to go. Filing in the back of her mind the fact that Juanita had suggested that she was willing to even engage in lesbian acts if need be to fulfill her hunger for blow.

"No turning back now," Walani thought to herself as she made a "B" line down Sutphin Boulevard toward 109th Avenue then back toward the "40".

In a flash she was there inside of the projects on the corner of 159th Street and 107th Avenue, "The Corner". Out of all the people standing there Hollywood made her feel the most comfortable because of the history he had had with Lance and with Lance telling Walani that it was his boys who had saved his life that fateful night years earlier.

"Hollywood, I need some really good blow. You know where I can find some?" Walani said sheepishly.

"Look no further little innocent church girl. I got whatcha need," sneer Hollywood, revealing his overlapping front two teeth which were gold capped.

"Let me get an eight-ball," Walani said trying to sound more seasoned in the art of street corner drug dealing than she actually was.

"Uh, how much is an eight-ball?" Walani said as an afterthought.

"Why lady blow, you don't know?" said Hollywood in a faked surprised way making fun of Walani's naiveté.

"An eight-ball is one eighth of an ounce, approximately three point five grams. This is a lot of cocaine for one person, it's actually enough to overdose on if they just started using. Are you trying to be a dealer church girl? Or are you using?"

Hollywood was well aware of his presumed loyalty to Lance, but shit Lance was gone and gone for a long time, and Walani was one hell of a good looking woman.

"Loyalty would have to take a back seat," Hollywood thought to himself.

"I'm buying it as a favor for a friend of mine who really needs a fix," Walani said shyly, trying to be almost flirtatious and concealing how much Hollywood made her skin crawl.

Hollywood made a big smile; then broke into laughter.

"NOW I believe you. You are not even talking about the right drug. A FIX is a term used by dope fiends who want diesel or heroin. People who are feign for COCAINE want a HIT," explained Hollywood sounding like a college professor.

"I think all you need is a gram, your money is no good with me," Hollywood said with a smile.

The going rate in 1987 for a gram was thirty dollars, but with being an old friend of Lance and hoping to one day get in to Walani's panties, Hollywood hoped that it really was for Walani. In an instant Hollywood made a green little envelope appear that was made out of a one dollar bill folded to look like an envelope. The gram made the envelope look really fat which of course really appealed to cocaine addicts.

"This is a gram?" asked Walani incredibly.

"Are you sure this is enough for an addict, I thought a gram would be like half the size of a man's fist?"

"That's an ounce," Hollywood answered with a tight smirk.

Walani turned in such a huff to get back to the church that she said "Thank You" looking in the other direction. Walani had tunnel vision trying to get her words together and wondering how to approach Juanita about her proposal. She was so deep in thought and walking so fast that she was almost hit by a police car as she crossed 157th Street in the Hole. Her heart was pounding wildly in her chest as the cruiser came to a screeching stop. Not because she was almost hit, but because she had a gram of cocaine on her. Walani had no idea about sentencing guidelines, as far as she knew a gram of cocaine would warrant ten years in prison which scared the hell out of Walani. Being that she was dressed in her 'Sunday Best" complete with the standard Baptist Crown *(that could easily cost a woman fifteen hundred dollars)*. The officers got out asking if she was alright.

"I'm just late getting to church," said Walani as innocently as she could.

"We're very sorry ma'am please be careful and have a nice Sunday," said the police officer cheerfully.

Walani was proud of herself at this point. "I'm going to get my Son that snotty little Black BITCH if it kills me!" Walani thought to herself and even laughing to herself as she realized how crazy her thoughts were and pleased that she was backing them up with action. To calm herself down she began to sing "Pleasure Principle" by Janet Jackson and then stopped; figuring that it would look out of place her dressed in her Sunday best singing such a wordily and hedonistic song on her way to church.

When Walani first entered the church she made a "B" line to the bathroom to freshen up and compose herself. Walani in a way felt beneath Juanita McDaniel even though she didn't think much of her. Making the kind of proposition she was about to make was borderline "Blackmail" and at the very least disrespectful and being from the projects it showed most of all that Walani did not know her place. Fortunately for Walani it was 1987 and Cocaine was being seen by the 'have not's" in South Jamaica, Queens New York as the great equalizer. Cocaine and more importantly "Crack" was doing something that not even the "Emancipation Proclamation" or a "PhD." could do for black people. Not only was it making somebody's out of nobody's, It was making SOMEBODY'S bow to NOBODY'S.

As the children were being led into the main part of the church, Walani noticed Juanita coming from the back office. The thought occurred to Walani that she might not have to bribe Juanita to allow her their children to intermingle; it occurred to Walani that she could just outright "Blackmail" Juanita to get what she wanted. Walani also thought that she could blackmail Reverend Burns for some extra cash, an extra prayer, or maybe just good measure. Walani quickly dropped the idea figuring that, "God didn't like ugly." If she got what she wanted, which was her son to be happy then she would just be thankful to the Lord for that and be thankful to the Lord for showing her the way.

As the McDaniel's took their seats in the pew, Walani and her boys took their usual seats in the front. Walani looked back and noticed Juanita leaving on her way to the bathroom. Juanita was twitching something awful. It was obvious that she did not scratch her itch and was probably going to attempt to make her way out of the church if need be in search of Fick or anyone else across the street at Big Mack's Deli who could scratch her itch.

Walani spewed a sigh of relief as Juanita turned right toward the ladies room. Walani entered almost on Juanita's heels and watched her put water up her nose and pat her face with cool water trying to turn the gorilla on her back into a monkey. Walani just decided to say what needed to be said.

"Do you get high Juanita?" Juanita spun on her heels in shock!

"What the fuck do you mean GET HIGH?" Juanita said shocked in the project girls insolence.

"I'm just a friend girl, trying to help. I know who you are and how respected your family is, but I know the signs. This is just between me and you."Walani started showing her underclass subordinate.

"Look......I'm struggling with a demon Walani, that's all and it's my business and No one else's!" Juanita said yelling in a whispering tone and not believing that she was having this discussion with someone so beneath her.

Walani sensing Juanita's weakness continued, "I can help you Juanita if you help me. You see my sons like to be in the company of your daughters and I want them to be happy. If you can find a way for them to interact, I can help you."

There was a long pause as Juanita struggled to understand Walani. At first she seemed a bit intrigued; then irritated.

"I can get it in check myself "Project Chick!" I don't need no damn rehab," said Juanita totally not getting the point.

Walani knew the time was right to pull the trigger. She held her breath and held out the green little dollar bill envelope.

"This is a gram and it's supposed to be very good. At least that's what I was told, but you be the judge," said Walani with a submissive smile of a slave girl to the mistress of the house.

Juanita snatched the little green envelope into her tightly closed fist and said, "You love your boys huh?"

"Very much;" said Walani with an icy cold stare.

Juanita started to sweat at the thought of getting some nose candy up her nostrils. Juanita had to have it now. Walani locked the door as Juanita leaned over the sink and unrolled the dollar bill envelope with expert precision then used her extra-long pinky nail to take little clumps of sweet nectar of the God's cocaine and sniff them like a bloodhound up her right, then left nostril. With the residue Juanita swiped it like toothpaste and messaged it into her gums like she was brushing her teeth, then like a starving animal she licked the dollar bill as if she were attempting to lick George Washington's face off of it. Then Juanita paused noticing that Walani had watched her entire unholy act up close and personal. Juanita then placed each hand on each side of the sink and hung her head to feel the sensation kick in and the bells go off.

"I'll see what I can do, but this is strictly between us, okay Walani?"

The fact that Juanita had called Walani by her name was a promotion in itself. No longer was she the "Hood Rat" and "Project Girl", but an equal; for starters. Walani turned to leave and smiled as she saw Juanita running cold water up her nostrils as chaser and cleanser. 'There's plenty more where that came from," said Walani with an evil grin as Juanita looked up in surprise once again at the project girl attempting to gain respect by talking to her in such a disrespectful way. In the black church this is referred to as "Sassing".

Walani headed back to her pew and hoped that her plan would work out. Walani had played the only hand that she could. Officer McDaniel had no weaknesses that she knew of except of course "Juanita" so that's where the play would have to be made. Walani who internally was agnostic sat there and found herself praying during the sermon.

"All I want is for my boys to be happy," Walani said at the end to herself and right before she said "Amen."

After Reverend Burns finished with his final words freeing everybody for yet another week, Walani and her boys rose and waited for their turn to leave the church. Walani walked with her head held high up the middle aisle with Gifford and Brian in tow with their heads hanging low and their shoulders slouched. Outside was different this Sunday. There was no cake sale going on. The congregation had gathered like school kids waiting for a three o'clock fight; waiting for last Sundays beef to pick up where it had left off. In the middle of a small crowd right outside the front doors stood Juanita, Capalitana, and of course Chinse. Officer Ralph McDaniel's sat in his white Maxima with a fake forged N.Y.P.D. parking plaque in the window grimacing in defeat as Juanita took control and greeted the "Cooks" with a big warm smile and said, "For now on you four will be in Sunday school together. I spoke to the Reverend and if your mother okay's it you're welcomed to join the choir. Rehearsal is every Wednesday night at 6:30 p.m."

Brian interrupted, "I thought you had to audition for Reverend Burns to be in the choir?" As Walani yanked on his sleeve Juanita just gave a sly grin and said, "Don't you worry about that, if you want to sing, you're in."

Walani watched with emotional glee as her sons stood up straight and tall. Feeling accepted and not shamed for once. Both boys looked at Walani and hugged her. The two of them knew that somehow someway Walani had used a little "Cook Magic" to make the impossible happen. Gifford and Brian wondered to themselves why there had been no cake sale, but not Walani. Walani knew that what she had said the previous week hurt Ralph's pride. Walani knew that Juanita had been selling that cake to help Ralph out with his overwhelming bills, and of course her ever growing cocaine habit. Everyone would have to wait a while to taste those delicious cakes again.

As far as Walani was concerned this was the answer to her prayers. Everything had seemed to fall into place, except for one thing. How in the world was she supposed to come up with enough money to fed Juanita's growing Cocaine habit; Walani figured that she had gotten as much as she could with twenty dollars and was appreciative for it. Walani also figured that if Juanita had done all of that for twenty dollars there was surely no need to give her more than twenty dollars' worth at a time, unless of course she had too.

Every morning Walani was handed a "till" at Western Beef with the exact specific amount of money inside needed to make change for customers as they purchased groceries as well as to cash checks at her register, on a two hour schedule her manager would show up at her register to collect from Walani's till and leave he with a specific amount usually the amount she had started the day with. The reason being was in case she was robbed the thieves would only get but so much money. The cashiers at Western Beef were allowed at these two hour intervals to either be five dollars over or under their expected amount of money in their tills according to their receipts. Incredibly Walani had always thought to herself there was always at least one woman who was always five dollars over her expected amount and would turn it over to the manager who was supposed to add it to the store's safe which surely never happened. Since

Walani was allowed to be five dollars short at the end of her shift Walani figured that would be the answer to her problem. Being as it would be embarrassingly suspicious she would for now on every day be five dollars short at the end of her shift. After a one day work week she would be able to squirrel away thirty dollars which is exactly what she needed to powder Juanita's nose. After school on Wednesday Gifford and Brian could hardly contain themselves. The two of them scarfed down their chicken wings and fried rice and put on their best clothes they had, which were matching rust colored Francis Giraud jeans, black and white "Kwame" polka dot shirts, and Air Jordan #2 sneakers. Walani didn't allow them to dye their hair like Kwame, but they felt as good as Kwame himself leaving out for church that night. Walani had planned to drop the boys off at church and then go searching for Hollywood, but was relieved to see him on the corner of 157th Street and 109th Ave as she prepared to cross the tracks into the "Hole". Walani handed Brian a single and instructed her sons to wait for her in the bodega in the 'Hole" after going to the back office behind the potato chip rack in the bodega, and asking the Spanish woman named "Silky" what the last number of the day was.

"Hello Hollywood, How are you this fine evening?" asked Walani as pleasantly as she could.

"It's better now," said Hollywood with a sly smile.

"Hollywood, remember what you gave me for twenty dollars last week? Can you give it to me again?"

Hollywood paused and said with a look of slight concern, "This is for your friend? Right Walani?"

"YES" Walani answered raising her voice at the slightest hint of accusation that the drugs could possibly on God's green earth be for her. Hollywood just listened and watched Walani with the eye of a drug dealer. Using the same calculations that a lion does when watching a heard then zeroing in on an individual wildebeest, watching for the slightest hint of weakness before sprinting into the open field in an all-out assault for what would be a delicious meal, but Walani showed none of these signs so Hollywood just minded his manners and hoped to see weakness sometime soon in the future.

"Too bad he can't look over Juanita like that" Walani thought to herself.

"He'd have himself some sure nuff blow top pussy"

Then Walani paused and became protective of her prey 'Juanita' as all dealers or tricks do when they are obtaining something from someone in exchange for drugs. Walani now wanted to make sure that no one else would give drugs to Juanita but her, and of course Fick and in time she hoped to squeeze Fick out of the picture so that she could have total control of Juanita.

"If Hollywood comes anywhere near the church or Juanita, I'll dime his ass out to the cops to keep him away" Walani thought coldly to herself.

The boys were bursting at the seams by the time Walani got to the store. "Come on Mommy we're going to be late," squealed the boys as Walani approached.

"The last number of the day was 9," said Brian as his mother grabbed each by their arm to head toward the church.

At the church Gifford and Brian rushed up to the front of the church and were greeted with mutual excitement by Capalitana and Chinse who quickly took them into the fold of other choir members who immediately exchanged pleasantries with the Cook brothers in front of the pulpit.

From the back of the church Walani paused for a moment looking at the McDaniel girls and her sons and began to imagine a double wedding and how beautiful it would be. This thought only fueled her attempt to gain complete control over Juanita, then and only then would this dream even have a chance of becoming a reality.

"Hey girl," Walani said cheerfully as she approached Juanita from behind as she was headed toward the back office to use the phone.

Juanita seemed nervous, preoccupied, anxious, irritated, and twitching, with her jaws clichéd tight she managed to give Walani a half of a smile and said, "I'm hurting Walani. Fick was supposed to have been here five minutes ago. I could really, really use some of what you gave me the other day."

"Does Ralph suspect anything between you and Fick?" asked Walani flatly.

Juanita showing complete weakness talked to Walani not even as an equal but as a superior confidant *(which is the beauty of drugs, it levels the playing field. Who was your boss yesterday could be your slave today)*.

I told Ralph that he's just a friend of the family, truth is we used to date, but ain't nothing going on now. Fick knows I'm married and would never disrespect a corrections officer. He just does favors for me hoping that I one day leave Ralph and consider dating him again.

Walani recognized this 'tell-tale" junkie behavior no matter what drug had their nose open. The belief that no one can see that they're full of shit meanwhile everyone does.

Walani recognized the perfect timing and didn't want to waste another second chancing losing her position to Fick and said, "I'll be able to hit the spot."

At the moment Walani reached out her hand and grabbed Juanita's, spun her around admiring her dress.

"OOOOWWWW that's a nice dress"

As Walani twirled Juanita she placed the green dollar envelope of cocaine in Juanita's palm. Juanita made a big broad smile as she was twirled and at the same time kissed Walani on the cheek in a way that let Walani know that she was willing to be more than a friend if Walani wanted. Walani just smiled and Juanita nearly ran into the bathroom with her prized nose candy. As Walani turned around to leave the back hallway she saw Fick come through the front entrance in a huff. He nodded and said, 'Hey Ms. Cook. You see Juanita around?"

Walani answered, "She's in the ladies room."

"Okay, I'll wait for her in the office, I see it's open".

Walani headed to the front of her church and tried not to laugh as she watched Gifford and Brian trying to sing and mostly lip syncing trying to fit in. It really didn't matter they were happy and everyone knew it. Gifford stared at Chinse the whole time as she shyly returned the look every now and then. The choir itself was very good. Their rendition of James Cleveland's 'God has smiled on me could move even the hardest anti-Christian'. Walani felt as though the song was being sung just for her and Gifford felt the same way. Before anyone knew it choir rehearsal was over.

Walani looked to the back of the church and was shocked to see Ralph McDaniel's enter looking round for Juanita. Although he was familiar with the church he was unfamiliar with its workings and expected behavior. Ralph had figured that the back office was off limits and assumed to not even knock on the door. Ralph figured that the Reverend would always be in there either in deep thought, deep prayer, or in the middle of writing a sermon. Thank God he didn't knock or enter or he would have interrupted his wife deep throating Fick after sprinkling a dime bag of coke on his penis.

Walani approached Ralph and said as calmly as she could, "Juanita went across the street to the store she should be right back. I'll get your girls ready and send them outside to you."

As Ralph left the building looking puzzled, Walani ran to the side office and began pounding on the door like there was a five alarm fire going on.

"YOUR HUSBANDS' HERE GET OUT NOW!" Walani yelled and whispered at the same time.

Juanita pushed pass Walani and ran into the ladies room as Fick struggled to pull his pants up he and Walani grinned at each other. Walani quickly closed the door as Fick knew to stay concealed and that this was a very dangerous situation indeed. As Walani turned to walk away from the office she saw Ralph come back into the Church.

"Hey you didn't see her? She came back in. She's in the ladies room"

Ralph gave Walani a hard stare and turned around to head to the front of the church.

When his daughters saw him coming they ran toward him up the middle aisle screaming "Daddy, Daddy!" Ralph made sure he also looked over their heads to give the Cook brothers a cold hard stare to make sure that they were in their place.

Walani slowly got her boys together and were the last to be leaving when she decided to go to the back office and let Fick know that the coast was clear.

"Thank you Walani for covering for us. I really appreciate it. If there is ever anything I can do for you just let me know."

Walani knowing it was dark answered, "You could walk me and my boys back to the projects, it is kind of late."

Fick jumped to his feet, "Not a problem Ms. Cook, at your service."

Walani stopped and thanked Fick on the corner of 157th Street and 109th Ave in the Hole and told Fick that she and her boys were fine from there. As Fick said good night the Corley brothers Rolls Royce turned the corner with Hollywood inside giving Walani a puzzled look.

"At least for now my sons are happy and everything seemed to be falling into place to keep them happy." Walani though to herself knowing that most importantly Juanita was on her side.

"Thank you sweet Jesus, you really do help those who help themselves, I am truly grateful, Amen."

Chapter 5

Captain Ralph McDaniel's goes too far....WAY too far

Things were going great, Gifford and Brian where able to see Chinse and Capalitana twice a week as well as talk to them on the phone. It didn't matter that Capalitana was years older than Brian the two seemed to interact because they were around each other so much and seemed to feel left out and a bit jealous that their siblings were so smitten with each other. This seemed to bother Walani but she just put up with it because it seemed to make everything in her world run smoother to do so. It felt good to Walani to feel like she was being a successful parent. The boys were doing great at school and staying out of trouble. All Gifford and Brian wanted to do was go to church and sing in the choir. What more could a mother ask for?

Just like with all people. There seemed to always be a piece of the puzzle missing in Walani's life. The piece that would make her life complete or perfect if you will. Some of us are afraid that if we attempt to force that piece of the puzzle into place that we would destroy the whole puzzle. So we deal with the imperfection as best we can and be glad that our lives are as close to perfect as it is, but sometimes that missing piece is such an eyesore that we have to do something about it even at the risk of destroying the whole puzzle.

For five years Walani had put up with occasional run-ins, insults, and endless un-pleasantries from Correction Officer Ralph McDaniel's. By 1993 Gifford had turned 13 years old. He had graduated at the top of his class and was attending Junior High School #8 at 10835 167th Street Jamaica N.Y. Brian of course had done the same thing and attended also. Gifford was still a little taller than Brian, but Brian was clearly stronger built and seemed much more mature. Brian looked so much like Lance that it made Walani's heartache at times. Walani had been receiving weekly letters from Lance, but only showed the holiday and birthday letters to her boys. She didn't want them distracted from their studies or feeling sad unnecessarily. Walani hadn't taken the boys to see their father once. Walani knew that eventually she would have to but didn't want the experience to negatively affect her sons. All of these conflicting thoughts really added up to the fact that she still loved lance and missed him terribly and with her sons looking more and more like him every day only reminded her more and more of that fact.

As much as Gifford tried to compete with his younger brother it was clear that Brian was the dominate one of the two. Gifford being the older brother felt silly looking up to his younger

sibling. Brian being so masculine and clearly being the 'man" of the house not only appeared to be a bigger brother but sometimes a father figure. This sometimes bothered Gifford and Walani. Although Gifford was better scholastically, Brian was far superior when it came to common sense. Both brothers favored their father however Brian was his spitting image down to his personality and logic. Gifford was happy go lucky and thought that everyone who smiled at him was his friend. It wasn't uncommon for Brian to demand Gifford's correct change at the corner store when Gifford just wanted to enjoy the snack he had just purchased trying to assure Brian that it must have had been an honest mistake. Nothing bothers Brian or Walani more than Gifford's tireless attempts to win Ralph McDaniel's approval. Gifford seemed to try every way possible tirelessly attempting to ingratiate or befriend Ralph McDaniel's and the more he tried the more he was given the cold shoulder even after Chinse had told him it was no use.
Ralph McDaniel's was a callus cruel man; who believed that being a bastard child no matter how the situation arose was a curse not a circumstance. That living in the South Jamaica Houses was a fate of the damned. That even though a chimp could pass a New York City Corrections exam or win a second place prize in a New York State lottery that would allow him to live out on Long Island. He thought he was better than all of the rest of the lower class niggers because he had been able to do so. To make Gifford's situation worse Officer Ralph McDaniel's had become Captain Ralph McDaniel's in July of 1992. At that point everyone had found him nearly impossible to bear.

On March 26th 1993 Gifford and Brian had been given a special assignment as per the Reverend. The Cook boys had been appointed junior ushers and were at the front door in their burgundy suit jackets, burgundy ties and white gloves. Walani had gone out of her that morning to secure white carnations in their handkerchief pockets. Each brother stood on each side of the churches front doors and Gifford insisted that he be the one to open the doors while Brian handed each parishioner the day's program as they entered. Chinse stood next to Gifford and Capalitana next to Brian with other teenagers gathered around laughing and talking as teenagers do; until the Reverend came out and said that everyone but the Cook brothers were to stand outside to make the parishioners comfortable as they came in. After all business was business. As the Cook brothers stood in front of the church rapping the words to the latest Tupac Shakur song, "Round and Round Round we go…I get around." Gifford noticed that Ralph McDaniel's was tending to his Gold 1992 Toyota Camry which appeared to have a flat tire. Ralph was so worried about his car that he sometimes skipped service to sit in the car to keep an eye on it.

"Good for his ass, he acts like that shit is a Rolls Royce or something," Brian said with a wicked smile.

"Maybe if we helped him he wouldn't hate us so much," Gifford said excited at the thought of gaining Ralphs approval.

Brian stood at Gifford's post while Gifford trotted across the street. Ralph had his back to Gifford as he made his way across Sutphin Boulevard. A car ran the Red Light and came roaring toward him, Gifford sped up and ran out of the cars way arriving at the other side of the street Gifford reached his hand out to Ralph's shoulder; Ralph was on his knees tending to the flat tire with his back toward Gifford. Unaware that Gifford was approaching to try to help and not a masked gunman looking to rob him of his meager earnings. As soon as Ralph felt Gifford's fingers on his shoulder; he did a textbook Maspeth Queens New York City Correction Academy Instructor Adonis take down complete with an elbow to the nose. Ralph then un-holstered his personal protection firearm and pointed it at the face of the "perp" who laid there on his back unconscious bleeding from his nose; to make sure that the extreme threat was under control. Cars stopped from every direction and a crowd started to gather as Brian ran across the street screaming, "You fucking asshole! My brother was coming to help you and you knocked my brother out!

At this point a New York City Police Sector R.M.P. arrived at the scene. The responding officers immediately called for a patrol supervisor and a bus *(ambulance)* and pulled their duty pistols and ordered this deranged looking black man to drop his gun.

"I'M A CAPTAIN!" yelled Ralph at the top of his lungs.

"DON'T SHOOT"

"Then you know the law!" The driving officer responded.

"Drop the fucking gun," The cop then said smoothly.

Ralph complied and dropped the gun, the officers then approached Ralph and spun him to the car to search him.

"I'm the one on the fucking job! He's the God damned perp!" Ralph yelled as the cops rifled through his pockets retrieving his wallet.

Before the cop could open the wallet the recording officer asked curiously, "Where do you work captain?"

"At O.B.C.C. on Rikers" Ralph said with overwhelming pride.

"You mean you're a Corrections captain?" said the recording officer now clearly pissed. "Why did you lie to us, you're not on the 'job' unless you're in the police department. You're not a cop."

The police officers stared coldly at each other and opened Ralph's wallet, then sneered at Ralph who started to stutter, "Well you know how it goes, corrections are like the marines and you guys are like the army, but it's the same job, you know." As ralph showed all his teeth like a good coon begging for mercy.

"WRONG!! You're a peace officer, we are police officers. You have no power of arrest. Now what the fuck is going on here "C.O." because it looks like you assaulted a young boy. First we're gonna deal with that, then we're looking at criminal impersonation of a police officer." Ralph started a tirade of how terrible the neighborhood was and how the cops should understand because they work with these savages everyday just like he has to on Rikers Island. He was ready to continue on his tirade when he was attacked with the full force of a protective black mother who came out of church and saw her son still lying unconscious on the ground with two white cops discussing his fate to a self-hating black corrections captain.

All ten of Walani's manicured finger nails seemed to disappear under Ralph's fleshy cheeks as Ralph let out a howl. Walani seemed to do all she could to tear Ralph's cheeks off and tears flowed down her own cheeks. It looked as though Walani wanted to scream but the sound could not come out. In seconds Ralph regained his composure as the police officers stood there in shock. As Ralph restrained Walani's arms the driving officer struck Walani on the back of her head with his P.R. 24 baton send her lifeless body to the ground. Not more than a millisecond would pass before Brian was on the back of the driving officer who had just knocked his mother out cold. Brian was trying to place his right arm around the officer's throat in a yolk hold when the recording officer used his own P.R. 24 to put Brian in the same mental state as his mother, and brother. At this point the entire congregation, approximately two hundred people watched in shock and horror from the front of the church. None of them could muster up the courage to even cry out for the Lord's help much less go out to the street and challenge two white police officers about the goings on with this horrific scene. Huge crowds of bystanders also started to gather on each side of Sutphin Boulevard with a total of four police cruisers now on the scene surrounding Ralph's car, Walani in her Sunday best laying on the ground with her legs agape with Gifford and Brian lying next to her in their burgundy usher suits, laying on top of each other with pedals of white carnations blowing in the wind all with blood flowing from open wounds.

"I WANT ALL THREE OH THESE GHETTO PIECES OF SHIT LOCKED UP!!!"
Ralph screamed over the sound of the sirens and jeers from the crowd.

"HA HA!! Assaulting two white police officers should put them away for years, Now they'll finally meet their piece of shit father!" Ralph continued with blood flowing down his cheeks.

"The boy only attacked me after I had to hit this woman who was probably his mother" The driving officer said through clinched teeth now furious with Ralph.
"Doesn't matter she attacked a cop! Just look at my face," declared Ralph showing his face in a matter of fact tone.

"SHUT UP NIGGER! You're not cop," the driving Officer responded staring Ralph coldly in his eyes.

"And you had damned well better have a good fucking reason to have had hit the boy in the first place, then drawing your gun on him," said the recording officer finally catching his breath and tending to Walani, Gifford, and Brian as they were being placed on stretchers and receiving medical care as the crowd was becoming hysterical.

"I need medical attention too. I get it first I'm a cop! Get over here E.M.T and tend to me first God damn it! Afterward I will make a complete report and submit to your precinct in person," said ralph as professionally as he could with his face completely covered in blood, now trying to compose himself as he looked across the street and saw Chinse and Capalitana hysterically crying and being held back by Juanita who looked high and confused.

"Oh is that so!?" said the recording police officer.

"Yeah really! I'm a captain and you're an officer and you will listen!" screamed Ralph, attempting to pull rank over an agency that he knew nothing about.

"You think you can tell a police officer what to do?" said the recording officer as his Sergeant finally walked on the scene.

"What do we got here Frank?" asked the Sergeant who was the responding patrol Supervisor.

"I'll let the "CAPTAIN" tell you what going on boss!" said the recording officer letting Ralph dig his own grave.

"Finally an equal ranking officer," declared Ralph as he began.

"Wait!"

The Sergeant interrupted. "I thought you said he was a Captain Frank?" the Sergeant now becoming upset.

"I'm a Corrections Department Captain!" announced Ralph clearly enjoying just the sound of it.

"Wait!" Once again the Sergeant interrupted.

"Just be quiet Corrections Captain and let me speak to my officers"

Ralph took out his handkerchief and began cleaning his face as the two officer huddled with their Sergeant which ended quickly.

"You're under arrest "CAPTAIN!" announced the recording officer.

"Now turn your BLACK ASS around and put your hands on the car! NOW!!"

Captain Ralph McDaniel's turned around and placed his hands on the hood of his precious Camry leaking blood down the windows.

The patrol Supervisor then said, 'Where is your gun?"

Ralph spoke up crying now, "It's holstered on my right hip. Look I'm a captain in the N.Y.C. Corrections Department can you please give me some professional courtesy. My children are watching, can you please bring me into your car un-cuffed?"

Ralph like other law enforcement officers who have faced similar instances was smart enough to not let the arresting officer know that he had a second Gun a .357 Magnum at home that wasn't registered known as a "throw away" that he bought in Virginia while on vacation. Ralph just overcome with emotion just bawled like a newborn baby.

"Is this your only gun? Is there another gun in the car?" responded the Sergeant completely ignoring Ralph's cries.

"That is my only gun," Ralph said each word in between sobs. Like a child getting a whooping.

The Sergeant was as cold as ice; white cops love to have a black man in this position. The arrest process seems to even slow down as they savor the moment. The moment is even more satisfying when it's a black man who thinks he's a "Somebody".

"I'm gonna call corrections to tell them your status, your gun will be vouchered by the arresting officer, who is the recording officer. Officer McDaniel's if you do have another gun at home you must turn it in after you are released on bail. Failing to do so will result in further charges."

Ralph wasn't too worried about this because the only other person who knew about his throw away was Capalitana. Who would never touch it unless there was an emergency as instructed by her father, not even Juanita knew about the throw away gun.

"Sir Please. I was the one assaulted I need medical attention," Ralph again managed to say through the tears.

"My boys will talk to you about your medical condition in the car," the Sergeant said coldly as he "Scratched" the officer's memo books of his officers, saluted then walked away.

As Ralph was being placed in the car he began to smile. Ralph saw each of the Cook brothers and Walani being tended to on their stretchers completely out cold, what made him smile was that they were all handcuffed to their stretchers and he was still not cuffed. The ambulances pulled way with everyone standing around begging for answers. The E.M.T's said that they were all going to Jamaica Hospital. The police car Ralph was in was the last police car on the scene. It was the focus of attention now. Juanita and the McDaniel's girls were at the window of the R.M.P. screaming as Ralph screamed back with his voice cracking.

"Daddy's okay, sweetheart. Its police business that's all, daddy's okay."

Ralph showed his daughters that there were no cuffs on his wrists as the car pulled from the curb heading north on Sutphin Boulevard.

"What about my medical care brothers in blue? I didn't get your names?" asked Ralph trying to befriend the officers.

"Listen Spade!" said Officer McDonald.

"I'm going to tell you how the police really work so listen good; you're under arrest. I'll read you your rights at the station house. If you insist on medical attention Officer Comiskey and I are going to make sure you REALLY need it, get me? If you make this smooth we'll give you professional courtesy and cuff you to a bench in Central Booking and not in a cell and expedite your paperwork to get you through central booking within eight hours. If not we're going beat your black ass to a pulp, sit on you in the hospital and whip your ass some more, then when we finally do get you to central booking and are sleeping on a floor by the toilet bowl in a jam packed bull pen. I'm going to put in a call for your paperwork to be lost down the elevator shaft, then it will be a week of bologna sandwiches and infections to your wounds on top of daily ass kicking from "Our" people before you see a judge. Understand Nigger?"

Ralph pulled himself together and said, "I decline medical attention. Can you please tell me what I'll be charged with?"

Mumbled Ralph now completely destroyed.

Officer McDonald began, "You'll be charged with assault in the third degree 120.00 of the New York State Penal law; a "A" misdemeanor."

Officer Comiskey sarcastically chimed in, "I bet they don't teach that in the Corrections Academy."

Both cops broke into laughter as Ralph openly wept in the back seat as the R.M.P. cruised toward the 103rd precinct.

Walani slowly came to in a Jamaica Hospital bed. She had an I.V. in her arm and bloody gauze over her left eye at her hairline where she had received seven stitches. Standing over her looking down as she blinked them into focus was Reverend Burns, Hollywood, and Fick. Reverend Burns explained that he was just glad to be there when the good lord bought her back to life. The reverend grabbed her hands together and said, "Praise God it's been two days." With a warm gentle smile he continued that he had to be leaving, that he had to report the good news back to the congregation who was busy holding an intense prayer vigil for Walani's safe return from purgatory.

Reverend Burns really didn't want to go, but was told by Hollywood and Fick that a message was to be given to Walani from Lance himself and that it would behoove him not be knowledgeable of such information.

"I don't know how Lance got the number, but Lance called my mother's house and told me to check on you until you woke up. Lance also somehow knows that I've been selling you drugs and demanded to know all that I knew. I found out that Fick was spending a lot of time at the church and the two of us put two and two together. Is it true that you've been feeding Juanita's nose just so that your sons could be friends with her daughter?"

Hollywood and Fick waited patiently and silently for an answer.

"You know how Long Island people see us," said Walani with her voice cracking ad lips trembling. "They see us as shit," Walani said in a soft voice as a tear rolled down her cheek.

Hollywood and Fick were both born and raised in Southeastern Queens and was well aware of the prejudiced attitudes of Long Island blacks toward Queens Blacks and nodded their heads in agreement, then Lance began to speak.

"Lance is a powerful man Walani. Lance helped put Queens on the map. A lot of people who came up with and under him are now doing long sentences for criminal enterprising after the Eddie Burns killing. Those people have a lot of influence and hold a lot of weight in our neighborhood. Those same people found out that I was selling you drugs, were very upset, and have given me an order. I am to deliver justice to you the way you want it word for word," explained Hollywood. "Matter of fact, Can I say something?" asked Fick.

"From what I hear killing a Corrections officer of any rank is 1st degree murder, just like killing a cop. If you ask me we wait to see if he's fired or do something to make sure he gets fired before we do anything."

Once again both men waited silently for Walani to answer.

"Where are my sons?" Walani said in a soft wounded voice.

Fick spoke up, "Since Ralph didn't claim any injuries there were no criminal charges filed against you or Gifford that's why your cuffs have been removed and we are allowed to speak to you. Brian on the other hand sustained a concussion, an injury sustained from a police officer in the line of duty. That cop had to justify his actions, so in turn Brian has been charged as an adult for assaulting a police officer. Brian is being held in Spofford Juvenile Detention center in the Bronx. Gifford was treated for a broken nose and a concussion. There was no one to turn Gifford over to so adult children services placed him in a group home until you are well enough to take him home."

Once again the two men stood there in silence patiently waiting for Walani's response. Walani lied there as tears welled up in her eyes and started to leak down each side of her face.

"What about hat piece of shit?" Walani asked with scorn.

Fick spoke up fast, "Ralph was charged with third degree assault. He's been suspended for thirty days. If found guilty he might lose his job and the most he would do as far as time would be a couple of months in jail. I know some correction officers who smoke crack; we could get to him once he's sentenced. Or we could just wait for him to get out and kill him. What I'm saying is by that point he would be an ex- corrections officer so no one would care.

Fick fell silent as Hollywood gave him a long hard stare. Hollywood kept the stare hard so that Fick would get the point. The only reason he was there was to give all of the facts, just the facts and of course his cooperation. Fick got the point that he was not to try to persuade Walani in any way on her final decision. The situation was made clear. The three of them were holding their own court. Black people in Queens couldn't care less about the law, all the black people of Queens' care about is Justice.

"How long would this trial last? I mean how long until he would be fired?" asked Walani, taking heed to Fick's warning.

"That could be as long as three years, he's out on bail already," Fick answered dryly.

"FUCK NO!" screamed Walani bringing a nurse into the room. Walani assured the nurse that all was okay and to please leave her alone with her cousins. Then Walani's voice fell low and as cold as ice.

"You tell my husband that we are struggling to survive out here. You tell him that he left us with nothing. His children are insulted all the time by this man, and if he considers himself a man and a man of his word he will stop the suffering. You tell my husband that if his so called friends could kill this cop Eddie Burns just to make a point then his so called friends could kill this jail guard for hurting his defenseless wife and children.

Both men nodded then both men said, "Understood."

"Now, what about my son's case?" asked Walani sounding more gangster by the second. "Depending on what kind of lawyer you get, depends on how his case would go. Reverend Burns has already agreed to write a letter of good character for Brian as well as put up church money for an 18B lawyer. You wouldn't want a legal aid lawyer; all the legal aid would do is plea bargain his assault on a police officer charge to third degree assault as a juvenile defender, which would send him to Tryon Juvenile Detention Center for six months," Fick said with as much sympathy as he could.

As Walani grit her teeth with fury she said in a calm tone, "I said what I have to say. I'm glad you two came by to check on me. I won't forget it. I need to rest now."

Both Men nodded quietly then left the room.

On Sunday April 2, 1993, Juanita McDaniel's dropped Capalitana and Chinse to Sunday school as usual. She then went to Rochdale Village, Circle 3 Building 10, and Apartment 13C and called her husband.

"Hey baby can you do me a favor?" Juanita asked Ralph as nicely as she could.

"Juanita, please don't tell me something happened to my car!" thundered Ralph. He was more protective over his Camry; than his own daughters.

"Mrs. Vickie Walker from church, I had to drive her home, she wasn't feeling well. On my way back to church the car broke down."

"WHAT!" Interjected Ralph

"How the fuck could my car break down *(with an emphasis on MY)*, you know God damned well my car is in excellent running condition and everyone knows Camry's don't break down!"

There was a moment of silence then Juanita answered back with a raspy aggravated voice, "Well it did!"

Ralph Thundered once again, "Where is my damned car Juanita? Where the fuck is it right now?"

Again a moment of silence, "It's on Foch Boulevard. I know you gave me money, but Mrs. Brooks asked me to borrow some so I gave it all to her. After all it is Sunday and I am a Christian. I wasn't going to walk through the projects back to church so I walked to my friend's house in Rochdale Village. I was wondering what in God's name I was going to do when I remembered it was your pass day. Can you please come get me?"

Juanita sounding more submissive now, there was an uneasy silence.

"Wait a minute, Who's house are you at?"

Ralph was a very jealous man and liked stories explained to the most prestige detail. Or else he would immediately think that Juanita was messing around and he was usually right.

"You know Kevin from church. Mrs. Walker's son, before I dropped her off she was saying that he was home, so when I broke down I knew he would be there if I walked fast enough. Kevin lives in Circle 3 Building 10 Apartment 13C," Juanita said knowing what the next line would be. Ralph was so predictable.

"I'll be right there. I don't want this "Kevin Walker" getting any ideas!" Ralph yelled into the phone.

At 10:43 a.m., Ralph pulled into Circle 3 of Rochdale Village. In front of Building 10 there was always an empty spot reserved for security and police vehicles. Even though his placard was in the Toyota Camry, Ralph pulled into that spot anyway. Ralph tried calling Juanita by recalling the number that she had called from. Juanita was smart enough to press *67 from the pay phone next to the security tower in Circle 3. Ralph became irritated because he was so focused on the fact that Juanita was in the company of a young man, that he hadn't remembered all of the information she had given him. Ralph remembered the circle and the building number but not the section. Every building number in Rochdale has three sections with all either being A, B, or C. That's what makes Rochdale Village's 20 buildings actually 50 buildings. The reason he didn't remember was because Juanita purposely didn't tell him. Juanita knew that by not telling him he would check all three thus irritating him more and making him lose focus and take more chances. Ralph had packed on the pounds over the last few years of free meals in the 'Keepers Kitchen" or 'K.K.' as corrections officers referred to it. Ralph resembled the police father from the TV show "Family Matters". Juanita was also instructed to do this so that Ralph would be tired and out of breath by the time he actually found the apartment.

"God damn it! Now I gotta check all three!" Ralph said to himself as he started to perspire at the very thought of all of that walking.

Ralph walked the long hallway to the back of the building along the waves of the green wall to the "A" section where he figured he start his search, and as all parties figured he would he arrived at section C, the correct section last and completely out of breath. On the elevator Ralph saw hammer slam marks that were black holes on the brown wood where years ago as teenagers Fick, Derek, and Steve Cherry vandalized the elevator on a drunken Saturday night.

"Fucking wild coons," Ralph mumbled under his breath.

It seemed like forever until the elevator reached the 13th floor.

"Now where in the hell is apartment C?" Ralph murmured through his pants to himself. N Now completely irritated and sweating nearly profusely.

Ralph then noticed that one of the doors in the hallway immediately to his left was ajar. Upon further inspection he saw the label 13C on the door. Out of breath, extremely irritated, and being blinded by jealousy makes for very hasty and reckless decisions.

Ralph drew his model 64 four inch barrel .38 caliber personal protection firearm and announced, "Police department! Your door is open, I'm coming in."

As Ralph walked down the long hallway of the apartment the same exact way reality had done nearly 15 years earlier he looked out on the terrace behind the living room. On the terrace Juanita was engaged in a conversation with a man who wasn't Kevin Walker. Juanita also looked as though she was being flirtatious with the man. Ralph thought that the man looked familiar but couldn't place the face.

Now fully enraged Ralph pulled the door open as if he were catching them in the act. Before he could say a word Juanita said, "Hey Honey. This is my friend Fick. Fick this is my husband Ralph."

Juanita then looked down to Ralph's gun and said, "Baby? What's with the gun?"
"Oh, I Uh, found the door open so I came in with my weapon drawn. It's standard procedure." Ralph said clearly upset but trying to gather himself. Ralph holstered his weapon showing off the length of the barrel so that Fick could see it.

"Where is Kevin?" Ralph said suspiciously.

"Oh, Kevin went to the store for me," Juanita answered nervously.

"Where's my damn car. I had to borrow the neighbor's car, a Chevy Malibu. I'm a captain now. I ain't supposed to be seen in no God damned Chevy Malibu," Ralph said with an air of superiority and glad that this Fick new of his rank guessing that Fick would assume he was a police captain.

"Fick had it towed to Star Auto Body on Liberty Avenue," said Juanita as if she was impressed with Fick to further annoy Ralph.

"Oh REALLY! You towed my car, and what was wrong with my new Camry Mr. Fick?" said Ralph now feeling tread upon and on the verge of openly challenging Fick physically.
"Calm down honey," said Juanita wrapping her arms around Ralph and giving him a big kiss.

"I gotta use the bathroom, I'll let you men discuss car stuff. Fick will explain to you everything the mechanic told him," Juanita said as she exited into the apartment.

"You came over to Foch Boulevard from here to pick my wife up?" Ralph asked probing Fick as if he were being formally interrogated.

"Why would I do that, Juanita broke down on Bedell Street by the power plant," Fick pointed over his shoulder with his thumb in the direction behind the building as if he were hitchhiking.

Now fully enraged by catching Juanita in a lie, Ralph moved in close to Fick's face and said while panting in a low deep voice, "What the fuck would my wife be doing parked on Bedell Street?"

"She was coming to get some coke and some dick. I've been fucking that bitch for YEARS NOW," Fick said "Years Now" very loudly as if it were a cue word.

Which it was and on cue Hollywood burst onto the terrace rushing Ralph, moving so quickly he removed the model 64 revolver with ease knowing exactly where it was thanks to Ralph telegraphing it earlier. With a quick easy motion Hollywood tossed the gun back into the apartment while Fick simultaneously put his left hand over Ralph's mouth and used his right arm to "half nelson" Ralph's right arm behind his head. Hollywood grabbed both of Ralph's legs and Ralph struggled wildly. Trying to scream through Fick's hand he turned his head toward the apartment and saw Juanita standing there with her hand over her mouth with tears rolling down her cheeks. Ralph reached for her with his left hand as Fick and Hollywood have the old, 'Heave Hoe" minus the three, two, one countdown launching Ralph over the side railing of the terrace. As soon as Ralph was launched over the side railing of the terrace, He started screaming on the way down. Fick and Hollywood ran back into the apartment closing the door and instantly heard Ralph's body slam on top of the Chevy Malibu. Fick said.

"Well I hope his neighbor's Chevy Malibu is good enough for him now."

No sooner than Fick finished his attempt at cold blooded humor did Hollywood shoot him in the right temple at point blank range with Ralph's .38 Model 64. As Fick's body fell lifelessly to the ground Hollywood heard Juanita scream as well as screams from bystanders outside crowding around the Chevy Malibu that had its roof caved in by Ralph's now dead body that lay inside. Juanita immediately tried to run to the long hallway out of the apartment once again the .38 Model 64 barked as Hollywood shot her in the back, then stood over her and put one in the back of her head. Hollywood as quickly as he could, pulled out a rag and wiped down the gun and placed in in Fick's hand. Hollywood then whipped the door knob down and ran down the 'B" staircase immediately to the left of the apartment. Hollywood knew that because of where the body landed the police where sure to be at apartment 13C in no time.

When Hollywood reached the ground floor he ran down the service hallway. Not the main polished hallway and out the back door and toward Bedell Street where his 93 Maxima was parked directly behind Ralph's precious Toyota Camry.

Chapter 6

Blessed are the meek.....

Walani woke up in her hospital bed on April 3rd because someone was tickling her toe. She was still in the hospital because she had developed brain swelling due to the head trauma she had received from the P.R. 24 hit. Walani was put under on April 1st to have the fluid drained and was told that she could be discharged on the 3rd to retrieve Gifford from the group home, go see about Brian's criminal case and somehow try and piece her life back together.

That someone who was tickling her toe was her childhood friend from 27 Cambridge Place named, Michael 'Mick-Man' Gourdine; he was a rookie Police Officer Tax ID #904062 Shield #31187 assigned to the 6-7 Precinct in East Flatbush Brooklyn, but was in full uniform at Jamaica hospital by Walani's bedside. Mick-Man had rolled over from the Corrections Department to the New York Police Department. Mick-Man had numerous relatives in the Corrections Department, State and City which gave him a lot of influence and access to people on both sides of the law. Mick-Man had met Lance in O.B.C.C. where he was a steady officer on the 3x11 tour in 8 upper. O.B.C.C. or the Otis Banthum Correctional Center; a state ready facility, meaning when a city inmate is sentenced he is sent to O.B.C.C. and waits for room in downstate, upstate New York which is the intake center for the State of New York. Most notably the location where an inmate now waits for permanent housing in a state facility; but sometimes it works in reverse.

When an inmate has to come back to New York City to stand trial for a past crime the state will transfer him to O.B.C.C. and have the inmate 'bussed' every day to and from court until his trial is over; then the inmate is returned to the state. This was the situation in 1990 when Lance met Mick-Man. One day when Mick-Man was doing his routine tour of the area, he passed Lance while he was reading a letter and looking at his pictures. Mick-Man noticed that it was Walani in the picture; the same Walani who lived at 45 Cambridge Place. The two hit it off from the beginning.

Mick-Man asked Lance if he knew of his Uncle Perry Burns and Lance told him that they were in fact good friends and went back a ways. Every day the two would talk about this history of the drug game and how the South Jamaica Cartel was really an extension of the Harlem Cartel. Mick-man enjoyed these stories and history lessons immensely.

In September 1990, a corrections officer who was considered a "Duck" by inmates and officers alike was nearly beaten to death for his wristwatch in O.B.C.C. What was to follow was one of the biggest prison riots to take place in the history of Rikers Island.

Rikers Island was locked down for five days, inmates locked the officers they liked in cells and fed them commissary while they took officers they hated and beat them mercilessly and sometimes worse. Captain Ralph McDaniel's was enjoying his vacation when this happened, luckily for him. Who happened to be during that time C.O. Michael 'Mick-Man' Gourdine, shield #12756. He was escorting 8 upper to chow when the alarm sounded. Mick-Man told his house to hit the wall as he ran to the roll call area where the "War Wagon" was pulled out and officers would suit up for battle.

As the officers headed back toward the chow hall, Mick-Man noticed that his house was gone, all 87 inmates where gone! The inmates had run into the chow hall with other inmates and were daring officers to come in and get them; which was the order that was given. As the "Goon Squad" entered into the chow hall all hell broke loose. Mick-Man was in the fourth row. All he saw was "Hats & Bats" and heard screams. Blood curdling screams that he still hears to this day. As Mick-Man passed a table he felt something grab his leg and pull him to the floor and under the table, it was Lance Cook and two other inmates.

"Be Cool and stay still little nigger," Lance screamed to Mick-Man who was more than happy to oblige.

The four men lied under the table until the fighting stopped. The officers had lost. There was screaming and blood everywhere. Mick-Man could see the entrance to the chow hall where Officers where lined up and ready to enter. Suddenly a voice came from a bullhorn, "We're going to release tear gas! If anyone wants to surrender come out now!"

Lance spoke into Mick-Man's ear, "Let us carry you out, look hurt and limp when we put you down."

Mick-Man nodded.

Mick-man then stood up from under the table waving his hands; and then fell down. Lance and the two inmates carried Mick-Man to the door way where Mick-Man was laid on a stretcher. Lance and the two inmates where cuffed and put on the wall face first. At the infirmary Mick-Man remembered to limp to the doctor. Where he told the story to A.D.W. Monroe how he gallantly went into battle and was struck down. Inmates were prepared to finish him when he was saved by Lance Cook.

Lance and the two inmates were transferred to Brooklyn Correctional Facility of B.C.F. and Mick-Man was treated and allowed to go home. Later that evening the riot took a turn for the worse and the lockdown began. There were inmates and officers alike whose lives where changed forever on that fateful days.

Mick-Man held Walani's hand and said that he would do all he could to help and told her that Lance had saved his life and he would do all that was in his power to help this terrible situation. Mick-Man placed a dozen roses on the window sill and told Walani that Lance had contacted him and told him everything. He assured her that no matter what; no one would put their hands on Walani or her children again. That He himself was her guardian angel.

"I don't know how my life got to this point Mick-Man," Walani started to speak.

"Love will take your life on a wild trip not knowing where it will end up, you just go with it. I remember you as such a funny little guy. I wished you were older so that I could have got with you myself." Walani smiled.

Walani was ten years Mick-Man's senior but Brooklyn was funny like that. The two had actually played skelly together a few times. Mick-Man was a street kid back on Cambridge Place and ran the streets all hours of the night. Sold the Daily News newspaper in the Wyckoff Projects on the weekend and had become a "Chili Pimp" in his middle teens as well as a small scale drug dealer. Walani was surprised when she had read in a letter from Lance that Mick-Man had become a corrections and then police officer. Mick-man seemed to want it all and nothing at all at the same time. He was always there for his friends and never forgot a favor. Walani was glad to see him, but knew that Mick-Man was always working an angle. Walani wondered if Mick-Man was looking to get into the drug game now that he was out on the street as a police officer and was sniffing around to see if Walani could get him some kind of drug connection in Jamaica, Queens.

Walani also remembered that Mick-Man always had his ear to the ground and always got news first good and bad. Some people even referred to him as the grim reaper. Not because he killed people but because he was always the bearer of bad news knowing that someone who was well-known on the street was dead before anyone else, even the Police. Walani sat up and recognized what he was really there for above all else, and that was to deliver a message.

"Mick-Man, why are you really here?" Walani asked with tears in her eyes welling up expecting to hear he worst.

"Today is your discharge day. I know you have a lot to do, but a lot has happened in the last week. Your boys are fine, but there has been a tragedy concerning the corrections Captain that assaulted your son."

Walani sat stone faced knowing that whatever happened Mick-Man knew what really happened and furthermore, knew that she was involved. Mick-Man continued.

"Yesterday Ralph McDaniel's followed Juanita to Fick's house in Rochdale Village. Ralph forced his way into the apartment. Ralph gunned down Juanita then he and Fick struggled over the gun, after Fick gained control over the gun, Ralph being the coward fell to his death trying to get away by jumping from one terrace to the other. Fick completely distraught over the death of Juanita decided to take his own life. The entire church is grief-stricken and holding around the clock prayer sessions to deal with this senseless tragedy. If anyone asks you about this incident act as though it's the first time you're hearing about it and don't forget to look sad. Remember you're just a meek church lady who was victimized by Ralph because he was losing his mind thinking that Juanita was having an affair. It's only a coincidence that he found out a week after your run in. I was told to tell you this, so that anyone who needs to know, now know that the case is closed and can continue on with their lives as you must now try to do."

Walani started to smile, now the visit made perfect sense. Mick-Man did have a message, but it wasn't for her. Mick-Man was there to tell her the news and how to respond, but the message was really for Hollywood, so that he would know that the police were not looking for him that the instruction he was given from the powers that be had been carried out to the letter and no one was the wiser.

"Here's my number, its 1-718-816-0273. If you need me for anything at all just call, and tell Lance I'm looking to get into something now that I'm in the police department; something other than the girls."

Walani motioned for Mick-Man to come to her and gave him a kiss on the forehead. "I'll be fine Mick-Man; be careful out there."

With that Mick-Man picked up his radio and turned to channel 9 and called for Nard to meet him in front of the hospital. Moments later Walani's hospital phone rang. It was the Good Reverend Burns.

"Have you heard the news child? I'm telling you the good Lord is testing us. We must pull together in this terrible time of crisis, just like Joshua did when he…."

The Reverend was interrupted by the doctor who politely said, "Excuse me Reverend, I'm terribly sorry to interrupt your prayer session, but I'm here to discharge Mrs. Walani Cook." The Reverend said, "It's alright doctor. Is there any special advice that Mrs. Cook should heed to, to further her rehabilitation?"

"Just get plenty of rest and take one 600 mg. tablet of Ibuprofen every six hours as needed for pain and recurring headaches." Walani nodded and hugged the Reverend who helped her to her feet, nodded and motioned that he was going to excuse himself so that Walani could get dressed and be ushered to the exit of the hospital.

"Reverend what was the sad news you were going to tell me?" asked Walani, while remembering Officer Gourdine's warning.

"Oh my goodness I never got it out, Ralph McDaniel's, Juanita, and Eric Fickland, are all dead. Apparently Ralph walked in on them and a struggle ensued, which resulted in the deaths of all three of them. Both of her daughters are in the custody of the bureau of child welfare as your Gifford. I'm telling you this week has almost killed me my child. My congregation has suffered terrible losses. Mr. and Mrs. McDaniel's services will be held at the church. I've elected to not hold services for Eric. His services will be held at J. Foster Philips Funeral Home on Linden Boulevard," with that Reverend Burns lumbered to his feet and exited the room.

Upon returning home Walani found apartment 3C just as she and her two boys left it a week earlier. It saddened her terribly that she had to find out where her boys where and that she had no idea how they were doing. Walani contacted the New York State Department of Juvenile Justice and found out that her Brian was being held in the 'A' building and was doing okay. She also found out that he would be there for six months, and visiting day was the following day.

Walani then called the Bureau of Child Welfare and found out that Gifford was at a group home on Heberton Avenue in the Port Richmond section of Staten Island. In the process Walani found out that Capalitana and Chinse McDaniel's had been taken in by Little Flowers Foster Care in Brooklyn Heights. They had been separated and placed with temporary families; in hope that a permanent family would be looking to adopt both of the girls together in the near future.

The case worker informed Walani that she could come to the office now if she wanted to and sign the papers to have Gifford released to her custody. Walani told the case worker that she was interested in the McDaniel sisters as well, that she was a fellow parishioner and that Reverend Burns would be her reference.

April 10th 1993 was a cold rainy day, a typical April day. Walani had given Gifford and Brian's room to Capalitana and Chinse; she had Gifford sleep on the couch. The apartment was solemn as Walani went from room to room making sure everyone looked their best. Walani then instructed Gifford to wait in front of the building for her and the girls. Walani wanted to speak to them.

"I know your father and I had some differences, but that doesn't mean that Ralph was not a great man, who loved his girls very much. We all loved him and feel terrible with him being gone. You're welcomed to stay here as long as you want. Capalitana you are seventeen years old now and will be an adult soon. All I want to do is help; the boys and I are here for you in whatever way you need. I will be by your side during the entire service." There was a moment of silence then both girls embraced Walani as tears began to roll down there cheeks.

For the first time the McDaniel's and the Cook's minus Juanita and Ralph walked together through the projects. Under the watch of sympathetic spectators they made their way to the 109th Avenue underpass into the Hole. The four of them walked with their heads down against the rain struggling to keep the umbrellas from turning inside out against the wind. When they made the right turn onto Sutphin Boulevard, Capalitana started crying very hard and said. "I can't do it! I can't go into that church knowing that my mommy and daddy are dead inside."

Everyone stopped, and then Chinse and Walani held Capalitana tight while Gifford held an umbrella over their heads. Capalitana sobbed very loudly, even gasping for air at times. Everyone remained silent until she found the strength to move on. When the four of them entered the church everyone stood up. Walani instructed Gifford to sit in the back while she escorted the McDaniel girls to the front where Walani was given unpleasant stares from the McDaniel family who somehow blamed her for this because of the incident she had had with Ralph two weeks earlier. Walani just leaned over and said in Grandma McDaniel's ear, "I'm very, very sorry. Even though we had our differences, this is a sad, tragic, terrible situation. You have my deepest sympathy."

Grandma McDaniel's just looked back with a blank stare and nodded. Everyone knew who Lance Cook was and what he was capable of, but this was a love triangle gone awry with terrible consequences. Walani then returned to her seat with her son and shed tears all the while smile and sometimes laughing inside.

After the services everyone attended the after pass or as some old school Christians call it the after party. Sometimes there's more than one that can go into the next morning at someone's house. The "After pass" was held in the basement of the church where Sunday school is held. People were eating some of the finest soul food a human being could possible taste when everyone stopped due to Capalitana screaming at her grandmother.

"What do you mean you have no room? We are your granddaughters! You're our father's mother!"

Capalitana then stormed off. There is no place where you will find more callous family, or un-Christian like behavior then the black church and Walani knew it with the nearly four hundred member congregation. If she didn't take these girls in then they would surely be place in foster care. That night Walani informed the McDaniel sisters that they would be getting her room and that she would be sleeping on a pull out bed that the Reverend had paid for that would be in Walani's new room; the living room.

That night Walani served the leftovers at her silent kitchen table. Everyone had been under a great deal of stress these past two weeks; emotionally and physically. The people at this table two weeks ago were complete adversaries and were now depending on each other for emotional strength and economic survival. Walani spoke up.

"Tomorrow I will be registering you two in school. Chinse you will be going to J.H.S. #8 with Gifford. Capalitana you will be attending Jamaica High School, you will accompany me to drop of your sister and Gifford then I will register you." Everyone remained Silent. Walani knew this would be a difficult transition for both. The girls had lost both of their parents and dropped a grade in the class system. The Girls had gone from Uniondale Long Island to the South Jamaica Houses. That is an extreme change in circumstance and surrounding. Girls had gone to private Catholic schools where they wore uniforms and prayed daily.

"This is going to be a difficult transition, but I'm here for you," Walani told the girls knowing full well that she didn't have to say no one else was going to be there for them. If there was anyone else who would have spoken up for them they would have gone with them in an instant.

"Why are you helping us?" asked Capalitana with a stone face.

"Because it's the Christian thing to do"

"Are you sure it's not because you son is so smitten with my sister?" asked Capalitana almost accusingly.

"I think all four of you were getting along fine. It would hurt both of my sons if the two of you were split up and cast to the wind with no one ever knowing what became of you. The foster care system is ruthless. B.C.W. treats black children like cattle. Most kids in their care are sexually abused and turn into drug addicts. Most are thrown away by their foster parents as soon as they turn eighteen and the check stops coming."

Capalitana interrupted, "Oh! So, there's money involved!?"

"Well the state does pay for adoptive parents to take care of children they take in. I have to fit a certain criteria and have credible references to meet those criteria. Someone is going to get the money Capalitana. It can be me. You live under the same roof with your sister, or you two can be split up, raped and abused and someone else get it. The choice is yours."

Capalitana got quiet again no matter what Walani's intentions where. Walani was clearly the best case scenario in this most dismal situation. The real reason for Walani taking them in was so that she herself would never be under suspicion for the McDaniel's and Fickland murders. Walani felt like Lance would be proud of such a calculated move and besides Walani had prayed that she could deliver these two girls to her sons and by God she had done it. If the four of them, two of them or even none of them would hook up would be up to them now. There would be no interference of class system, skin complexions, or even zip codes. Their fates were now entirely up to them. Walani then continued.

"On Tuesday, Gifford and I have to go see his brother. My baby is suffering and it is no one's fault in this room. Things are as they are and we just have to deal with it."

Two suitcases had been delivered to the church before the funeral that had belonged to Chinse and Capalitana by their grandparents. It was a small collection of the vast wardrobes both of them once possessed. A small plastic bag of toiletries were thrown in the suitcases as well. This was the last of their worldly possessions; as the two girls readied themselves for bed on the new bedspreads that waited for them in Gifford and Brian's bedroom. Gifford couldn't help but watch them in the bathroom while the door was ajar. Gifford could not believe that these two saintly creatures that he once saw as goddesses where now humbled to the point of squeezing together for space in his tiny little bathroom. That their backsides were going to sit on the same toilet as his, that they were actually going to sleep on his bed. Gifford was amazed at how his mother had transformed his bedroom for the two of them with some new bedspreads and curtains and a thorough cleaning. The room smelled like pine sol, and looked "Fluffy" to him. Gifford felt a sense of pride; he knew that in a way he would be the envy of all the boys at school and church. These two heavenly creatures lived under the same roof as him.

The next morning Gifford was awaken by his mother who had allowed the McDaniel girls to completely get washed and dressed before waking him. The two girls were in the kitchen eating grits, scrambled cheese eggs and bacon as Gifford walked half asleep through the foyer. Gifford looked into the room and fantasized about laying his head on the same pillow, the one he used to own that Chinse had placed her head on to sleep. Gifford felt his attraction and desire to possess Chinse begin to grow. Gifford wondered if she felt the same. Chinse had been withdrawn and saddened by the tragic events that had occurred.

"Which was to be expected," Gifford thought to himself.

Gifford thought he would wait a while before trying to recapture the magic that they shared before this whole situation erupted two weeks earlier. Walani, Gifford, Chinse, and Capalitana arrived at J.H.S. #8 and went directly to the general office. As Walani showed all of Chinse's paperwork to the Principal, Mrs. Erica Brooks in the back office and explained what had happened. The three children sat on a bench in next to the huge green counter in the main office. No one said a word. Chinse was glad that Gifford was silently by her side. She could feel his passion for her, she knew he was trying to silently support her in any way that he could. Both Gifford and Chinse knew that Capalitana was not pleased about the whole situation. Capalitana being older felt as though this public school was beneath her little sister and although she wasn't speaking it was written all over her face.

Walani walked out of the back office with the principal Erica brooks in tow.

"This is little Chinse?" said the Mrs. Erica brooks, trying to sound as pleasant as possible.

Chinse now thirteen was small for her age. Chinse had not developed as quickly as Capalitana and was thin, pretty much looked like she was all dimples. What Chinse lacked in size she made up with confidence and assertion. Chinse spoke up loud, loud enough to startle everyone.

"Yes I am Chinse. How do you do Ma'am?"

"We are very pleased to have you in our school Chinse. I understand Gifford has to escort his mother on business, but I will have him show you to your class which is now in art class, Room 315. Your sister and Mrs. Cook will wait here for Gifford."

"That sounds great," said Chinse who seemed so bubbly and full of life that Gifford went into a trance. Chinse then did something that put him on a cloud. Chinse extended her hand for Gifford to hold. The room seemed to go into slow motion to Gifford who eagerly accepted it. When the two hands met everyone standing there knew that it meant much more than just two kids holding hands. The moment seemed to be the indication of a destiny that was meant to be. The moment felt magical to the both of them. Chinse being more mature knew to try to downplay it. Gifford however seemed to be in a dream state.

The next thing Gifford knew Chinse was saying, "This is it Room 315."

Gifford let go of her hand, but he wanted to immediately wanted to hold it again, he wanted to ask if it would be okay to hold it again later, but knew better not to. Gifford stood there as Chinse was introduced to the class and then told to take a seat. As Chinse made her way to an empty desk in the back Gifford noticed boys in his class looking at her flirtatiously. Gifford was immediately enraged. His face turned beet red. Gifford went to the back door of the class and made an okay signal to Chinse. Gifford then got the attention of his classmate Eric Heckstall and made the hand gesture with his finger to his eye then to Chinse to "Look out for her".

The scene was much more tense and unpleasant at Jamaica High School. As the trio approached the school walking up Gothic Road, the School seemed enormous. There were four white columns in front that made it look liked The White House on steroids. There was a crowd outside the school, on the steps that looked like it never thinned out or left the front of the school.

Gifford had never been to a high school and was glad that it was not him being dropped off because it looked like a rough crowd. As the trio got close, Gifford noticed that he knew nearly all of the people in the crowd. They were all "40 projects" people, which put Gifford at ease. Gifford was able to relax his shoulders by the time Walani, Capalitana, and he made it to the front steps. Walani was holding Gifford's right arm and Capalitana was holding the left as if Gifford was the man and they were his women. Both women seemed to be stunned but pleasantly surprised that everyone seemed to know Gifford's name. The three were met with smiles and pleasantries. Gifford freed his right arm from his mother to give numerous neighborhood students and tough guys 'daps', 'pounds' and different variations of the "brother shake'" all while Capalitana clutched his left arm; which made Gifford feel like a very big and important man, and for the first time attracted to Capalitana. Not the same way as he was attracted to Chinse.

Gifford was developing love for Chinse. This feeling he felt for Capalitana was lust, and Walani saw it too but said nothing figuring that all boys Gifford's age felt love for any female they could get their hands on. Inside and after Capalitana was registered, Capalitana stood in the hallway to say goodbye to Gifford and Walani. Gone was her arrogant snooty attitude. Capalitana appeared as a scared little girl for the first time alone, and just a week after having both parents murdered her fear and confusion showed in her eyes. Unlike Chinse, Capalitana was tall like Walani and dark like her too. Her facial expression didn't match her size and demeanor. Capalitana seemed to revert back to childhood right in front of Gifford and Walani's eyes. Capalitana's shoulders hunched an as she exhaled tears welled up in her eyes. Walani couldn't help but feel sorry for her. Walani moved forward outstretching her arms like a protective mother would to an injured child as Capalitana said, "Thank you Mrs. Cook. I'm sorry for my sister and me burdening you. I don't know where we would be without you."

Walani said, as she felt Capalitana's tears upon her cheek, "Try and be strong. We're here for you. I'm not trying to be your mother. No one could ever take her place. I will be for you what you allow me to be. Try as best you can to settle in and make friends."

With that Capalitana stood back and wiped away her tears, smiled, then waved as she head down the hall looking down at her program card and the numbers on top of classroom doors. Walani felt like a new mother, a mother of daughters she always wished she had. Walani also thanked God that the McDaniel girls did not know that it was in fact her doing that their parents were dead. Walani felt immense regret that Juanita was dead also. She did not ask for Juanita or Fick to be killed, but Walani was aware that that was the way it went in the streets. When the thunder is called down on someone, sometimes the people around them are struck by lightning too, especially if it is beneficial to the person doing the killing. Walani promised herself that the girls would never know. Not because she wanted them to have pleasant memories of their parents, but because deep down inside Walani wanted the McDaniel sisters to trust her and her sons and hopefully love her and her sons as well.

After taking the 'E' train all the way to 42nd Street in Manhattan and transferring to the #6 train going uptown; all the way uptown, Walani and Gifford finally arrived at the Longwood Avenue Station then had to walk the arduous journey all the way down Longwood Avenue to Spofford Avenue then through the imposing front door. To a search area where they were both patted down. Walani and Gifford where then seated at a green plastic table with three green plastic chairs. The room looked like it was possibly the cleanest room in the prison, for appearances sake of course. After about twenty minutes of waiting Brian showed up at the entrance door to the room dressed in blue jeans, a blue, sweatshirt, and blue pony sneakers that were prison issued. Brian was held at the door momentarily and given a stern talking to by two juvenile detention officers. By the way the officers talked and their demeanor the first person Walani and Gifford could think about was Ralph McDaniel's. Both mother and two sons stared with every officer there with contempt and the age old New York City hatred between Blacks and law enforcement was mutually felt by all parties in the room. For the first time Walani and her sons realized that Ralph McDaniel's was not original or even being himself. Ralph was being what he was brainwashed to be, a self-hating drone, without the ability to freely think or express himself. About 80% of all blacks in law enforcement suffer from a ranging degree of this, and the other 20% feel trapped and figure that they will make the most of their dismal situation by becoming corrupt and 'Getting theirs" out of this trap in the city of the damned called New York City.

Brian walked as fast as he could up to his mother and the two embraced long as Walani began to cry. Walani sobbed into Brian's shirt.

"I'm so sorry my big man. You were just trying to protect me, who was trying to protect your little brother."

Gifford sensed for a minute that this whole situation might be his fault and that certain people including his mother might be blaming him for the entire situation and possibly the deaths of Ralph, Juanita, and Fick. His fears lessoned when he saw Brian hold his mother's face and kiss her on the cheek. All three took their seats and Brian said, "That's my job. I would do anything for the two of you. We are a family. Whether we rise or fall, sink or swim, we will meet our fates together."

Walani sat dumbfounded not only had Brian's voice gotten deeper and more harsh over the last two weeks making him sound damned near like Lance. Brian was quoting and exact favorite saying of Lance's. Walani wondered had he been this large or had he grown in the last two weeks.

"Where did you hear that saying?" asked Walani nearly choked up feeling like she was looking at Lance himself.

"I've been getting letters from my father," Brian answered proudly.

Walani wanted to ask how the two had gotten in touch then figured that if Michael 'Mick-Man' Gourdine had found her then anything was possible. Besides Walani knew that the visit was only for one hour and wanted to make the most of it.

"How are you doing? Is anyone bothering you? Are you eating okay? I'll make sure to put money in your commissary, okay honey."

Walani was trying to say as much as she could. Brian held her hand and said.

"Everything is alright Mommy; The C.O.'s were just giving me instructions. I have one hundred dollars in my account; how it got there I don't know. Other than that warning they just gave me I've been treated very well here, kind of like a V.I.P."

Walani's mind went back to Officer Michael 'Mick-Man' Gourdine. Walani was well aware that his reach was far and wide. Officer Gourdine's mother was a Warden in the Department of Corrections which further lengthened his reach especially within the prison system.

Brian then turned to Gifford and said, "Well you said that if you tried to help old Ralphie boy that he might like you. You were hoping that helping him would deliver Chinse to you gift wrapped. Well Big brother, at least you were half right."

All three sat silently after that remark and were well aware of what that statement could signify, and what ideas that could put into people's heads. Walani raised her hand, and then lowered it slowly signaling to stop talking about Ralph being gone in any way that wasn't sympathetic. Brian just shrugged then punched Gifford in the arm.

"How is everything "Big Brother", have you spoken to your girl?"

Walani spoke up, "The girls live with us now, in fact Capalitana sleeps in your bed." Brian's eyes lit up in surprise, and then he looked to Gifford with a big broad smile, "I bet you ain't sleep a wink since they been living there huh?"

Gifford blushed a little bit as Walani started to giggle. Walani held both of their hands and said, "You are right Brian, we are going to meet our fates together, we will overcome all obstacles, and get what's coming to us in this world. God deals with those who mean us harm. God doesn't like ugly, and the man up top way up north, has a special justice system for the wicked and wretched."

Gifford and Brian nodded knowing what their mother meant, and knowing that she was telling them that justice had been served, that swift and brutal retribution had been exacted, and not from the lord above but by their father upstate.

The visit was very helpful to all three of the Cooks. Their re-bonding after being separated for the first time since they were born was needed and necessary. On the #6 train back home, Gifford rested his head on his mother's shoulder, then remembered how "Manly" Brian had looked and lifted his head up and placed it on the window behind him. Walani figured that the thought of Brian was the reason he decided to do so. Walani had noticed the change in Brian also and wondered just how much he would change by the time he would come home, would she have to treat him differently? Would Brian get into a rift with the McDaniel girls? Only time would tell. In a situation such as this all Walani could do was pray, but even the most staunch Christians, especially the black one know that God may set the stage, but he does not write the script. Walani prayed for peace and serenity, that all four of the children in her care would make it to adulthood and live happy, healthy, fruitful and prosperous lives. Walani hoped that the good Lord would watch over them, and if he couldn't then please make it possible for Lance to do so.

Walani then did something that she had never done before. Walani reached out to the devil. In her mind making sure her lips where still as she sat on that train with Gifford sleeping she wanted to make sure that no one heard her, "Lucifer, Devil, Satan, whatever your name is, I need help. I need my boys survive and do well. If you can provide a way for them to make it to adulthood and live happy, healthy, fruitful, prosperous lives, then you can be my "Holy Ghost". If you Satan deliver these things then you can have my soul. If God refuses to show us the path to attain what the White man has here on earth then he can't blame us for being lost. I will cast my faith behind which ever super power helps my boys."

Walani then looked around to make sure that she had not spoken out loud, hoping that no one heard her thoughts and then whispered, "Amen."

Chapter Seven

With the Lords help nature takes its course…...for everyone

It took three weeks before things felt slightly normal in the now Cook, McDaniel household. Walani, who never had a daughter, appreciated the "women's" touch the McDaniel sisters put on her apartment. They fixed up the apartment with curtains, throw rugs, new dishes, and a new dinner table in the kitchen designed to seat five. A new bunk bed was placed in Walani's room where she and Gifford slept until Brian came home. This way she could keep an eye on Gifford and make sure that he and Chinse were not having late night rendezvous or at least not yet, then Walani planned to make the living room her room with a new sofa bed. The money to pay for this came from donations made to the church by people, who saw the news story on NY1 news, by people at the church, The Corrections Captains Association, and Hollywood.

For the past three Sundays, Hollywood had arrived at 9:30 a.m. sharp to drive the kids to Sunday school in his new 93' Acura Legend. Hollywood would then return and drive Walani to church at 11:00 a.m.; he would then wait outside to drive everyone to Carmichaels on Guy R. Brewer Boulevard and waited outside for them while they ate. On this Sunday, Walani invited Hollywood to eat with them. He was just the touch the newly formed family needed.

Hollywood was a character. Everyone laughed for the first time as Hollywood mocked Reverend Burns with an extended sermon before they ate. Hollywood told jokes and all the while remained respectful and reserved. After the meal Hollywood took everyone back to the projects and made his way to 143rd Street in Harlem to meet with Police Officer Michael Mick-Man Gourdine, who did not work there yet, but had made a "connect" and informed Lance Cook who was incarcerated in Attica Correctional Facility that he had an endless supply of heroin and cocaine. Lance introduced the two and things were beginning to flourish for all involved.

Capalitana and Chinse seemed to change right before everyone's eyes in the last few weeks they went from suburban sheltered church girls to hardened tough talking still ladylike, but street girls. One could tell that the two of them were used to either wearing catholic uniforms, or church clothes. Now they were wearing jeans, Jordan's, riding boots, Tommy Hilfiger jackets, and thanks to Walani had gotten their hair braided like Janet Jackson in the movie 'Poetic Justice". The McDaniel sisters even walked and moved differently. Gifford felt strange about the change. Gifford didn't like the fact that Chinse was treating him like a brother at school. Gifford's favorite time of day was the walk to and from school. Chinse had started to talk to him and listened to him talk. The two would talk about their views of the world, religion, teachers, their favorite subjects, and what they wanted to do in the future. While walking and talking Walani would catch Gifford staring at her hair, teeth, and clothes, in awe; he would just blush and smile. Gifford hated when neighborhood boys would "cat call" to Chinse who seemed oblivious to his jealousy.

After week number four, during lunch Gifford was shocked and infuriated that Chinse was sitting with another boy in the lunchroom. Gifford not knowing what to do very awkwardly took his tray to another section of the lunchroom and tried not to stare. Gifford felt a sensation that he had never felt before. It felt like there was a knife in his heart that was stuck, that couldn't be removed.

After school for the past four weeks, Gifford had waited for Walani across the street from the front entrance. On this particular day Gifford watched Chinse walk out of the school nearly arm in arm with the same boy from the lunchroom. The boy was in the seventh grade and his name was Sean Wilson. Even though he was in a lower grade he was still larger than Gifford due to the fact that he had been held over three times. Gifford was familiar with him because he was in Brian's former class. If Brian was home this would not have been a problem. The Cook brothers had always been known in the school, they had never had any confrontations of any kind after all they were "neighborhood" boys.

Gifford had never had this sort of problem before, he felt like Chinse was his girl and due to circumstances beyond his control he had somehow become her brother, and he wanted this situation to stop right now. Chinse looked across the street to Gifford and motioned for him to come across the street.

"Gifford this is my friend Sean," said Chinse in a joyful tone.

Gifford answered sharply, "I know who he is, what does he want?"

"What I want is Chinse, and she don't have a problem with it so why should you?" answered Sean, causing people to stop and stare.

"That's her business then, I don't have to like it. Ya'll just walk and I'll fall behind. I have to make sure she gets home okay," answered Gifford clinching his teeth as he bowed down knowing that Chinse had lost respect for him. Gifford stayed calm knowing where Sean lived figuring that it was time he let Chinse know how he felt about her after Sean went about his business on the corner of 109th Ave and 164th Street since Scott lived at 40 164th Street, but that did not happen as Sean kept on walking with Chinse. Gifford lost his cool and decided to lay his cards on the table.

"Chinse! I thought we were supposed to be going together? Everybody thinks so, why are you even talking to him!" Gifford said as he walked out in front of the two as they were walking; bringing the three of them to a standstill.

"Gifford I thought you didn't like me anymore after what my father did to you and your family. I though you quit me?"

All three just stood still as Gifford tried to find the words to explain himself, but that's hard to do when you're thirteen and have been through as much as he had been in the last few months; besides Brian had always done the talking for both of them. Gifford tried to speak when the next thing he knew he was on the ground holding his nose. As the blood spilled down his shirt Sean stood over him and said, "Your brother ain't here no more, little yellow nigger! If I'm getting at a female whoever she is, that ain't none of your fucking business, understand!"

Gifford stood up and looked at Chinse Who had a look of shock on her face. Chinse screamed, "You ain't had to hit him Sean! I told you he's like my brother, that wasn't called for!"

Sean got calm and said to Chinse, 'Look, let me just walk you home and we'll talk about it"

Before he couldn't finish the sentence Chinse had turned her back and was walking toward the projects with Gifford making his way to his feet and Sean walking behind Chinse trying to talk to her. Gifford crossed the street as Sean turned around to make sure Gifford was not trying to attack him from behind. Gifford ran past both of them and into the projects holding his nose with tears pouring down his cheeks. Chinse saw this and stopped to talk to Sean. The two talked back and forth for about fifteen minutes. Sean had convinced Chinse that no man should attempt to stop another man for getting with a female, that is was her choice to choose who she wanted and Sean made her believe that it was him. That all it took was to walk up to Apartment 3C, ask Gifford to come outside. Sean would apologize and Chinse would advise Gifford that she would be Sean's girlfriend and there would be the peace.

As the two came to the corner of 160th Street and 109th Avenue to make the left turn toward building #6, the block was strangely empty. The two continued down the block to the building and up the stairs. Where no one answered the door, then suddenly there was the noise of a large crowd outside of the building. The two looked through the hallway window and saw what appeared to be a lynch mob in front of the building. Gifford screamed up to Chinse, "Stay in the building Chinse! Scott bring your ass down here faggot!"

Chinse screamed out , 'Gifford he wants to apologize, and I want to talk to you"
Before Gifford could answer back the mob had already made it to the third floor. They seemed like a mad clan of gorillas. The first one of the two of them tackled Sean to the ground like a linebacker "sacking" a quarterback immediately or by someone pulling the winner of the race up to his feet and followed by at least twenty people stomping and kinking from every direction. It looked as though Sean had disappeared under a mountain of "Timberland" boots that were stomping Sean ears together. Sean had made a terrible mistake and had put his hands on a bona fide resident of the "40" projects and he did not live there himself. The consequences; were always enacted swiftly and justly whenever this infraction occurred which didn't happen too often. The truth is the neighborhood of South Jamaica is stronger than the South Jamaica Houses, but no way near as close knit, only in the matter of business would the neighborhood flex its muscle, when it came down to violence, the projects would stand together all for one and one for all.

Chinse was grabbed by the arm and lead pass the crowd of young men screaming insults and warnings as Sean was squirming and crawling on all fours; being kicked on both sides of his ribcage, legs, back, and head by steel toed Timberland boots. Chinse was hand delivered to a waiting Gifford and told "Take a walk and talk it out, go now the police are coming!"
Gifford grabbed Chinse and walked into the projects as everyone ran past them scattering into different buildings and the squad cars came to a screeching halt in front of building #6.

The two walked on 109th toward the Hole. Gifford held his breath and just started talking figuring he would just speak from the heart and forget about how cool he sounded doing it.
"I Love you Chinse, since the day I first met you. I can't take the thought of anyone else being with you. I couldn't find the nerve to say it before, but now I have to. If you want to be with Sean, I'll understand."

Gifford felt like a ton of weight had been lifted off of him. The fear of saying that and being rejected was far worse than the fear he felt of Sean's revenge or even the police for what happened to Sean.

Chinse didn't even speak; she just held his hand as they walked out of the projects and to P.S. 48's park. In the park Gifford asked Chinse if she would be his girl and Chinse nodded. In South Jamaica this is an oral contract that among teenagers is taken very seriously, deadly serious, as serious as a marriage. Gifford held her two hands by his own and pulled her close. The tension of their lips meeting almost caused him to faint. Chinse lips were as soft and delicate as Gifford had dreamed and imagined while sitting in class or church. Gifford felt like he would do whatever he had to, to secure these lips and the young woman attached to them for him-self at all costs. Gifford was firm in his conviction to kill whoever stood in his way of doing so.

After hours of kissing until their tongues throbbed, cooing into each other's eyes, and swearing undying devotion to each other the two held hands and walked back into the projects. They walked for the first time as a couple under the pleased and approving eyes of all of the residents of the South Jamaica Houses. Chinse was hereby recognized as Gifford's girl and all who challenged this was sure to meet ferocious resistance. People screamed from windows, "Gifford, you alright? I'm glad your girl is okay?"

This made Gifford feel as though he had proven himself, and that he had the support of his people. The people of the South Jamaica Houses and the '40' projects had shown him love. Right or wrong they had his back and that made him feel secure and like he could defend his woman if he had to.

Chinse did feel this love for Gifford, but was a little uneasy. Gifford had after all overridden her feelings, and her choice in the matter. Chinse's survival and being close to her sister did depend on the Cook's giving them a place to live that was seen as fit by the bureau of child welfare. Needless to say that that was the deal breaker, with Gifford she would have to be. As the two entered their apartment Walani, Capalitana, and Hollywood were sitting at the table. "Loving you" by Mary J. Blige was playing on the radio which made the apartment feel mellow. Everyone looked down to Gifford and Chinse holding hands, and then to Gifford's swollen and bloody nose.

"The police where here, and so was the Wilson family," said Walani with a smile.

"Do you two love birds mind telling us what happened?"

"It's a long story mommy, but we love each other and want to be together. Some people don't like the thought of that."

"Tell me something I don't know," said Walani as the room broke into laughter.

"Can you tell me how Sean Wilson came to be found unconscious by the police in our hallway?" said Walani with a smirk.

The room fell quiet, by this point Walani had been completely filled in on what had happened, she just wanted Gifford and Chinse's take on it. Walani knew that she had to be "Ginger" about the situation. Using tricks that black woman are legendary for; Walani knew she could get her way. Approaching this situation like a square could make this whole situation blow up. Walani had to make sure Chinse knew or at least make Chinse think that she has a choice of which young man she wanted to court. First, by making Chinse see the benefits of choosing Gifford, Walani hoped that she would choose Gifford, and if she didn't choose Gifford then and only then would she let Chinse see the other side of sweet little Walani. So Walani decided to have a little alone time with Chinse to see exactly where her head was and how this whole situation was going to play out, and if this situation needed to be coaxed into being played out the correct way.

"I see you were hurt, are you okay Gifford?" Walani asked with motherly concern.

"Yes Ma, I'm okay just a little stressed out, I 'ma go wash my face."

As Gifford walked up the hallway which is exactly what Walani figured he would do Walani turned her attention to Chinse. "Chinse, can I talk to you in the hallway please?"

More like telling Chinse to follow her out of the door than asking her, Chinse just instinctively followed with her shoulders hunched making an "OOOH I'M In TROOOUUBBLE" face to a smiling Capalitana and Hollywood.

"Chinse, do you want to be with Gifford? Tell me now; don't be afraid, you won't have to leave if you don't want to be his girl. Gifford will just have to understand," said Walani with all the buttery syrup of a southern bell spinning her black widow's web which Chinse recognized because she after all had Juanita as a mother. Chinse recognizing this instinctively knew that she was being put on the spot, to test her loyalty.

"I'm fine with Gifford. I was just confused because I thought Gifford blamed me for what happened to Brian. The two of us hadn't talked much since the whole situation happened a month ago. I do love him deeply Mrs. Cook," waid Chinse with the upmost sincerity, which made Walani break into a big broad smile.

"You two have to take it slow, okay? Don't let the case worker know about this when she comes around, okay?"
Said Walani all excited and 'Giddy"

The two went back inside and found Gifford, Hollywood, and Capalitana sitting and talking calmly to "Freak like me" by Adina Howard playing in the background.

"We have a situation we have to deal with," said Walani making everyone quiet down and pay attention.

Hollywood then spoke up.

"I grew up with the Wilson's and Sean has asked for a "fair one". We have to go over to the 164th Street basketball court and handle this."

This was South Jamaica Queens, New York City 1993. The police played no part in family disputes, crimes of passion, or any kind of disagreements at all. This was before O.J. Simpson had caused there to be billions of orders of protections to be served, before "D.I.R.'s" or domestic incident reports were written. When the police arrived, Sean was able to pull himself to his feet and walk it off. Sean told the police that some he had been chased by a gang of thugs who were trying to rob him, that he had nowhere to run and tried to hide in the building where they found him. The police drove him home, Sean's mother told the police that there was no need for a report and that Sean would be okay, the police marked the job a "10-90 Yellow", which means that writing a report wasn't necessary and that they themselves, the police had handled the radio call.

Gervaise English known in the neighborhood as "Pudden", Sean's mother immediately called her childhood friend "Hollywood" and asked him to find out exactly what had happened. One hour Gervaise and her boyfriend Charles Minter met with Hollywood in the projects and court was held. The only way for there to be the peace was for the two concerned parties to have a "fair one" that means that Gifford and his people would be able to walk out of the projects and to the 164th Street basketball court which was the territory of people who, lived east of the projects, for Gifford and Sean to fight hand to hand without any interference, then shake hands and go home. This situation however was slightly different. Sean was under the impression that

Chinse was still his "Girl" and Chinse had to go along to confirm otherwise, to satisfy the Wilson family that she was not being held against her will and was no longer the property of Sean.

"Are Ya'll ready to go?" asked Hollywood.

Part of Court being held and the request for a "Fair one" was the understanding that this request could not be turned down. By declining such an invite would label Gifford a disgrace and lower him to the caliber of being nearly a homosexual, by both sides. That meant that if you turned down this invitation you couldn't hold your head with any dignity in your own neighborhood, much less in the neighborhood of the person who challenged you. You and your family would now be outcasts.

"Yes we're ready," responded Gifford with the new sense of self-confidence that only first love can give.

Walani beamed with pride at how fast Gifford spoke up for himself.

Everyone then rose and headed down the stairs to the lobby and up to 110th Ave. As the small crowd of five turned from 160th Street to 110th Avenue they were joined by fifteen people from the projects who were tailed by a small crowd of teens and even smaller children who would witness the fight and be popular in school the next day for being able to report what happened with complete artistic freedom to twist the facts of the event to whatever they chose to and in some cases would even put themselves in danger for such exaggerations.

Gifford and his entourage approached 164th Street they could see in the darkness a large crowd assembled on the corner and inside of the basketball court on 164th Place and 110th Avenue. As the two crowds met everyone fell silent as Hollywood and Charles Minter a.k.a. "Guess" met face to face and shook hands to a 'Brother shake" completed with a half hug.

"Where's Sean's Girlfriend?" asked Guess; while motioning for Sean to point her out in the crowd, which he did. Sean immediately sensed a change, and an unfamiliar stare from Chinse's eyes and facial expression as his eyes met hers. Yes this was Juanita McDaniel's daughter alright. Chinse was getting used to picking sides based on whatever situation suited her best. It didn't hurt that she genuinely had feelings for Gifford, but even if she hadn't Gifford was clearly her best suitor. Chinse was learning basic survival skills fast. Chinse spoke up, "I ain't his girl. I'm going with Gifford."

Sean looked hurt and betrayed.

Guess then said as he shrugged his shoulders.

With that settled I guess we can settle our business then. Hollywood and Guess motioned for the crowd to pull back making a circle, at which point a marked R.M.P. (police cruiser) pulled up on the scene with its lights on giving a "Whoop" with the cars bullhorn. Hollywood excused himself from the crowd and went to the cars window and said.

"Yeah it's me, Hollywood, ain't nothing going on, just some kids going to fight to settle a disagreement over a girl."

The Cops smiled and shook Hollywood's hand and drove off.

Hollywood returned to the front of the circle and motioned for Gifford to come inside the cleared circle where Sean and Guess were already standing. Hollywood and Guess then fell back right across from each other but not as far back as the rest of the crowd to serve like "Corner Men" in a boxing match.

"Alright do it," both men said simultaneously.

Gifford and Sean threw up their hands boxing style and approached each other. The first couple of punches thrown by each young man resembled what that first round of a professional boxing match is supposed to look like. This is always the case in "Street Fights". Then as usual within seconds this jousting deteriorated into a slug fest, then scrapping, which is wrestling with occasional punches thrown when one of the fighters had a free hand. Usually it is hard to tell who is winning or at the end of the contest who has actually won, unless one of the two fighters gets the other in a ghetto headlock otherwise known as a "Yolk"; that his opponent cannot get out of. The fighter holding the 'Yolk" will always be declared the winner no matter what the damage to his face was during the fight.

So far in this fight the slug fest was going on longer than usual which benefitted Gifford. Gifford being two years younger and at least three inches shorter was not supposed to last this long in a slug fest with a man the size of Sean.

"KICK HIS ASS GIFFORD!" Walani screamed, which gave Gifford even more steam. Gifford then connected with a crunching right hand, followed by his elbow, which stunned Sean causing him to stumble forward grabbing on to Gifford's waist.

"NO! Don't let him grab you!" Hollywood yelled.

But it was too late, the scrapping had started as Gifford tried to turn away and being pulled to the ground by Sean. Scrapping is an art and the trick is not to panic. By not panicking one might be able to see a bottle, a brick, a stick or something they might be able to use as a weapon. For some reason during the jousting, or the slug fest this is seen as cheating, but not during the scrapping time in the fight. Like during the fight scene in the movie "Friday" between Ice Cube and Debo. Gifford however was panicking and breathing heavy as Sean's weight was becoming overbearing. In the struggle Sean was able to turn Gifford on his stomach, squirm up his back and administer the dreaded "Yolk".

The crowd is always worked to frenzy by this point and security is needed the most during this period, as it is difficult for family members and friends to witness a loved one struggling to breathe and sometimes begin to beg for mercy. This is when the metal of a prospected young man is tested.

As Gifford face turned cherry red, with blood and snot running down his nose, Gifford continued to struggle refusing to give in and preferring to let his lights turn off before surrendering in front of Walani and Chinse. Gifford's lips started to foam as his eyes began to roll in his head.

"BLOOM! BLOOOOM!"

Thundered Capalitana's 357 Magnum straight up into the air. Ralph's 357 that she had bought with her from 808 Fullerton Avenue, when she and her sister were taken into foster care. The entire crown fell low as some ran in panic. Capalitana immediately handed the gun to Hollywood who put it in his pants over his penis and motioned with his hands saying, "Everybody be calm! It's alright!"

Guess and Pudden stood before the crowd staring furiously at Capalitana as Sean's victory was spoiled by everyone watching him tremble in terror behind his mother and Guess.

"She just panicked; she's not from around here," Hollywood said apologetically because bringing a gun to a "fair one" is a strict violation of ghetto rules of conduct.

Gifford struggled to his feet and resumed his fighting stance signaling he was ready to continue. The police came 'creeping" up the block. Hollywood waived to them that everything was okay; the police turned their headlights off and stayed on the block this time. Hollywood asked if Sean wanted to go again.

"DAMN RIGHT HE DOES!" answered Pudden, not taking her eyes off of Capalitana.

Sean came from behind his mother and put up his hands. Both young men moved forward throwing punches with everything they both had left in them. In South Jamaica these were known as "HayMakers." Gifford landing one and Sean landing two causing him to fall

125

backwards. As Gifford rolled onto his knees he was met with thunderous kicks to his ribcage, payback for the kicks Sean had received hours earlier. After allowing Sean to regain his glory lost by Capalitana's outrageous antic Hollywood then nodded to Guess, who nodded back then both men moved in to 'fairly' separate the two fighters. Who were then instructed to shake hands, it was clear that Gifford had lost the battle, but won the war. Gifford walked away with not just his girl on his arm, but her sister who was not only willing to go to jail for him, but possibly kill someone. Gifford would from now on be seen as someone to respect and it was clear that Chinse and Capalitana where two new girls in the neighborhood who would be a force to be reckoned with. On the way up 110th Avenue a police car pulled to the curb and Hollywood went over to speak. The car looked like a normal N.Y.P.D. cruiser, but to everyone who paid attention to detail the tags where unusual to the rear along the center of the car 'Queens' police cars always had tags like "QNTF", but this car had "67 Pct.", which meant that the car was from Brooklyn.

'Everything alright?" asked Officer Gourdine.

"Thanks for coming out, I had a feeling this might get ugly. I'm glad you were working tonight," answered Hollywood looking relieved.

"I told some of my friends in the 1-0-3, that I would handle this that's why they fell back. I'm glad everything worked out okay," said Officer Gourdine, as he extended his hand to shake Hollywood's who gladly accepted it.

Officer Gourdine then sped off into the night and Hollywood rejoined the Cooks, and McDaniel girls on the corner of 110th Avenue and 160th Street. Nature had been allowed to take its course in more ways than one. Gifford had been so preoccupied with his own trials and tribulations that he had failed to take notice of the world happening around him. When Hollywood made it back to the crowd, Walani threw her arms around him and gave him a big kiss on the lips. Gifford was completely shocked, but too exhausted to contest the situation. Gifford lead the way holding Chinse's and walking along the curb *(which was something all men did back then)* Capalitana walked on the inside of Chinse, while Walani walked directly behind with Hollywood walking along the curb, which meant that he was "claiming" her.

Back at Apartment 3C, Walani let everyone in and asked Gifford to talk to her outside. "Hollywood and I spoke to your father, your father said that it would be okay, that he's at peace and that it was my decision."

Walani stalled for a moment and took in the rage on Gifford's face.

"Look I'm the mother here and what I say goes. You'll still have your room. Hollywood has his own place in Rochdale; he won't be staying all the time. Hollywood and I spoke to Reverend Burns who expects us in church on Sunday. The Reverend has also given his blessing. Don't forget Hollywood was the one who had your back out there tonight?"

Walani was saying all that she could to take the pain off of Gifford's face, but nothing seemed to work. Gifford felt betrayed, like all the Cook men had been betrayed. Gifford had to learn to understand that nature takes its course not just with him, but with the world.

"I'll be okay Mom," Gifford said as he turned to go inside, while doing so Hollywood was coming out and put his forearm up against Gifford's chest turning him around and saying, "Walk with me to the store?"

Walani knowing it was time for them to talk said noting and went inside as the two men headed down the stairs.

"Look Gifford, I go back with your parents a long way. I'm not trying to take your fathers place. I'm here for you if you need me, but don't worry about me trying to run the house or anything like that, we cool?"

Gifford realizing that Hollywood was the only male figure that he had in his corner said, "Of course we are Hollywood, and thank you for having my back out there tonight."

Hollywood replied, "That's my job Gifford, besides loving your mother, I love your father, and owe him my life."

Hollywood said this while putting his arm around Gifford shoulder, and there was the peace.

In the fall Brian was told to pack his things and that he was going home. Brian thought that he would be escorted all the way to the street by a guard, but was turned over to a police officer at the front gate.

'Hi, I'm Officer Gourdine and this is my partner, Nard. I'm a friend of your father's, I'm here to take you home"

Brian being very nervous looked to the juvenile guards who said, "It's okay Brian, good luck!"

Brian turned and shook Officer Gourdine's hand and turned to have handcuffs put on.

"Naw Brian, you're free, I'm taking you home"

127

In the car Officer Gourdine spoke to Gifford who sat in the backseat "Are you okay, did anyone mistreat you in there?"

Brian smiled and said, "Now I know why nobody gave me a hard time."

Officer Gourdine broke out laughing and nudged his partner.

"Now look, a lot has happened since you've been gone. I've been asked to tell you a few things so you won't be shocked when you get home."

Brian's face tightened to hear what he knew would be unsettling news.

"Relax, all of your people are okay, there was however a terrible incident involving the man who hurt you and your family, turns out Juanita McDaniel was having an affair, that's why Ralph McDaniel was so crazy. Ralph walked in on her and another man, kills Juanita, lost his gun in a fight and jumped off of a terrace to get away and died. The man, whose name was Eric Fickland then shot himself in the head; their daughter Chinse and Capalitana where adopted by your mother and now live in your house with your brother, mother, and sometimes your mother's boyfriend, Hollywood sleeps over."

Officer Gourdine paused because of the stunned look on Brian's face.

"That's a lot of changes," answered Brian.

"What about my father? You said you where his friend. You don't have a problem with Hollywood staying there and seeing my mother?"

There was a long pause while Officer Gourdine looked at his partner then turned around to face Brian.

"I'm sorry Brian; things are the way they are. It's not my place to decide who sees who. From what I understand your father gave his blessing. Your mother is a person Brian and your father will be gone a long time. Don't you want to see her happy?"

Brian just stared straight forward and remained silent. Officer Gourdine could see that his little sermon did absolutely nothing to quell Brian's obvious fury so, Officer Gourdine figured he's going to let him stew over it silently for the remainder of the ride, then give him some more words of wisdom at the drop off. Officer Gourdine of course did not give a damn who, slept with who as long as the money continued to flow out of the projects and into his pockets. Officer Gourdine did feel sorry for Brian. However, Brian had gotten a raw deal, so Officer Gourdine tried to be as nice as possible.

"Are you hungry?" asked Officer Gourdine.

"Just take me home please," answered Brian with an extra heavy layer of attitude.

Officer Gourdine then looked over to his partner, Nard and shrugged. Voices the came over the police radios on both officers waists, "Sector Adam......Sector Adam," Said the voice.

Officer Gourdine then picked up his radio, "Go ahead central," he said.

"Are you still out 10-63" said the voice.

"No central you have a job?" asked Officer Gourdine.

"You have a 10-10 suspicious male, Black male, blue jeans, Black tee shirt, black timberlands, on the corner of Nostrand Avenue and Martense Street, suspect believed to be carrying a 9 millimeter handgun and threatening people coming from the "Chen Chow" Chinese restaurant," said the voice.

"Copy that central, will advise;" said Officer Gourdine as the R.M.P. (radio mobile patrol) made a right onto the Bruckner expressway headed toward the Whitestone Bridge to Queens.

As the R.M.P. stopped in front of building number 6, Brian looked around. Even though he's only been gone six months, it felt like a lifetime to Brian. Officer Gourdine turned around to face Brian.

"If I were you, I'd try to get along with everybody, and give Hollywood a chance. He's not such a bad guy," said officer Gourdine as the voice came from his radio again.

"Sector Adam, I need to mark the last job?"

Officer Gourdine in a haste picked up his radio and said, "Yes central of course, mark that job a 10-90 yellow, and please show me on a car stop on the corner of Avenue D and east 92nd Street, will advise!"

"If you need anything Hollywood will contact me for you okay?"

"Okay" said Brian as he exited the vehicle dragging his bag along.

As Brian knocked on the door, the door flew open as Walani wrapped her arms around him. Walani lead him to the new kitchen table where Gifford, Chinse, and Hollywood were seated waiting for him. Capalitana stood by the cake that read "Welcome Home Brian."

Brian approached the cake and smiled. Gifford rose from his seat.

"I missed you little brother!" Gifford screamed as he hugged Brian.

Brian then looked to Chinse, Hollywood, then turned to Capalitana.

"I see a lot has changed, huh?"

Walani spoke up, "I'm sure officer Gourdine told you everything. We are all here now, and we all love you Brian."

Brian turned to his mother who he loved dearly and saw the "pleading" in her eyes. For peace's sake Brian then decided to go along with the present situation as long as his mother was happy. Gifford then looked to Chinse and held Capalitana's hand."

"I heard about your parents, I'm very sorry to hear about what happened. I'm also sorry I got into it with your dad. I hope you like it here."

With that everyone smiled and kind of breathed a sigh of relief. With Brian's approval life could continue as it had been for the past six months. Capalitana had been the "5th" wheel the whole time and patiently waited for her man, four years her junior to come home. Although Brian was only 12, he sure didn't look it. Brian was nearly a head taller than Gifford and had filled out from countless push-ups in Spofford. Brian stood nearly as tall as Capalitana and they appeared to be a good match. Capalitana pulled Brian close and gave him a deep kiss making sure there was no doubt as to how willing she was to be Brian's woman. Everyone cheered and clapped in approval of this display of open affection and confirmation that there were now officially three couples in the house. Brian asked Gifford to walk him to the store to catch up on each other and Gifford gladly obliged.

"It's good to see you Brian, I really missed you man," said Gifford as the two hit the street headed toward the bodega on 110th Avenue.

"I'm glad to be home big brother," said Brian looking down on Gifford.

It was clear that Brian was showing respect out of love. Brian was clearly the "Big' brother in more ways than one. He was at least six inches taller and had filled out the frame making him man sized. Brian's voice was deep and harsh. All of Brian's childish traits were gone. If someone walked past they might even assume the Brian was Gifford's uncle much less a big brother. Gifford was threatened, and felt challenged by this, but tried hard not to show it. It made him feel a lot better when Brian referred to him as Big Brother.

"You ready to start school?" asked Gifford trying to gauge Brian's mindset.

"I'm ready to go back, mommy told me I was promoted and I'll be graduating this year. I really don't want to go to school anymore though. I want to get money now."

Brian paused to see what Gifford would think about his statement.

"Money for what?" asked Gifford.

"What the fuck you think for?, to live. What you think we going to be with Mommy forever. Jail done opened my eyes Big Brother. All we could think about before was the two Bitches sitting up in our house now. That's what caused all this mess, when we should have been thinking about money that whole time. Mommy risked her ass to give Juanita drugs just to hand deliver those bitches to us, did you know that?" asked Brian with anger growing in his eyes.

Gifford was stumped; he had never stopped to think of what chasing behind Chinse and Capalitana had done to these families lives. The risk that everyone took, the price that everyone paid, in both families, Gifford himself was damned near beaten to death fighting over Chinse, Walani being beaten and Brian going to jail. Gifford started to feel like a fool.

"How do you know Mommy gave Juanita drugs?" asked Gifford in a shy voice.

"Because I paid attention God damn it, while all you could do was, think about Chinse." shouted Brian as they approached the corner of the store where old friends where standing around selling crack, coke, and heroin.

Both ceased hostility to put on a good front for the neighborhood fellas, who greeted them both and hugged Brian welcoming him home and offering him a beer as a sign of entering into manhood. In Queens as in the rest of New York City going to jail for the first time is like a ghetto "Bar'mitzva" you are seen as a man when you return home. You are giving respect that others are not given who have not been to jail. Gifford was shocked at Brian's acceptance of the beer which was a forty ounce of Saint Ives. Brian grabbed a snicker bar and a bag of onion rings as the two left the store justifying their visit in the first place, then both left and resumed their conversation on the corner. As Brian poured some beer out, "For the homies that ain't here."

Gifford watched in amazement as Brian guzzled the beer. Brian had never drank before and seemed to drink it like a pro.

"Where did you learn to drink like that?" asked Gifford, wondering if he should attempt to stop Brian as a big brother should.

"Inside we get beer sometimes," answered Brian with an air of arrogance.

"By the way, with all this trouble we've been through, have you even fucked Chinse yet?"

Gifford was insulted that Brian would even use the word fuck and Chinse in the same sentence.

"You heard me nigger....Fucked...have you fucked that bitch yet?"

Brian reiterated seeing how insulted Gifford was, that not only had he used the word fucked, he also referred to Chinse as a Bitch.

"Don't call my girl a bitch Brian!" Gifford said now seeing Brian as another Sean Wilson.

"Whatchu Gonna do!?" said Brian in a challenging tone. Gifford looked around and was glad that the two of them were two blocks away from the store and had no audience.

"Look Brian, you're my little brother and I'm glad your home. Let's not fight okay? I love you and I'm just glad to see you," said Gifford in a surrendering tone.

"Yeah okay, that's a bitch move, but okay," said Brian as he put his arm around Gifford. Gifford felt his heart racing. Brian was intimidating and menacing. Gifford was really afraid.

Gifford also felt as though he didn't know Brian anymore. That he would have to get to know this person. Brian sure wasn't the little brother anymore.

Chapter 8

Watch ye therefore: For ye know not when the master of the house comet, but who is the master?

One thing that is guaranteed in South Jamaica Queens New York City is change, often swift, brutal, and not usually for the best. What people do is always try and find a silver lining to the new cloud that has suddenly appeared over their heads. If that silver lining in raining gold they try and find a way to keep the cloud where it is....even if it's blocking out the sun. Change in South Jamaica Queens is most often caused by a governing body (meaning which ever drug crew is running the area at that time) being locked up in total, just its leadership, or even the cops protecting that governing body being locked up. Sometimes although usually rare, but more drastic and usually cataclysmic change is created by a "heavyweight" or big shot returning to South Jamaica after a long stay in prison.

This was the case in 1995, after a couple of years of tumultuous but prosperous years for the Cook's and McDaniel's a true heavyweight was returning to the neighborhood after ten years in prison. For the safety of this writer, I will refer to him as "Your Highness".

Your highness was in prison at the time of the Police Officer Eddie burns murder, but because then President George Bush put South Jamaica under a national spotlight, "Your Highness" and several other high profile Kingpins in Queens were given lengthy prison sentences for damn near nothing, including, Thomas Mickens aka Tony Montana who was given a thirty five year sentence for income tax evasion. Now in 1995 several of these heavyweights were returning to Queens and were re-establishing their old connections, and claiming their respective territories. This of course, was bad news for Police Officer Michael Gourdine, Hollywood, the Cook's, and the McDaniel's sisters. At best all one could hope for was to secure a fruitful position in the new administration that was formed by such a dramatic shift in structure in the neighborhood. Hollywood immediately notified Officer Gourdine that although "Your Highness" was not in control of the inside of the projects, he would be supplying the projects so Officer Gourdine's Dominican connection was no longer needed except for in cases of a "drought" in the neighborhood. "Your Highness" also re-connected with corrupt police officers in Patrol Borough Southern Queens who quickly cordoned off the neighborhood to all other cops. 'Your Highness" informed Hollywood that he would now be working for as a street soldier and not a supplier. Hollywood was reduced to corner street sales like he was doing when Walani was supplying Juanita with cocaine. This really hurt the income in Apartment 3C as well as their status in the neighborhood. In a way it was done just to show the neighborhood that those were in control for the past few years no longer had any status at all. When shifts like these happen, these changes are accompanied by spikes in crime, all crimes. Usually as the heavyweight is re-entering his kingdom a series of seemingly random murders will take place, some to get rid of people who were a threat whether real or imagined, and some murders are committed just to send messages that any thought of resistance by anyone in the entire neighborhood is at best a moot thought and any hope for overthrowing the new administration should be abandoned.

Robbery usually surges because people who were used to a certain amount of money being made because of the absence of such ruler or governing body refuse to live within the means of their now meager earnings and insist on 'keeping up with the jones" in their neighborhood. This feeling of 'keeping up with the Jones's" is compounded by the feeling of despair setting in by the constant display of decadence by those who are now making the money that this demoted person used to make. Some of these robberies are small i.e. Check cashing joints, small supermarkets, or maybe even a tractor trailer at J.F.K. airport, but in some cases more extreme measures are taken, like the robbery of distant drug dealers or even more suicidal the kidnapping of a Kingpins wife or child.

Hollywood felt humiliated by his meager wages being made under "Your Highness", the money being made was shameful compared to what he made under Lance Cook thirteen years earlier. Lance was being paid by "package commission" now. Hollywood would stand in the lobby of 97 W 159th Street with a package of two thousand dollars' worth of crack in a mailbox and actually deal hand to hand on the corner like a fourteen year old. Out of this $2,000.00 package he was allowed to keep $400.00. The thing was by 1995 the crack game was beginning to slow down except "Your Highness" was not aware of this and since "Your Highness" had corners sewn up down in Washington D.C. that were making a million dollars a week he didn't want to hear that the same couldn't be done in New York City. To make matters worse "Your Highness" put three dealers on that corner making it hard to sell a $2,000 package in a single day. Hollywood was lucky if he made that $400.00 a day equaling $2,800.00 a week. Hollywood couldn't even afford to pay off cops like he once had.

Gifford and Chinse were now attending Andrew Jackson High School in Cambria Heights and down the street from a home recently purchased by Officer Gourdine at 116-27

Francis Lewis Boulevard who was suffering terribly as a result of the shift in power in Queens. Both Gifford and Chinse were sophomores and doing well in school. Being members of the choir and making church services every Sunday kept the two pretty balanced. The two still hadn't taken their love for each other to the next step mostly because of Gifford's inexperience in taking the initiative. Chinse seemed more than ready, but was content in waiting for her knight in shining armor to be ready him-self. Brian who was just a year behind them rarely showed up to school and was busy spending days and sometimes weeks in Capalitana's dorm room at Old Westbury College in Nassau County. Being only a year behind Gifford meant nothing to the years ahead of him that he was mentally, physically, and most definitely sexually. Capalitana had taken Brian to "School" in more ways than one. The McDaniel's grandma paid for her tuition and food card, so Capalitana felt like Walani couldn't tell her anything. Capalitana had even experimented in Bi-sexuality and had had threesomes with Brian. The two had even developed small cocaine habits in the two semesters that she had been there. Walani was terribly worried about Brian as everyone silently was. Walani tried to have Hollywood talk to him and it went nowhere. Hollywood had lost all the meager status he had and was even looked at like a joke in some circles. It is very hard to be treated with respect when your peers at work are fourteen years old. This also took a toll on Walani and Hollywood's relationship. The only thing that made Hollywood feel like somebody was the fact that he still had Apartment 13C in building 10 of Rochdale Village. The gift he received for the job he did on Juanita and Ralph McDaniel. Hollywood was bringing in a respectable income, but in Queens respect is not only given for money, usually your power and status in the neighborhood are respected more than your monetary worth.

      This caused Hollywood to begin to relieve the pain of his diminishing status by sniffing a few lines himself, especially on long cold nights on 159th Street and 107th Avenue while knocking off packages. Hollywood's appearance showed the effects of his usage immediately. People often wonder why someone who has been in the drug business for so long would decide to start using as their approach middle age. There are many different reasons, but Hollywood's was the most common. Losing power and prestige is worse than never having any power and prestige at all, that loss is unbearable to people. It takes a strong person to move on from that. Being sent off to prison a millionaire and coming home to nothing is no way near as bad as being demoted and reduced to soldier in the street when you felt like a boss and millionaire.

Hollywood simply wasn't strong enough to handle this. To compound the situation Hollywood felt like he was getting old and someone feeling the depression of being at bottom of the totem pole and being around people who were younger than half his age made the temptation of instant relief too great.

Hollywood was selling crack, and knew that crack readily hastened the demise of all users. Hollywood had known people who only 'Sniffed" powdered cocaine and were able to function for years before they would graduate to the pipe. Heroin made him feel lazy and out of it, so Hollywood decided to sniff blow, and besides it made him feel up, really up, twenty five years younger. After trying it a few times Hollywood decided to pull back. Cocaine is a great and misleading drug that way. You can actually go a few days without using it making you feel like you actually aren't addicted. You can even turn it down when it is being offered to you giving you a feeling of superiority over the drug.

Things got so bad that Walani had to return to work. Walani got a job at New York Fried Chicken on Merrick and Farmers Blvd. Hollywood would seem to be on the corner all of the time and would never have any money. Brian would even show up at the drive through window, which also was a 'Walk up" window and would ask for money from Walani from time to time. Walani would come out and beg him to come home and go to church, but Brian seemed distant and lost. Walani would look into his eyes and just couldn't seem to reach him.

One night Brian and Hollywood showed up at the drive through window together asking for food and something to eat. This made Walani almost feel hopeless. Things were falling apart fast. Walani could see the decline and was wondering if everyone else could. Walani decided to say no. Hollywood erupted in rage.

"BITCH! After all I've done for you and you're no good fucking kids! You do me like this"

Walani and Brian stood there in shock by such a statement

Walani looked to Brian who had been sent to jail protecting her and waited for a response. There was none. Brian just stood there with his eyes on the ground.

"Look both of ya'll get the fuck out of here! I ain't giving ya'll shit!" screamed Walani from the window. Hollywood slammed it with his hands a few times before saying.
"Come on Brian! This Bitch ain't doing shit for us!"

As the two of them walked off Walani caught Brian's eyes and it was as if she didn't know him.

About two hours later the phone rang at New York fried Chicken. It was Chinse hysterically crying.

"Walani they're going to kill him I swear! Please come home!"

Walani called the police and then called Officer Gourdine who was working Midnights at this time. Officer Gourdine was sitting or guarding a hospitalized prisoner at Brookdale Hospital and had to abandon the prisoner and take his own car to Queens.

When the police arrived Gifford was laying on the ground, Hollywood and Brian had beat him to a pulp for the three hundred dollars that Walani had stashed in a can over the refrigerator. Officer Gourdine arrived on the scene and asked what was going on. The officers explained and so did Gifford. Chinse said that she had also saw Capalitana outside the building waiting for them. Officer Gourdine left the scene and drove straight to 159th Street and 107th Avenue. When Officer Gourdine pulled up the corner was rocking. Officer Gourdine stepped out of his car in full uniform and walked up to Hollywood, Brian, and Capalitana and asked to speak to them in his car.

"OH, I thought you was going to try and start some shit, you would have gotten your ass whopped, police uniform and all!" said Brian as the four of them walked to Officer Gourdine's car.

"What happened?" asked Officer Gourdine, while ignoring what Brian had said and all four sitting in Officer Gourdine's brand new Mitzubishi Eclipse.

"Look man this is family shit! You need to mind your fucking business!" said Hollywood staring hard across the front of the car into Officer Gourdine's face.

"Look Hollywood, I came out here because I thought you might be in trouble. I'm trying to look out for all of you. I didn't even know ya'll were having problems with each other?" asked Officer Gourdine and starting to realize the changes in the appearance and demeanor in his people from Queens.

"There was no problem until that bitch tried to hold out on us," said Capalitana from the back of the car in a real cold voice.

Officer Gourdine took a long breathe and said, "What do you mean holding out?"

"That bitch gets money for me and my sister every month and wouldn't give Hollywood and Brian a dime when I sent them to her job to get some money for us," said Capalitana.

"So that's just a misunderstanding," said Officer Gourdine remaining calm and realizing he was talking to three junkies that were stinking up his car with every second they sat there.

"Look you know people Mick-Man, you talk to my father. We need to get paid here. The powers that be are starving us out. Hollywood even tried to talk to the Big Man so I could work a package and was fired for it. We can't get any product and even if we could we have nowhere to sell it," said Brian from the back seat into the rear view mirror not realizing that he was permanently on Officer Gourdine's shit list for his earlier statement.

"Ya'll looking for work. Okay, okay, I'll ask around and see what I can do. I'm hurting too. Ya'll know I depended on ya'll for years for me to eat. So the least I can do is asks around," replied Officer Gourdine, now trying to just get these junkies out of his car.

Officer Gourdine returned to the apartment and sat down with Walani who had ran home losing a night's pay, Gifford and Chinse and were relieved that they were at least drug free and had clear minds.

"Look, here's three hundred dollars you lost. You have a bad situation on your hands. We care for all of them and must try and be there for them okay?" said officer Gourdine in a pleading voice as he noticed Gifford's shiner.

"This niggers always getting his as whopped," Officer Gourdine thought to himself. Feeling like every time he gets a call to come out here more often than not, Gifford had a black eye.

On Monday October 23rd 1995, a police radio call went across the airwaves in Brooklyn South. "Sector George we have a call for shots fired no "MOS" involved in Apartment 2A, 506 East 96th Street corner of East 96th Street and Church Avenue.

"This is Sector Adam I'm a block out I will respond," answered Officer Gourdine surprising his partner Willie Reed who never knew Officer Gourdine to volunteer to work. As the two cops approached the doorway to the building on 506 East 96th Street, they noticed Sector George parked all the way down the block waiting to back them up.

Upon entrance into the building at 0330 hours a woman who knew Officer Gourdine simply pointed up the staircase, as she stood there with several others.

"Anybody see anything?" asked Willie Reed.

No one answered.

Upon reaching the second floor both officers noticed red footprints on the ground and found the door to apartment 2A ajar. Officer Reed went to grab his radio when Officer Gourdine grabbed his wrist and shook his head. Officer Gourdine then motioned for the two of them to go inside, both officers drew their weapons and flashlights, placed one over the other as trained and entered. The apartment was pitch black which made it scary and officer Gourdine could smell that there was "fresh" blood in the apartment. There were bloody footprints and several bloody one hundred dollar bills strewn along the long hallway to the opening to the living room, where lying on the ground was a bloody safe, a portable safe that had been opened by a key. Both officers noticed the living room window open and connected to a rope that led to the neighboring building then to an even lower building which was the Brooklyn Public Library at 9612 Church Avenue.

Officer Gourdine and Officer Reed looked deeply at each other knowing that something wasn't right, both spun around quickly and "Fanned" apart toward the bedroom, before the bedroom was the bathroom where they found "Tiger", a well-known Jamaican drug dealer in east Flatbush face down on the ground and handcuffed behind his back with a massive gunshot wound to the back of the head. Both officers then noticed that they were standing in blood. Officer Reed then again reached for his radio and again was stopped by officer Gourdine who whispered, "let's search this motherfucker, might be some money in here?"

Officer Reed nodded then put his radio away.

When nothing could be found Officer Gourdine, came out of the apartment and went to the roof where they found the bedroom window to Apartment 2A was opened and that the neighboring window was closed with the light on. Officer Reed wanted to go down and knock on the window, but Officer Gourdine stopped him.

"Now make your call," said officer Gourdine headed for the rooftop staircase back into the building.

"Since Officer Gourdine answered the job he should be made to sit on the body!" Demanded Officer Mangano of Sector George as Sergeant Chititus was determining who had to wait with the deceased for the meat wagon from the Brooklyn medical examiner's office to come pick up the body. There's only one per borough in N.Y.C. and with Brooklyn being the biggest there was always at least five dead bodies to pick up a night which meant whatever cop had to wait; the wait was going to be at least six hours. Some cops love this and fight over it, because it meant overtime, but in 1995 with the midnight tour being so corrupt in the 6-7 pct. on the "A" squad, NO ONE wanted overtime.

"I got it…..No problem," relented Officer Gourdine.

All of the officers started to leave as Officer Gourdine started the first part of the "Wait" which is dealing with Brooklyn South homicide coming to investigate. All cops hate this especially black or Latino cops from Brooklyn, because all of the homicide detectives are only detectives because they have connections to the hierarchy of the police department, which means that they are Irish and live in the Rockaways or Lido Beach, Long Island. They all have cocky attitudes and treat the black or Latino cops like shit and are made to sit on the body. These detectives know absolutely nothing about the dealings of the streets and swear that they're "Kojack", Officer Gourdine found them comical. These detectives even show off their callousness and lack of care for black people by playing with the dead body, but Officer Gourdine didn't care, he wanted them to destroy the crime scene on this night. The detectives tore the place apart.

"Damn, the killers didn't drop single dollars, that's unusual," Detective Capra said smiling at Officer Gourdine while standing on top of poor dead Tiger.

"I know that is unusual," answered Officer Gourdine before the 2nd Grade Detective ordered Officer Gourdine to go outside the apartment and ask if anyone heard anything. Officer Gourdine was also commanded to knock on every door and ask.

"You didn't hear anything right?" asked Officer Gourdine, at every door he knocked on as the terrified faces all shook their heads no. Not terrified at what happened, but terrified by who was asking them. Everyone in the neighborhood except for the clueless detectives knew who Officer Gourdine was and what he was capable of. Every door was knocked on. Officer Gourdine saved Apartment 2B for last which was right next to and almost touching the door of 2A. No one answered in 2B only the peep hole shifted.

After all the detectives left Officer Gourdine was left all alone with poor "Tiger" and had to wait for the 'meat wagon'. All cops take advantage of this time to see if the deceased has anything good to eat in their refrigerator, or call Chicago on their house phone and thing is that nature, because it's not like tiger had to worry about the phone bill anymore and certainly wouldn't care about who ate his jerk chicken. Officer Gourdine sat down on the couch and every time he heard a noise he would go to the door. People would come and go; the family usually comes and is told that this is a crime scene. If the officer wants to be nice he will move aside and let the family see the dead body sprawled out on the floor. Gourdine was one of these "Cool" officers, but tonight, Latonya R. Reid was knocking, just to talk and hang out. Latonya lived in the building and was a casual acquaintance of Officer Gourdine.

"You know nobody left this building……right" said Latonya in a low voice shifting her eyes to Apartment 2B.

Officer Gourdine told her that he knocked already and no one was home in Apartment 2B. Latonya shrugged her shoulders and walked away.

As officer Gourdine stood there he looked down and noticed that the bloody footprints leaving the apartment were actually coming to the apartment.

"None of these "genius" detectives noticed this"

Officer Gourdine chuckled to himself as he also noticed that the foot prints disappeared, which only meant that they stepped across the threshold of the apartment around to Apartment 2B. A white person would never notice this because their minds don't think this way. Officer Gourdine went down to the lobby to wait for the meat wagon, and then lead them upstairs. When poor 'Tiger" was taken out of 2A; Officer Gourdine, put the yellow police tape around the door sealing it and left.

That night Officer Gourdine got off work and decided to check on Walani feeling bad about the whole situation. Hollywood greeted him and was all smiles.

"Look Mick-Man, You've been very good to everyone here over the years. Thank you for everything. Here's something for you." Hollywood handed Officer Gourdine a brown paper bag. "I just want everyone to be alright, ya'll have always been good to me," said Officer Gourdine.

Officer Gourdine saw that Hollywood had no shirt on and the lights were off so Officer Gourdine just left. Officer Gourdine opened the bag in his car and there was $25,000 in it. Officer Gourdine just shrugged and pulled off wondering why Hollywood had given him the money.

The next evening at work, Officer Gourdine's name was the buzz of the 6-7 Precinct. Numerous Officers approached officer Gourdine to tell him that all day long threats were being called in to the "T.S" desk at 718-287-3211. Officer Gourdine was accused of taking over one million dollars from a safe from "Tigers" apartment.

"Yo Goldie, your name is everywhere man, people are saying you took a million dollars out of Tigers house!" said Officer Dawn Dowling as Officer Gourdine walked up the back ramp to head toward the male locker room.

"The safe was a little beige portable safe Dawn, there was a few bloody twenty dollar bills laying around and I changed those this morning to pay my damn phone bill, whoever killed that mother fucker is spreading lies, they ain't get no more than maybe $100,000.00," Officer Gourdine said annoyed.

"I don't know Goldie; the whole East Flatbush is even saying that "YOU" killed him for it!"

Dawn reiterated giving Officer Gourdine her little crooked smirk she always gave him when she knew he was lying.

"GOURDINE! The Lieutenant wants you in his Office....NOW!" Sergeant McDonald screamed from behind the desk.

Dawn gave Officer Gourdine a look like "OOOOOOOH YOU IN TROUUUUUUBBBLE!"

Officer Gourdine went to the Office wondering what the hell was happening.

"Officer Gourdine is there anything you want to tell us about last night?" asked Lt. Brown from the "C" squad.

"No Sir, nothing, I wrote in the report exactly what happened, just ask Officer Reed."

"We will, he had off today and has been ordered in, in the meantime you'll sit on an 'E.D.P." at Kings County Hospital.

Officer Gourdine just saluted and left.

At about 0100 hours as Officer Gourdine was nodding in the "G" building sitting on a nut behind the half a wooden gate when the bell rang, it was Officer Reed.

"Goldie, what's going on? They just questioned the shit out of me, I told them exactly what happened," said a confused Willie Reed.

"Good, nothing more and nothing less," answered Gourdine which was his trademark reply as a police officer.

Officer Willie reed then gave Officer Gourdine a handshake and hug as they always exchanged, shrugged his shoulders and left.

As Officer Gourdine sat there, he reflected on the $25,000 given to him the night before by Hollywood and where it might have come from. More importantly the fact that Hollywood might be in possession of over one million dollars had his brain clicking even more. Officer Gourdine remembered when he helped the Homicide detectives turn Tigers body over his face had been brutally tortured. Officer Gourdine now realized that the small safe was left open with bloody twenty's laying around to throw off the scent of what had really happened.

"Hollywood was now a full-fledged crack head and was dangerous with that kind of money. Hollywood knew a lot of secrets about everybody. This situation was bad." Officer Gourdine thought to him-self, then nodded off to sleep as the crazy people did a 'Soul Train" line in the 'G" building figuring he'd work on it the next day.

The following day was a Wednesday, which meant that there would be choir rehearsal for Chinse and Gifford. Walani would be working at 1800 hours, which left the three musketeers the apartment and all the freedom to run amuck unchecked in South Jamaica. Officer Gourdine figured he drop in on them to see if he could sniff something out. Junior Mafia's song "Get Money" the remix was playing as Gourdine turned his car on and headed toward Queens. Officer Gourdine made sure his Glock 19-nine millimeter was fully operational. He also made sure to switch gun barrels with a buddy in the locker room. Officer Gourdine made sure his back up Model 64a was also at the ready as he drove onto the Belt Parkway headed toward Queens not knowing what to expect, but by the way Brian had spoken to him the night before he was certain that no matter what happened he was going to shoot Brian square in between the eyes. Officer Gourdine also made a mental note to pay Lance Cook a visit to make him aware of what was happening to his family.

As officer Gourdine pulled up to building 6, he saw the 1993 Acura Legend parked in front of the building with Brian sitting inside. Brian had started mixing heroin with his coke and had also started shooting up. When Officer Gourdine approached the car he was in a full nod.

Officer Gourdine knocked on the window startling Brian who broke into a wide half dazed grin.

"Hey Officer Mick-Man," said Brian with a slur.

"Where's Hollywood?" asked officer Gourdine.

"We was driving around looking for Capalitana, my girl been missing a lot of school and my mother wanted us to find her and take her back while she was at work. I fell asleep; he went upstairs to use the bathroom. Let's go up and get him," replied Brian. Matter of fact when the two arrived at Apartment 3C the door was ajar, both walked in on Hollywood riding Capalitana doggie style on the living room sofa bed.

Hollywood jumped up and tried to explain to a shocked Brian who couldn't even get his words together. The look of shock and hurt on his face said it all. To add to his pain Capalitana was so out of her mind on smack that she didn't even notice what was going on and said in slurred speech, "What's wrong baby…..don't stop hitting this asssssss."

Capalitana then half realized what was happening because she jumped up staggering toward the bathroom, with Brian running alongside her crying, "How could you do this to me bitch, I love you!"

Brian continued to yell this very line as Capalitana threw up into the toilet bowl.

Hollywood fixed his shirt and zippered his pants as Brian walked toward him ready to fight knowing Officer Gourdine would get in the way.

"You just a boy Brian, that bitch need as man," Hollywood exclaimed with pride.

Officer Gourdine was mad to be in the middle of all of this, but glad at the same time. He needed them at each other's throats. The thing with drug addicts is if the infraction against each other's trust isn't severe enough it will be forgotten by the next time the three of them were jonesing for some get high, but this was severe.

"Look, Capalitana thought it was you, can't you tell?" said Officer Gourdine, chilling Brian out for a second.

"Yeah, but what about this motherfucker? I'm gone too man, you know me. I sniff coke and maybe smoke a little crack, but that bitch gave me something, I think some diesel (heroin). You better check you bitch man she tripping."

Brian then switched his focus back to Capalitana which is what Officer Gourdine and Hollywood hope their bullshit lines would do to this poor lost little idiot.

At this point Capalitana stumbled back out of the bathroom and gave all three of them a 'Wicked" smile.

"Brian, Officer Mick-Man, ya'll don't think I know what happened to my parents? This fake as drug dealer told me everything."

Officer Gourdine, Brian, and Hollywood sat there shocked and now scared.

"Look, I'm here to check on ya'll and ya'll fools is tripping. You know what, I'm out," said Gourdine, as he turned and headed down the stairs, knowing it was only a matter of time before Capalitana was telling everybody something he knew nothing about, and didn't want to know nothing about.

Officer Gourdine went through the drive through at New York Fried Chicken and told Walani all that had transpired and was worried that Gifford and Chinse were now in danger because of these crazed "Hypes".

Walani didn't show any emotion. She just kissed Officer Gourdine on the cheek, "You've done all you can look-in' out for us, for my husband, Thank you."

Officer Gourdine drove back to Staten Island where he was staying at the time not knowing what to expect next. Officer Gourdine slept with his phone in his hand wondering who was going to call and why. If the cell phone rang it could be a heads of by fellow Officers, if the house phone rang it was bad news. If there was a knock on his door at 82 Arlo Road in Grimes Hill, then he was in trouble. If the door was rammed in he was in serious trouble. That was a very restless night for Officer Michael 'Mick-Man' Gourdine.

Officer Gourdine woke up at 1300 hours surprised that nothing had happened. He got dressed and drove to Queens and just drove around trying to see if there was any signs of what may be happening to him or any of the people he knew. Officer Gourdine even drove by Andrew Jackson High School and asked the school safety officer if Gifford and Chinse were in school that day, they indeed were and all seemed fine. Surprisingly he saw no one. At 2300 hours Officer Gourdine stood roll call without incident, not even a second look by his Sergeant. Officer Gourdine was assigned to a patrol sector and he was happy about that that meant he would be in a police cruiser allowing him to drive to Queens. As he drove up to the New York Fried Chicken his heart was in his throat, he was expecting for Walani to tell him only God knows what, to find out she hadn't come to work shocked him because Walani never missed work. Officer Gourdine and his partner Willie Reed then returned to Brooklyn with Officer Gourdine completely confused.

"Well, okay, just gotta wait and see what happens?" Officer Gourdine thought to himself.

Two days later on Saturday morning, Officer Gourdine got a phone call form Gifford.

"I haven't seen my mother since she left for work the other night, We keep your number in the kitchen drawer in case of emergency, I'm afraid something may have happened to her, can you look into it Officer Mick-Man?" asked Gifford sounding scared.

"Alright Gifford, I'll check it out," answered Officer Gourdine completely confused.

Officer Gourdine was R.D.O.'d that night which gave him the whole day to be awake so he figured he ride out to Queens again and have a sniff around. Officer Gourdine stopped for some food at R.C.L. soul food on Rockaway Blvd. and proceeded to Baisley Pond to eat his food. As Officer Gourdine was tuning his radio to the song "Touch me tease me" by Mary J. Blige and Kase, he notice the unmistakable 93' Acura Legend parked in the lot across from August Martin High School. He could see Hollywood and Capalitana kissing in the front seat and what appeared to be Brian in the back seat asleep. Hollywood and Capalitana then heated up some heroin on a spoon and loaded up a spike through a swab of cotton. The two actually where shooting up in broad day light in a parked car. Officer Gourdine put his food down and waited a few minutes to make sure their "High" was setting in good before pulling his car into the parking lot. With his hand on his gun Officer Gourdine approached the car and knocked on the driver's side window startling Hollywood.

"What's Good Mr. Police Man?" asked Hollywood with a slur.

"Everything is fine Mr. Hollywood, have you seen Walani anywhere?" asked Officer Gourdine.

"Maaaan, I don't know, That bitch be tripping," answered Hollywood with a wide intoxicated grin.

"Yeah she done tripped alright," slurred Capalitana.

At which point Hollywood turned and slapped her in the mouth.

"Yo don't hit my girl yo," hissed Brian from the backseat as he drifted back into a nod, now sporting half a front left tooth courtesy of Hollywood who had been seen beating him in public in the past week.

"Shut the Fuck up Brian! She done told you she's my Bitch now, and about to start turning tricks on south Road.....Just go back to sleep little Nigger, before I have you selling your ass!"

Half of Hollywood's statement fell on deaf ears because Brian had fell into a deep nod before Hollywood could finish. Now there was a silent stare down between Officer Gourdine and Hollywood.

"Are you going to tell me where she is or what?" asked Officer Gourdine giving Hollywood a murderous stare.

"Man, kiss my ass COP!" said Hollywood as he screeched off in the car. As the car screeched by Officer Gourdine heard a thump in the trunk.

Officer Gourdine ran back to his car and drove to Apartment 3C and was glad to find Chinse and Gifford there. Officer Gourdine nearly drug them to his car and drove them to Staten Island. Along the way on the Belt Parkway Officer Gourdine tried to explain.

"Look, Hollywood is tripping; I don't know what he's capable of."

"Hollywood and Capalitana have been gone since Thursday night, Brian cried in the bathroom all last night before he fell asleep in there. I have no idea why he would fall asleep in the bathroom," said Chinse.

"I don't know what's going on, but they have all been acting weird lately, I don't think mommy is with Hollywood anymore, I'm starting to think he's with Capalitana," Gifford said looking scared and confused.

Officer Gourdine was afraid, most of all of Chinse hearing from Capalitana first-hand what happened to her parents by Hollywood. In a way Officer Gourdine was trying to save their lives.

Officer Gourdine made them comfortable in his apartment he gave them his 'R.C.L." order of Oxtail, collard greens, and macaroni with cheese with the candy yam juice poured on top of the collard greens. R.C.L. always gave you enough to feed a family so the food which was known to split the Styrofoam container in half was more than enough to have Gifford and Chinse stuffed for a while. Officer Gourdine then stepped outside to make a few phone calls to try and somehow get a grip on what was going on.

"Hello 113 pct. I can't call central for your division because I'm out of state, I'm an M.O.S. (member of the service) but a 10-21 approximately forty five minutes in the past took place on the corner of 155th Street and Baisley Blvd. in the parking lot of Baisley Pond Park. The woman approximately 5 foot 11 and dark complexioned was robbed of her jewelry and forced into the car at gunpoint the car is a 1993 white Acura Legend with Virginia plates AZA 1342.

The perpetrator is one Alfred "Hollywood" Gatin, approximately five foot nine, one hundred and eighty five pounds. Alfred is in possession of a Glock 19 service pistol that was stolen from the voucher room in the 6-7 pct. located at 2820 Snyder Avenue, Brooklyn, New York."

Officer Gourdine was sure that action would be taken because the "T.S." operator was a rookie police officer who had called the 'D.O." who was Lieutenant Brown over to the phone and was listening to the conversation; he had already raised sectors from the radio on the wall. Once Officer Gourdine heard all of that happening he simply hung up the phone without once identifying himself.

Officer Gourdine had always tried to be careful, but everyone makes mistakes. Officer Gourdine realized that he had bought Hollywood to his apartment in the past and now felt as though he and everyone else were sitting ducks. Not sure of the visiting schedule at Great Meadow Correctional Facility, Officer Gourdine called his cousin, Barclay "Sandy" Cook who was a New York State Correctional Officer and asked if it were possible to see Lance Cook on an unofficial visit in the "Salley Port" of the prison for questioning by a police officer conducting an investigation.

"Cuzz I need a favor?" asked Officer Gourdine

"Sliiiiiiick!" In a low voice as Sandy always called him

"What can I do for you Cousin?"

"I need to meet with you know who, you know where," said Officer Gourdine, in the code the two always spoke under.

'No problem, when you coming up here?" asked Sandy.

"Give me the usual four hours, it's an emergency," said Officer Gourdine.

"I'll be there, if you slow you blow, I don't even want to know," said Sandy in his usual witty rhyme.

Officer Gourdine got Gifford and Chinse in the car and told them to try and get some sleep, that it was a four hour ride to Comstock, New York.

"Who's up there?" asked Gifford.

"Your father," replied officer Gourdine.

Gifford was elated and saddened, he knew that if they were going to meet with his father the things had taken a turn for the worse, but at the same time he was elated that he was going to see his father for the first time in nearly ten years. He struggled to remember his father's face, all he could think about was the pictures on the wall at home in Apartment 3C. Gifford was on pins and needles for the whole ride upstate. Chinse being exhausted fell asleep as 'Brown Sugar" by D' Angelo played on the radio.

On Route 22 as you make a left turn through the gates there's and orange building. In that building was Lance Cook escorted there by some Correctional Officers that owed Officer Gourdine and several family members' favors. Officer Gourdine told Chinse to stay in the car and bought Gifford with him. Everyone was jovial and hugged once inside except Gifford. Gifford couldn't stop staring at Lance Cook who looked unusually young for his age. Lance stared hard at Gifford as well; as Officer Gourdine laughed and joked with the Corrections Officers whom he was also "Kin" to. The Officers then went to the doors and became silent as they kept look out for superior Officers or Officers that they did not trust. In the corner of this Garage behind a large New York State Corrections Bus, were a table and three chairs waiting for them to sit down and talk.

"Lance, shit is pretty bad back home. I need you to tell me how things should be handled and how you want them handled?"

Officer Gourdine opened up the discussion by getting right down to the point, not realizing that Lance and Gifford were locked in a stare down with Gifford streaming tears down his face.

"I love you son," said Lance in a low tone and matter of fact, which seemed to lift a ton of weight off of Gifford's shoulders.

'I Love you too daddy," said Gifford who then started to openly cry with a curled up face.

Lance stood up and outstretched his arms. Gifford rose and came around the table and the two embraced. Gifford sobbed as Lance assured him that everything would be okay, that there wasn't a lot of time to catch up but the two of them would make time in the near future.

"Let's have a seat, and remember Officer Gourdine is the only one besides your mother that you can absolutely trust. Things may start to happen that will confuse and possibly sadden you, but we are going to make sure everything is okay, aren't we Mick-Man?" said Lance as he hugged his son.

"Absolutely," responded Officer Gourdine with the tone of a loyal soldier.

Gifford re-took his seat and gave the floor back to Officer Gourdine.

"Things have taken a turn for the worse. I have to say things that might not be good for Gifford to hear. I knew he wanted to see you so I bought him in."

Officer Gourdine then continued, "I have to tell you both that Walani might be in the hospital. If she is hurt bad Gifford and Chinse have to be in the custody of someone else until she gets better. I have a friend in adult children services named, Carmella Breedlove who can arrange for the two of them to be in my custody. I could put them up in an apartment and check on them every day. What do you think?"

Lance stared hard and long at Officer Gourdine.

With that being said by Officer Gourdine, Lance raised his hand like a child in a school room asking a question and a corrections officer was there in a flash.

"Please take my son back out to the car?" directed Lance. Whose direction was carried out immediately.

Officer Gourdine and Lance then continued to talk for about twenty minutes. Officer Gourdine also told Lance that he had made calls in an attempt to have Lance be granted an early "conditional parole". Officer Gourdine had friends in high places in the New York City Corrections Department who had friends all over the state.

"My pockets are killing me Lance. I lose half my check to taxes and I'm damn near broke."

Officer Gourdine belly ached to the only person who both knew could help him.

"For starters, I can have you ordained a Reverend therefore your federal tax probe would then be settled."

Officer Gourdine gave a big broad smile.

'That would be great! Thank you Lance," answered officer Gourdine.

The two men talked intensely for another hour, sometimes even joking about things that happened when they were officer and prisoner back when, Officer Gourdine wasn't even old enough to buy alcohol; but held the power of life and death in his hands on Rikers Island.

On the way back Chinse and Gifford joked and laughed. Gifford attempted to ease Chinse's anxiety, which impressed Officer Gourdine.

"He's becoming a man."

Officer Gourdine thought to himself. Knowing it was needed now more than ever.

Officer Gourdine, Gifford, and Chinse arrived back in New York City that night actually 2:00 a.m. Sunday morning. Not knowing what the hell was going on Officer Gourdine checked the three of them in at the Staten Island Motor Inn on Victory Boulevard and got them some take out from the Applebees next door. Although Gifford and Chinse were only thirteen years old he treated them like adults and gave them their own room. Officer Gourdine told them to stay in their room while he made some calls from downstairs on the pay phones to make sure his cell number wouldn't show up anywhere by mistake. Officer Gourdine also made sure to use *67 so that no calls could be traced.

"Hello Reverend Burns?"

"Yes this is he?" answered Reverend Burns sounding as if he was going to break into the I have a dream speech by Doctor King at any minute.

"This Is Officer Michael Gourdine of the New York City Police Department. I've been told to inform you that I was to be ordained as a Reverend and given all of the proper paperwork especially the "Federal Tax Exemption" paperwork as soon as possible."

"Who on earth informed you of that?" asked Reverend Burns as if he were having a "Con" ran on him.

"Lance Cook," replied Officer Gourdine.

"Don't talk anymore over the phone come to the church or my home as soon as you can at 193-36 Foothill Ave in Holliswood Queens."

"I will Sir, I greatly appreciate the opportunity to serve God."

Reverend Burns sighed and said, 'God does work in mysterious ways."

Officer Gourdine then went upstairs and went into his room and decided to try and get some sleep.

Right next door, something way overdue was happening. Something that some would consider pre-mature, in the old south it would have seemed appropriate one would guess. Officer Gourdine had told Chinse and Gifford on the way home that his own grandmother "Retha (Dorothy) Cook" had given birth to her first child "Lynette" at the age of twelve. This of course made Chinse feel that maybe it was time. This hotel room had by far been the most romantic place the two of them had ever seen.

"Do you love me Gifford?" asked Chinse, staring into Gifford's eyes on the terrace of their twelfth floor balcony.

"Yes I do." answered Gifford.

Chinse then lead Gifford back to the bed. Chinse stood Gifford up as she sat down and said, "Then be my man, and take me as your woman."

Gifford had never been in this situation and was not quite sure what action, taking a woman would require.

Chinse then slowly and as seductively as a thirteen year old virgin could took her clothes off and laid there waiting for Gifford to do the same. Gifford stood there in amazement staring at every nook and cranny of Chinse's dark chocolate body that he could see under the moonlight.

Chinse finally laid on her back completely naked in the near dark on the bed.

"Close your mouth and take your clothes off silly," said Chinse giggling.

Gifford figuring that men don't "Strip" like a woman would simply drop his pants and undressed. Gifford then crawled up to Chinse until their bodies where face to face on top of each other and kissing passionately on the bed. The feel of Chinse's pubic hairs up against his was a strange and fantastic feeling to Gifford who was overwhelmed with a hard on could have been used a door-jam during a robbery of Fort Knox's safe.

The two kissed until their tongues throbbed as Chinse waited for Gifford to finally grab his own penis and insert it. This did not happen. Chinse finally frustrated reached down and grabbed Gifford penis causing him to flinch. Not hesitating Chinse inserted Gifford penis into her throbbing vagina that had become so wet her thighs and bed sheet were now soaked as if Chinse had "Squirted". Chinse delicately held Gifford in place while he began to stroke and hump naturally as Chinse followed his rhythm receiving and complimenting each thrust with intense kisses. In what felt like an eternity on a tropical island but was actually two minutes and thirty six seconds in the Staten Island Hotel, Gifford exploded inside of Chinse who spontaneously did the same; completely soaking Gifford's stomach and testicles with feminine ejaculation that carried enough fluid to match the birth of twins in a delivery room.

The next morning Officer Gourdine was well aware of what had happened just by the smell of the room.

"If you two have any problems; I will handle it understand. I mean unwanted pregnancy or anything. I have added you two to my G.H.I. health plan as dependents already okay. So just let me know."

Gifford and Chinse both nodded recognizing Officer Gourdine as their new Guardian whether official or unofficial.

"Have you found my mother yet?" asked Gifford.

"I haven't heard anything. I'm still checking. I'm sure she is fine."

As officer Gourdine said this, he noticed Chinse grabbing hold of Gifford's hand as if she knew exactly how Gifford felt when she herself was waiting for news on her own mother.

"I got to go to work tonight. You two just stay here like grown-ups. I should know something by tonight. If the room phone rings answer it. I'll have food delivered to you. Don't go anywhere," Officer Gourdine said in a stern voice.

Upon showing up at the 6-7 Pct. Officer Gourdine was met again at the back ramp by Officer Dawn Dowling.

"Goldie, you should try and take lost time! Everybody on the street is saying you killed Tiger for a million dollars."

Officer Gourdine just shrugged and waived Officer Dowling off like he had better things on his mind.

After being assigned a hospitalized prisoner, Officer Gourdine walked to Nostrand and Church Avenue to buy some sweets to have with him at Brookdale Hospital when all of a sudden he was hit in the head with a brick and stomped repeatedly. As Officer Gourdine fade to darkness all he heard was.

"Bloood Clot!!! You killed me Man Tiger, for the loot! Murderer!!! Murderer!!!"

Officer Gourdine woke up in K.C.H Hospital with his fellow officer standing around him. Officer Dowling said.

"Your boy is in I.C.U. barely alive! No One Fucks with the 6-7 Pct. and don't get what's coming to them; you're going to be alright, just a concussion and some stiches. Boss said you can get "Lost Time" go home spend the night or whatever you want."

"I'll go home, but only after I put in another U.F. 57 and a request for an administrative transfer for the safety of my life," replied Officer Gourdine, while reaching for his clothes.

"Come on let's go then," answered Dawn Dowling as she helped Officer Gourdine to his feet.

Back at the station house officer Gourdine was informed that the "Duty captain" Captain Materrazzo wanted to see him in his office.

"Is there a problem you want to make us aware of Officer Gourdine?" said Captain Materrazzo as he invited Officer Gourdine to have a seat in his office by the front door at the 6-7 pct.

"No sir, all I hear are the same rumors the rest of the station house is hearing," answered Officer Gourdine.

"And they are just rumors? Correct?" prodded Captain Materrazzo.

"Of course sir, had I got my hands on a million dollars that night, I would have quit the next day. Sir, you're well aware of how things work in East Flatbush. If anyone is accused of anything whether it real, imagined, or seen in the spirit world by the Haitian High Priests, everyone believes it and it could cost anyone their life, black white, or Puerto Rican. I was just doing my job like any God fearing man, and now I might lose my life over it."

The captain just stared intently then made a face that showed sympathy toward Officer Gourdine and his sad situation, as officer Gourdine sat there looking pale, disheveled, with stitches sticking out of his hair.

"What can I do to help Officer Gourdine? Do you want to stay here, transfer, take some of your vacation days now to think about it; tell me what you want?"

Officer Gourdine sat for a second and said, "I think my days here at the 6-7 are done if I want to remain alive, Sir. I would like a transfer to Manhattan North Narcotics. I'm planning to move to Rockland County, and I'm interested in making detective. I heard from Sergeant Chititus that they were looking for officers there. I have ten days on the books. I would like to use them to get my affairs in order."

"You got it," said Captain Materrazzo smiling at the fact that he was able to get rid of this problem so easily. Had officer Gourdine insisted on staying he would have had to been given a police radio to take home, be specially monitored for his own safety and a bunch of other nonsense that would have made the precinct a "Spectacle" in the community.

When Officer Gourdine got back to the Staten Island Hotel, he found Gifford sobbing in Chinse's arms on the bed.

"What happened?" yelled officer Gourdine to the two of them.

"We called Reverend Burns. I know you said to stay off the phone, but I was desperate Officer Mick-Man. We are worried about my mother and brother, and Chinse is worried sick about her sister."

"What did he say?" said Officer Gourdine lowering his tone and bracing for the news.

"They found Hollywood's car on 155th Street and South Road. A white Acura that had been reported to have been involved in a crime; and in the car's trunk…….and in the car's trunk…..WAS MY MOTHER!!!!!!" screamed Gifford as tears spurted from his eyes and he dropped his head back into Chinse's bosom.

Officer Gourdine wanted to grill Gifford for more information, but knew not to push it. Officer Gourdine himself was saddened by this. Walani Stevens after all was his child hood friend. Officer Gourdine had known her longer than anyone in this whole scenario. He stood there thinking about him and Walani playing "Hot peas and butter, and red light green light" as children and it weighed heavy on him. Officer Gourdine then approached the two kids who jumped up and hugged him as if they were his own children even though they were only ten years apart in age.

"MY MOTHER WAS STABBED 32 TIMES OFFICER GOURDINE!!!!"

This stunned Officer Gourdine, but he knew by the sound of the viciousness involved that the murder was done not only by Hollywood, but by Capalitana, only someone scorned, who knew a very ugly truth about someone could kill with such ferocity. "Overkill" is always a sign of a "revenge killing".

Officer Gourdine was just worried now about Chinse finding out that awful truth and somehow blaming Gifford yet ruining their future together and even their lives, because they personally might not psychologically survive this without each other. Officer Gourdine stood over them and began to speak.

"Look, we are going to stay here. I'm going to go to the Reverend and find out all I can. I will bring your brother and sister back here, and plan services for your dear mother. I will find Hollywood and place him under arrest for the terrible murder. I need you two to pray for my dear friend Walani's soul. I will also contact your father, okay Gifford?"

Both kids nodded at officer Gourdine who quickly went to his car and headed toward the Staten Island Expressway eastbound. Officer Gourdine knew he had ten days to get things in order; he didn't want a cloud over his head when he began to work at Manhattan North Narcotics. He wanted his life in order and his head clear. Gifford and Chinse were his responsibility and he wanted them squared away. Officer Gourdine's money was tight, but was elated by the news of a potential win fall given to him by Lance at the visit. Officer Gourdine reached deep down into his "connections" list to find the name of one Chief Damont who was a friend of his mother's and held a lot of weight in the New York City Corrections Department. Chief Damont also owed Officer Gourdine a favor for helping him with his little brother who was charged with a crime in East Flatbush and Officer Gourdine made all the witnesses catch amnesia. If Lance could get ordained as a Reverend by Reverend Burns himself and granted an early parole, courtesy of Chief Damont's connections then there was ample opportunity for money and protection from the Jamaicans in Brooklyn, but first it was imperative to find Capalitana, Brian and most importantly, Hollywood. Officer Gourdine was able to contact Reverend Burns and made an appointment to meet at the church. At the Church Reverend burns and officer Gourdine talked fondly about Walani and how much they would both miss her. Officer Gourdine knew he would have to do this alone in case things got messy. Brian was a junkie for sure by this point; Capalitana was also to add to this dilemma. Capalitana knew the awful truth that even included Officer Gourdine himself.

"Any word on Hollywood, may even try to blackmail me, the son of a bitch," Officer Gourdine thought to himself as he exited the 150th Street ramp off of the Belt Parkway.

First Officer Gourdine pulled in front of building 6, Brian and thought Capalitana?" "Here we go again, I hope I make it out of this alive….again."

As officer Gourdine saw no life in the apartment he drove through the neighborhood. Remembering that Hollywood mentioned "pimping" Capalitana, Officer Gourdine drove to 155th Street and South Road since the sun was starting to come up, and sure enough there they were…all three of them. Capalitana was wearing a bra and panties with Walani's Sunday high heels on as Brian laughed at her "high fiving" Hollywood screaming, "PIMP HARD MY NIGGER……PIMP HARD!"

As Hollywood counted the money in his hand out loud over and over again saying "My Bitch gets MONEEEEEY!"

Officer Gourdine decided to follow them as they walked back toward the projects. There was no rush since they were undoubtedly going to score some smack before returning to 3C to shoot and sniff.

Officer Gourdine decided to pay the church a visit to make plans for Walani's funeral with money that he was instructed was in a safe in the Church that Reverend Burns thought EVERYONE had forgotten about.

"Reverend? This is Officer Gourdine; can you please meet me at the church to make plans for our departed and beloved Walani Steven's"

"Officer Mick-Man we are all in shock, this is just terrible news. It is awfully early, but I'll be there in short order."

Officer Gourdine parked on 149th Street and waited until he saw the Reverend's black Mercedes pull into the parking spot around the side of the church.

As the two men walked down the pew Officer Gourdine said, "The money in the safe secreted in the wall downstairs will cover the funeral, the rest will stay where it is until Lance comes home," Officer Gourdine said flatly.

Reverend Burns turned in shock.

'I didn't hear anything from Lance."

"You just did mother fucker, and another thing I need papers stating that Lance and myself are now ordained ministers in the Burns Memorial Church."

"Okay no problem, I didn't know Lance was coming home, boy how the Lord does work in mysterious ways."

"I'll need the paperwork right now"

"Insisting," asked Reverend Burns.

"I haven't heard anything," replied Officer Gourdine with tears in his eyes.

"I think it's time," said Reverend Burns.

"For what?" asked Officer Gourdine looking confused?

The reverend just nodded and motioned for Officer Gourdine to follow him to the side office by the rest room. Where he pulled the forms, stamped, and signed them.

"Now you'll have to go down to 1 Centre Street and get a register number as proof that you're now a "Minister" Officer Gourdine."

Both men just nodded at each other as Officer Gourdine headed toward the front door. Upon circling back around 160th Street, Officer Gourdine parked and collected himself to prepare for the drama. Officer Gourdine then exited his car and walked to the corner. Using a pay phone on the corner he said calmly into the phone.

"Central be advised that a man known as Alfred "Hollywood" Gatin who is wanted for murder is in Apartment 3C, 6 160th Street. He is armed and extremely dangerous."

Officer Gourdine then called the "T.S." operator in the 103 Precinct, and said that he was an "M.O.S." with the same exact description of Hollywood; to make the call an "85 forthwith".

Officer Gourdine then went into the building and performed an old "cop" trick. Officer Gourdine placed a .25 caliber handgun or "Saturday night special" in front of Apartment 3C, pounded on the door and then ran to the roof.

Brian answered the door in a half nod and picked up the Gun and just stood there, as the Cops reached the second floor, Brian just stood there like a deer caught in the headlights as Hollywood peaked his head out of the door, at that moment Officer Gourdine let off two rounds, in a project hallway the deafened everyone sounding like a cannon, giving no one no idea where it came from.

Brian and Hollywood never knew what hit them as they were shot over thirty times a piece as Officer Gourdine scurried across the roof top and down the next building, and out to his car.

"Two down and one to go," Officer Gourdine thought to himself.

"Well at least Hollywood control, grip, and mastery of the situation are over with".

Chapter 9

When the Lion lies down with the lamb, true Jubilation

"Do you accept Christ as your Lord and savior?"

"Absolutely yes I do."

"Then I pronounce you Reverend Michael Victor Gourdine II"

Reverend Burns then handed Officer Gourdine papers to sign.

"Take this to your payroll department and you will be exempt from federal taxes. Your federal exemption code certifying you in the State of New York is on the top of the paper. Lance called here earlier and told me to bring you in the basement.

In the basement, in a back office was a picture of Jesus on the wall, behind that picture was a safe that Lance had installed fifteen years earlier.

"Lance said to give you two hundred and fifty thousand dollars of the money to make sure his kids are alright. Lance said you had a good friend named Carmella Breedlove in the bureau of child welfare who could get them placed with a good family. Since you're a Reverend here now the safe is yours to use as well, for whatever reason you like."

Officer Gourdine nodded his head and stood up as did the Reverend and both men embraced.

Reverend Burns loaded the money into a satchel with a letter inside for Officer Gourdine. "I contacted Walani's parents, they instructed me to make whatever arrangements I wanted. Mr. and Mrs. Stevens declined to attend Walani's homecoming services because of her involvement with a criminal. Tell me something, why did you consort with such a man, Officer (slash) Reverend Gourdine?"

Officer Gourdine stared into Reverend Burns' eyes and said, "because Lance Cook saved my life, I couldn't count on one immediate family member to have done what Lance Cook did for me, maybe my cousins the 'Cook's" in Connecticut, Edwardo "Mans" Gilbert, and his little brother my cousin Brady "Fats" Gilbert, but I have no family or friends like Lance Cook. I'd die for him; much less kill for him. Black people need a Lance Cook in their lives. There is no sense of order or protection in America for a black person. All of us without exception latch on to a lance Cook if we're lucky enough to meet one. Where would you and your church be without him? You let him know his children will be fine. He has my word, and my word is bond."

The reverend said, "I know all that you have said already, I just wanted to hear it from you. You said exactly what I feel. Saint Michael cast Lucifer from heaven for the Lord. Some would say that Saint Michael was an evil entity. I say Saint Michael performed a necessary evil for the betterment of the universe.......do you hear me Saint Michael?"

Officer Gourdine just nodded understanding that is was now his job to protect the church from harm by any and all evil doers in the universe.

When Officer Gourdine arrived back at the Staten Island Hotel he found Chinse sitting upright on the bed and Gifford with his head lying in her lap quietly weeping as the two of them watched an episode of Martin Lawrence's TV show "Martin."

"You two must be starving let's get something to eat," said officer Gourdine.

"We both want to go to Queens. Gifford wants to see and be near his mother," said Chinse sounding more like a wife by the minute.

"That's a good idea. I identified your mother at the medical examiner's office already. Your mother, God rest her soul will be at the church the day after tomorrow," said Officer Gourdine trying to be accommodating and still treat the two of them as children.

"I also want to find my brother and tell him what has happened. I also want to know what he knows," said Gifford as he rocked back and forth staring at the TV intensely. Officer Gourdine and Chinse locked eyes as if they both suspected something and was not telling each other.

'Well let's head out, I'll stop at the McDonald's drive through on Forest Avenue before we hit the road," said Officer Gourdine trying to cheer them up. Going to McDonald's had always lifted his spirits when he was a child; it didn't seem to work on these children though, Maybe because they weren't children anymore, Officer Gourdine thought to himself.

While driving on the Belt Parkway eastbound traffic came to a grinding halt at the draw bridge near the Jamaica Bay Riding Academy. There was a thick black smoke coming up from the Canarsie swamp that early morning. The trio sat in the car wondering if they and the rest of all the cars on the Belt Parkway might be in some sort of danger. Officer Gourdine noticed lights ahead signaling that it was "Highway 2", an officer got out of the car and approached the highway cars that were parked at the edge of the highway looking down at the water where the horses usually crossed on their daily routes through the swamp. Officer Gourdine noticed Officer Farina and asked what was going on.

"Hey Joe, How's it going?" asked officer Gourdine seeing his friend.

"Hey Mike? It's going all right; a typical reply from a fellow officer."

"We got a car fire again; we're just putting it out and making sure there's no "body" in it. We've had four of those this month."

The smoke turned white which was a clear sign that it would soon be extinguished and traffic would be moving along. Officer Gourdine and Farina then saw an officer waive them down to the car. The car was unidentifiable, completely charred and so was the body in the back seat. Through the smoke and eerily appetizing smell of BBQ was the body of a young man, charred except for the half a front left tooth which officer Gourdine noticed immediately. Officer Gourdine made sure to keep his 'poker face" on to keep the highway cops in the dark about his intimate knowledge of this grizzly crime.

"Is anyone else inside?" asked Officer Farina to the highway cop on the scene.

"We're waiting for the car to cool off so that we can open the trunk," replied Highway Officer Jeffery Poje.

By this point there were dozens if not over one hundred people looking from the upper parkway down to the swamp wondering what in the hell was taking so long for the road to be re-opened. Finally the "ESU" unit arrived and pried the trunk open and found a Female in her late teens not too badly burned. Officer Gourdine recognized Capalitana McDaniel's immediately. It made his heart skip a beat that Hollywood could be such a monster. Capalitana was wearing the same clothes she had been wearing nearly a week earlier, was brutally beaten although still recognizable, Officer Gourdine knowing how bad he would look to his fellow officers and superiors if he reported who and how he knew who these two dead people were, knowing that he was as dirty as a dirty cop could get, that he himself might be implicated in numerous crimes. Officer Gourdine knew that there was only one person he could tell and hope that justice would be served swiftly and absolutely. Officer Gourdine was praying that Gifford and Chinse had not seen Capalitana in the trunk from the parkway. It seemed amazing that the car could be so badly charred and that Capalitana seemed as though she was just sleeping.

"What's going down there," screamed Gifford with Chinse by his side from up on the parkway.

"Stay up there!" screamed Officer Gourdine noticing that it was already too late, Chinse was on her way down with a horrific look on her face that no one would ever forget who was standing there that day.

"MY SISTER!!!!! MY SISTER!!!!! OH GOD CAPALITANA!!!!!"

Chinse rushed to the car with Officer Gourdine trying to stop her. Chinse was able to get passed and hug Capalitana and as she did everyone noticed the multiple stab wounds on her lower neck and upper chest. Officer Gourdine then released her and stood there, as did everyone else including the firemen. It was terribly sad. Gifford just stood next to her as a "Man" would and was simply there for her as Chinse heaved and sobbed cradling her sister's head in her arms. Officer Gourdine made eye contact with Officer Farina, and Poje who were definitely interested in the fact that Officer Gourdine knew God damned well who that poor girl was and had said nothing, and why was Officer Gourdine down there in the first place?

"I was driving my niece and her boyfriend home, I thought it might have been her sister but wasn't sure," said Officer Gourdine to the duty captain at his interrogation at Highway 2 on Flatbush Avenue.

"Well Ms. Chinse Mcdaniels said that you were hiding her and her boyfriend on Staten Island because her mother's boyfriend had gone berserk and that you feared for their lives," said Captian Kean staring intently at Officer Gourdine.

"This actually looks good for you seeing that someone obviously did go berserk because her adopted mother, Walani Cooks' son Brian, and most tragically her sister is now dead, and all just three years after her parents were killed in a tragic murder suicide. It also turns out that you are a recently Ordained Reverend at the church where all parties involved have been parishioners for over a decade and between me and you I heard that the Cook boy's father "Lance Cook" ordered Capalitana murdered as payback for Walani and Brian being killed. I'm an Old Irish Man and a fourth generation police officer and I know when a cop is dirty, just be careful Mike, understand?" Captain Kean was smiling broadly and Officer Gourdine who sat stone faced.

Officer Gourdine sat in the back of the church as Chinse and Gifford sat in the front row with in laws and tried as best they could to console each other as Walani, Brian, and Capalitana's coffins stood side by side at the triple funeral. Officer Gourdine paid for caskets known as the "Gonzales Special" because these coffins where used to bury his first cousins, and entire family with the last name Gonzales, Lawrence Anthony, Lang Tina, Lance Phillip, and Lawrennia Markel, Uncle Felix, and Officer Gourdine's Maternal Aunt Ida Gonzales.

Reverend Burns gave a touching eulogy and summarized the tragic tale by blaming the devil for encroaching on South Jamaica and causing all this Chaos. At the end of his sermon the N.Y. State department of Corrections arrived and interrupted the service by walking Lance Cook down the middle aisle as everyone stared. He was sat in the front row. Gifford came over to him and they hugged tightly.

"I'm sorry Son.....I'm sorry," was all that Lance could say as tears flowed down his cheeks.

Three weeks later on a Sunday morning Reverend Burns was giving his Sunday sermon while Reverend Gourdine was counting the collection money in the back office when the phone rang. Officer Gourdine had to leave immediately. People wondered what; all the huff was about as he rushed passed with a big smile on his face.

"I can't believe my mother was able to pull this off"

Officer Gourdine grinned to himself.

Warden Gourdine, Officer Gourdine's mother was always his ace in the hole. She was able to pull off incredible favors on his behalf and this one was the biggest. Lance Cook had been granted a conditional parole and released into the care of Reverend Burns. This was Reverend Gourdine's big surprise. All he had to do know was make it to the Port Authority Bus Terminal on 42nd Street and Eighth Avenue and return with Lance before the service was over, where an additional surprise was waiting for Lance.

As Officer Gourdine and Lance entered the church everyone was in shock as the two of them approached the pulpit; where Reverend Burns revealed the surprise.

"Everyone here is going to witness a miracle today! God has chosen yet another disciple and I am going to anoint him in front of thee!"

"Do you accept Christ as your Lord and savior?"

"Yes I do," answered Lance in a stone cold voice.

"I hereby ordain thee, Reverend Lance Cook"!

The entire congregation erupted in applause as Officer Gourdine and Lance hugged, then everyone came forward to hug Lance and congratulate him.

Special Thanks

Ron Chepesiuk, Carmen Nieves, Capalitana Micronia Buie, Chinse Daniels, Shabazz Maldrey, Phoenix Michael Gourdine, Cesar Victor Gourdine, Adonis Valentino Gourdine, Valear Usina Gourdine, Aunti Vickie Walker, Kevin Walker, Carmella Breedlove, Alexandra Passe, Tita Diaz, Latonya Reid, Nadine Lusardi, Annette Rowe, Yolanda Daniels, Kelly Braithwaite, Erica Brooks, Eric Heckstall, Siri Jolie Azor, Sharonda Hardy, Uncle Perry Burns, Curtis Scoon, Byron "Spoon" Howard, and Lorenzo "FAT CAT" Nichols.

Back page....

In this touching time piece, two sisters who are dark skinned meet two brothers who are light skinned in early 1990's South Jamaica Queens New York and in spite of all of the black races obstacles including self-hate, drug abuse, prostitution, and murder try to find love, safety and God.

Their biggest obstacle however is Capalitana and Chinse McDaniel's father N.Y.C. Correction Captain Ralph McDaniel's who moved his daughters to Long Island hoping that they would never fall for young black men from the ghetto, who will stop at nothing to keep that from doing so.....even if it means murder.

- Michael "Mick-Man" Gourdine